Siren Suicides

Second Edition

Ksenia Anske

*To Cyril
from the wet city
where sirens live in
rivers and lakes...
xoxo Ksenia*

Also by Ksenia Anske

The Badlings
Irkadura
Rosehead

Siren Suicides

Copyright © 2016 by Ksenia Anske
http://www.kseniaanske.com/

All rights reserved.

This work is made available under the terms of the Creative Commons Attribution-NonCommercial-ShareAlike 3.0 license, http://creativecommons.org/licenses/by-nc-sa/3.0/.

You are free to share (to copy, distribute and transmit the work) and to remix (to adapt the work) under the following conditions: you must attribute the work in the manner specified by the author or licensor (but not in any way that suggests that they endorse you or your use of the work); you may not use this work for commercial purposes; if you alter, transform, or build upon this work, you may distribute the resulting work only under the same or similar license to this one. Any of the above conditions can be waived if you get permission from the copyright holder. For any reuse or distribution, you must make clear to others the license terms of this work.

ISBN-13: 978-1519598103
ISBN-10: 1519598106

Dedication

This book is dedicated to my daughter, Anna Milioutina, who gave me a new purpose in life when I became a mother at eighteen. At seventeen, I escaped the violence of my home life by running away. I was a suicidal teenager, the result of an abusive father. Then, at seventeen, I got pregnant. Giving birth to a baby girl drove the suicidal thoughts out of my mind and filled me with new life. I am forever grateful for her.

This book is also dedicated to my partner, Royce Daniel, who believed in me as a writer and helped me finish this book by painstakingly reading and commenting on my writing every single day. At thirty-three, I was suicidal again, from revisiting my adolescence and discovering that my father sexually abused me. Becoming a writer and writing out my pain in Siren Suicides gave me the will to live once more.

Above all, this book is dedicated to every single human being who has ever wanted to take his or her life and leave this world. If you are thinking about killing yourself, please, don't. Life is beautiful, and it's even more beautiful with you in it. It might seem like there is no other way out at times, but, please, hang on to it, hang on to me, hang on to this book. It gets better. There is love everywhere, if only you're willing to stretch out your hand and ask for help. I know how hard it is; I know that it's nearly impossible. I know how painful it seems to continue living in your body, continuing an existence that you hate. Please, ask for help. I know you don't want to, I know you don't believe anyone cares. I do. E-mail me at kseniaanske@gmail.com, tweet to me at @kseniaanske, and I'll respond back as soon as I can.

If you'd rather talk with someone anonymously, you can also call the US Suicide Prevention line at 1-800-SUICIDE (1-800-784-2433) or visit http://www.suicide.org/.

This book is available for free, forever, as a download from my website, http://www.kseniaanske.com/. Why? Because I have a secret wish. I wish that my novel will help save a life, or two, or more.

Contents

Chapter 1. Marble Bathtub 1

Chapter 2. Bathroom Door 17

Chapter 3. Aurora Bridge 27

Chapter 4. Lake Union 37

Chapter 5. Lake's Bottom 49

Chapter 6. Brights' Boat 57

Chapter 7. Blake Island 64

Chapter 8. Stern Trawler 81

Chapter 9. Fish Factory 91

Chapter 10. Wet Lab 102

Chapter 11. Dry Lab 114

Chapter 12. Padded Cell 122

Chapter 13. Lifeboat 136

Chapter 14. Allen Bank 144

Chapter 15. Salmon Bay 153

Chapter 16. Fremont Bridge 164

Chapter 17. Fremont Canal 173

Chapter 18. Mount Rainier 184

Chapter 19. Paradise 201

Chapter 20. Nisqually River 209

Chapter 21. Douglas Fir 219

Chapter 22. Mud Lake 227

Chapter 23. Cascade Range 237

Chapter 24. Brights' House 248

Chapter 25. Marble Bathtub 258

Epilogue 271

"The Sirenes (Sirens), daughter of the River Achelous and the Muse Melpomene, wandering away after the rape of Proserpina [Persephone], came to the land of Apollo, and there were made flying creatures by the will of Ceres [Demeter] because they had not brought help to her daughter. It was predicted that they would live only until someone who heard their singing would pass by. Ulysses [Odysseus] proved fatal to them, for when by his cleverness he passed by the rocks where they dwelt, they threw themselves into the sea. This place is called Sirenides from them, and is between Sicily and Italy."

—Pseudo-Hyginus, Fabulae 141 (trans. Grant)
(Roman mythographer C2nd AD)

Introduction

I was breaking my head over how to write the introduction to this second edition. I looked at heaps of books and read heaps of introductions and none of them really helped me with what it is I wanted to say, so I thought, "Fuck it. I'll just say it how it is."

Why second edition? Why cut the trilogy from 249K words down to 88K? Well, number one, Siren Suicides was never a proper trilogy to begin with. The story simply didn't fit in one book and I chopped it in three parts and published it that way (back then I didn't know any better). Later I started getting comments from readers like "Great book! But it sort of ends abruptly…" and without batting an eye I would reply, "Oh, it's meant to be that way." Still later I noticed that many people read the first book but hardly anyone reads the second or the third, and the message at the end of the third book is lost. In fact, the whole point of the story is lost as it's sitting snugly in the very last chapter.

It wasn't only me who was thinking this. Lots of readers in their reviews mentioned it, the idea that editing it down could make it better, and I thought, "Okay. All right. Fine. Let's dive back in and see what we can do." And we did, or, rather, it was mostly my new editor Sarah Grace Liu. Sarah sliced and spliced and stitched and mended important parts together, and I wrote a sentence here and a sentence there to fill in the gaps, which weren't that many.

What you're holding in your hands is the result of this work and the hope that this story will reach more readers and speak to them as it spoke to me when I wrote it, back when I traded suicide for writing books, this being my first. On the next page you will see the original dedication that has been trimmed just a little, and after that, the sirens will greet you with their cold pitiless gaze.

And now, lots of thanks to lots of people who made this book happen.

Thank you to all my readers who have encouraged me to republish Siren Suicides as one book. There are too many of you to list here. You know who you are. I love you. Thank you to my Patreon supporters. You guys are supporting the printing of this book and the giveaways and the shipping costs and much more. Thank you to my daughter Anna Milioutina for designing the new beautiful cover that keeps the original covers' color scheme intact—the grey Seattle skies, the rain, the water. I adore it. Thank you to my editor Sarah Grace Liu for taking the time to shrink this sprawling beast down to a neat orderly tale AND NOT LETTING ME BUTCHER IT (I tried). Thank you to Colleen M. Albert who edited the original trilogy and made me believe in my story. Thank you to my formatter Stuart Whitmore for making the interior of this book crisp and readable. Thank you to my partner Royce Daniel who once more proofread the whole thing just in case some mistakes have been overlooked. And, above all, special huge enormous THANK YOU to Katya Pavlopolous and Christi Frey who have offered their help in identifying the parts that could be cut and who have painstakingly commented in red ink and in neon yellow highlighter and in black pen and in tears (I'm sure) on the printed manuscripts and then shipped them to me and I shipped them in turn to Sarah. You girls have started it all. You rock. I hope you like the result.

Chapter 1

Marble Bathtub

I chose to die in the bathroom because it's the only room in the house I can lock. And because water calms me. I have to be calm to pull the plug on my life. Nothing would irritate my father more than finding his sixteen-year-old daughter on the morning of her birthday, floating in his beloved antique marble tub—a ridiculous Bright family relic. Each corner is held up by one of four carved sirens, their mouths open in lethal song, their hands turned up in worship to the Siren of Canosa, a bronze faucet figure. How fitting. Ailen Bright, the deceased, guided into the afterlife by a tap. *Do you hear me, Papa? This is my morbid joke.*

Eight. Nine. Ten.

Ten seconds since I took the plunge, submerging into the bathtub full of water, wearing faded jeans and my favorite bright blue hoodie. Big white letters spell *Siren Suicides* across the front; they're my favorite band, because their music kicks ass, because they make me want to sing.

Blue is my favorite color. Three is my favorite number. It

Chapter 1

takes three minutes for an average person to drown. Only two minutes and fifty seconds left. I hold my breath.

Six years ago today, my mother jumped off the Aurora Bridge. I heard Papa scream at her, heard her run out of the house slamming the front door. And that was it. I hadn't seen much of my mom during my childhood, but after that day, I lost her forever. For this, and for all of the pain he's caused me, I want to hurt my father the only way I can—by sending him a message as twisted as his soul. By ending my life in the very place he delivered me, on a rainy September morning.

The tub is a central feature in our large bathroom; its plumbing is hidden beneath the floor, and its lack of a shower curtain adds to its authenticity. In some perverted sense, as far back as I can remember, its carved sirens were the sisters I never had. While I hid in the bathroom during my parents' fights, I talked to them for hours. I even had fitting siren names from mythology for each one.

Pisinoe, the one with the persuasive mind, is the youngest of the five. We both want a pet, so I like her best for that. Teles is the perfect one; her cute, yet slightly chubby, face makes me like mine so much better, thank you. Raidne symbolizes improvement. With hair that's long and curly, it's the envy of my life; my hair has been dubbed "chicken-feathers" by the kids at school. Ligeia is the shrill one, perhaps due to her voice. Her perfect breasts were the source of my secret admiration since the day I understood that being flat-chested would be my fate.

These are my four marble sisters. They stand two feet tall. Their bare bodies protrude from four corners of the tub, their knees on the floor, their arms spread wide as if they're the wings of birds getting ready to fly. At the head of the tub, with long hair covering her body and legs dangling from the rim, sits the Siren of Canosa, my big bronze sister. The way the others worship her says she's the boss. Her left hand holds the faucet, and her right arm is raised over her head in a gesture of mourning. She's the funerary siren whose job as a mythological creature is to lead the souls of the dead into the afterlife. But I'm forgetting to count.

45. 46. 47.

My clothes feel oddly warm and clingy. I close my eyes. I press my hands into the sides of the tub to keep myself from floating up. *I can't do this, I can't. I'm scared.* I sit up and gasp, grabbing my head with both hands to prevent it from spinning. No, to prevent the bathroom around me from spinning. Water rushes down my face. Wet cotton sticks to my skin in thick, soggy layers.

I hear the doorknob as someone tries to turn it. Then, after a puzzled pause, it rattles several more times.

Click-click-click.

"Ailen?" Papa's voice.

My muscles constrict as if freeze-dried. My heart attempts to beat through layers of ribs, exploding in my head with a pounding migraine.

He shouldn't be up so early. Damn it. And another thought. *I should've jumped off the bridge. Why the fuck am I so afraid of heights like Mom was? What do I do now? The whole bathroom stinks like weed.*

He knocks. I hold on to my knees, watch the early morning light stream through the window, listen to his footsteps. He's probably checking my room.

He'll be back.

All at once, I panic. A thousand needles of terror prickle my skin. The impossibility of facing my father, the impossibility of getting out of this bathroom in one piece floods me with renewed force. The bathroom stops spinning. Reaching a place of calm, a moment of soundless emptiness, I decide to try once

Chapter 1

more. I don't feel sorry for myself. I've thought of everything there is to think about while smoking away the night. There is no other way out for me except death.

I hear Papa open the door to my room and shout my name. I ignore him. I can do this. I'll have to think of something to distract myself. Everywhere I look, my mother's face floats up—the distant memory of her smile, her long brown hair and blue eyes, and a thousand freckles on the bridge of her nose. Like mine. I blink and focus on the towels. There she is again. I look at the sink. Same. I squint my eyes and shake my head hard. That does it.

I conjure a memory of Hunter to replace her. There, that's better. Hunter saves the day, as always. He's my best friend, my only friend. While everyone else shuns me at school, he obliviously calls out to me in the hallways, making obnoxious gorilla noises that have me snorting into my fist.

Whenever Papa leaves on his boat trips, we get stoned in my bathroom. It's the only room in the house that has a fan and a window. Last night I came way too close to telling Hunter my plans. We were blowing smoke rings, listening to Vivaldi's *The Four Seasons*, which Hunter makes us listen to whenever we get stoned, under the pretext of *cultural enrichment* and a *divine experience*, because classical music supposedly makes you feel higher, or something. Hunter touched one of the marble sirens, tracing her open mouth with his finger.

"What would you do if you met a real siren?" he asked, his head cocked to the side, his long skinny legs spread out wide on the tile floor, ending in two poorly laced sneakers.

He didn't know I talked to them, that to me they were real. When I raised my finger to touch Ligeia's mouth, she winked her marble eye at me. I jerked my finger away, thinking she might bite.

"Not the mythical kind. I'm talking about a real siren. The

killer kind. The one whose gaze never sits still. The way she walks, the way she talks. Every man wants to hear her velvety song, the song to die for."

"You're stoned," I said.

"Yeaaah, but, no. Listen." He sucked in on his joint, his slender fingers dancing across it. "Real sirens are among us. They're the girls who come out at night, in the fog, to sing their pain. Their voices make you do things. They command you to come close to them, and then they sing your soul out, ignite it."

"And then what?"

Hunter passed his free hand through his hair, bunching it up into an uncombed mess, before exhaling. "Then they put it back. Burning and smoldering."

"I thought sirens killed people."

"Those are the lucky ones. Those ones? They find them dead in the morning. They can't say what happened. It looks like their heart stopped. What's creepy, though, is that they're smiling. Dead, but smiling. Like they were their happiest just before they died."

"You say it like you've met one."

"A siren? Maybe I did."

I squinted at him. "You're such a liar."

He laughed, causing the whole room to vibrate. It vibrates now, in sync with Papa's steps returning from my bedroom.

I grip the sides of the tub.

Three short knocks on the door.

"Ailen? I know you're in there, sweetie. What are you doing in the bathroom so early? Open the door, please."

I whisper, looking up at Canosa to get her approval for what I'm about to do. *Nothing, Papa. Just killing myself is all. Because one minute of fantasy is better than nothing.* My head starts spinning again and I don't know if I imagine it or not, but she nods her head. It's time.

Chapter 1

I dive in, this time face first. For whatever reason, I imagine how our bathroom ceiling looks behind me, how it reminds me of a giant face. Its long, intricate ornaments look like wrinkles, its décor a bad impression of a Roman bath designed for the gods themselves. That white plaster type, a dirty shade of a cleaning lady's absence. I think I must clean it, but then I remember I need to count.

One. Two. Three.

My face is submerged in the water, my legs free-floating, the tips of my naked toes barely touching the end of the tub. Who in their right mind has an eight-foot marble bathtub? That's the Bright family values for you. Not love, but plenty of beautiful things to admire. I hold my breath until it feels like I can't hold it anymore.

Twenty seconds go by. Papa shakes the door.

I exhale. Bubbles trace my cheeks, rising to the surface.

"Ailen? Whatever it is you're doing in there, you have one minute to finish. If you don't open the door, I'll force my way in. Do you hear me?" His voice is muffled, yet strangely amplified, by all this water.

Perfect. It's been thirty seconds. Plus, one minute of waiting, and surely more than one minute to break down the solid oak door. Thank you, Papa.

The last of my air wants to come out through my nose, and I let it go, feeling a growing heaviness in my chest and an urge to inhale. Panic rears its ugly head again, but I drive it back into its dark corner. There is no other thread of sanity to hold on to except my last conversation with Hunter.

"Have you ever wanted to kill yourself?" I asked.

He choked on his spit and coughed. "What?"

At least his mom was still alive. I pulled myself closer to the tub and propped my feet right over Ligeia's face, to stop her from winking, and to make sure I couldn't see her naked breasts.

Marble Bathtub

I tightened my mouth saying each word slowly. "I said, have you ever wanted to kill yourself?"

"Are you out of your fucking mind, Ailen? What kind of a question is that?"

"God, it's just a question. Relax. You're telling me stories about sirens singing out people's souls and I can't ask you a simple question?"

"Of course you can. It's one hell of a loaded question though. Are you all right?"

"Idiot. I'm fine. Just wanted to know is all." I closed my mouth in an attempt to shut up, but my curiosity won, as always. "Okay, let me rephrase it. *If* you ever wanted to kill yourself, how would you do it?"

He blew out a coil of smoke, and studied the ceiling for a moment, his face lax.

"Don't tell me you've never thought about it; I won't buy it for a second."

To my surprise, after a minute of empty gazing, he answered. "I'd get my hands on the fastest motorcycle out there, hop on a highway, and ride as fast as I can."

"And then?"

"Then I'd crash!" He grinned and turned to look at me, his eyes full of mischief. I imagined Hunter mounting a bike, gunning its throttle, and whizzing past cars heading up a twisty, mountain road. Riding higher and higher, speeding toward the safety rail on some cliff—beyond which there is only empty air and jagged, mountain rocks all the way to the bottom.

I've been underwater for one minute and twenty seconds now.

I spread my arms wide, forming a perfect bridge from one cold marble wall to the other, trying not to lift my head and inhale air. *I have to stay down, I have to, I have to.* Circles begin swimming in front of my eyes, and my throat tightens further.

7

Chapter 1

Another few seconds and I'll be inhaling water.

"Ailen, your minute is up. Open the door, now." Papa is always impatient. Hearing his terrible voice warbled by water makes me more determined than ever. Yes, that will be worth it. Except I wish I could see his face when he finally breaks down the door and sees me floating here. I imagine it contorting in surprise, then horror, then regret. Priceless.

One minute, thirty-one. One minute, thirty-two. One minute, thirty-three.

"I said, open the damn door!" My heart pounds in my ears and I begin spinning as if headed down a whirlpool; except, when I look down at the plug, it's not moving.

The door rattles under his fists. He shouts, "Open the door!" again and again, slamming his fists harder. A strange calm spreads over me. I let out one last air bubble, staring into the marble. Long, delicate silver lines form a pattern—an otherworldly landscape with its own slopes, hills, forests, and mountains. All cold and distant, as if covered with a layer of snow.

I touch it. It's cool, like the water around me. I hope to feel something for myself, some sort of pity or agony before dying, anything at all. But there is nothing left.

I turn numb, numb like marble, numb like the bathroom door. I hope it proves hard to break. It's the only door in the house that can remain shut for longer than one minute, under the pretext of my monthly "girly" problems: stomach cramps, nausea, mood swings, tampons. All of the things Papa doesn't want to hear about because he's not my mother. If only I could see her one more time. I will. I know I will. This is my chance.

Do you hear me, Papa? I'm moving out. I'm going to live with my mom and you can eat shit. Unable to suppress the urge to breathe any longer, I open my mouth and inhale.

It's not air that I inhale, it's water. There is no other way to describe it except that it feels like inhaling liquid flame. It burns my throat, burns my chest, fills my ears with ringing. In that instant, I change my mind. I want to turn back, but it's too late. My larynx shuts down in one violent spasm, cutting off the flow of water into my lungs. My mouth clamps shut with an audible clicking of teeth. Time comes to a standstill. I reach that moment of tranquility I've been craving all along. A land of no pain, no yesterday, no tomorrow. A land where everything exists as a sequence of single snapshots of *now*.

This is what I see.

A bright light blinds me, like a photographic flash that illuminates the scene. It's my hand floating in the water, yet at the same time, in sharp clarity, it's a wide expanse of freshly freckled soil. Iridescent circles form in my peripheral vision, then another flash makes me wish I could shield my eyes. I see my wrist up close, with a forest of hairs shaking lightly. I look down the length of my body. The brilliant blue of the hoodie is too intense, making my two feet, dangling at the far end of each leg, look whiter than they are. Then it all turns fuzzy.

I can't tell up from down anymore. I close my eyes and listen. I hear something faint. Thump. Thump. Thump. It's my heart. I'm still alive. I feel confused and disoriented—is this how one feels when dying? What if the afterlife, or whatever you want to call it, what if there *is* something out there, on the other side?

I want to know what happens next. But my body thinks otherwise. It says, *Get the hell out of the bathtub!* I want to tell it to stop shouting, but my tongue won't move, caught between rows of my clamped teeth. My body says, *This is it. I've had enough of your stupidity. I'm getting you out.*

Unwillingly, I bend my knees. My feet touch nothing, as if I'm in deep water. I throw up my arms in one desperate stroke. There should be two polished-marble rims to grab—smooth, solid, and secure. Instead, my fingers close on water. The bathtub is gone.

Chapter 1

I open my eyes to find myself vertical, drifting deeper down into some kind of murk. The liquid around me turns muddy and greenish, with flecks of tiny fuzzy plants hanging here and there. I thrash around, watching the greenish tint of the liquid turn ultramarine. Blue is my favorite color. Three is my favorite number.

An insatiable need to breathe propels me upward. After a dozen strokes, I surface, gasping for air and coughing up stale water. I shiver, inhaling one lungful of air after another, hyperventilating and sobbing hysterically at the same time. It takes me a moment to calm down and look around.

The water is clear and blue, reflecting a cloudless sky. I'm in the shallow end of a lake. It's overgrown with lilies. Their stems touch my legs, their sweet and fruity smell overpowering me.

All thoughts vanish, all feelings desert me. I can only stare.

On the edge of the lake sits the Siren of Canosa. My big bronze sister. The boss. Only she's not bronze anymore. She's real and as tall as I am. With real skin, real hair, and a real body. She pins me with her practiced, innocent gaze that I've seen so many times in the bathtub. Without realizing it, I exhale a long sigh of awe.

She's a beautiful thing. The early morning sun paints her pale face a golden hue. Warm wind lifts a strand of her silvery hair. Yet as she smiles, I taste bile at the back of my throat, and a sinister feeling penetrates my core, as if something in this perfect picture isn't right. It hides rotten secrets inside. There is a lie in the air, and I feel like I'm about to buy it.

She locks her piercing green eyes with mine and begins to sing. At once, I'm spell-bound, unable to retreat, listening with my ears, my skin, my everything that can absorb her voice.

"We live in the meadow,
But you don't know it.

Marble Bathtub

*Our grass is your sorrow,
But you won't show it."*

My mind wants to reject the tune, categorizes it as false sorrow—pitched a little too high, a quarter note off, a hairline away from a genuine song that makes your heart beat faster with its beauty. You're not real, I want to say. You're just a bronze bathroom figure. Your song is fake, it's a tool. You don't care for me. It's your job to transport me to the other side, right? And you probably hate your job. When was the last time you got a raise? But I keep listening, mesmerized.

*"Give us your pain,
Dip in our song.
Notes afloat,
Listen and love.
Listen and love.
Listen and love."*

I notice other sirens now, my marble sisters. They crawl out from behind bleached logs and join Canosa, singing together with her. I want to drown in their melody. Its thrilling notes reach to me, like a stretched out invisible hand, pulling me closer. Water lily stems tangle around my legs as I wade through the lake toward the beach, wanting more, drinking in their sorrow, gorging upon their gaze.

*"We wade in the lake.
Why do you frown?
Our wish is your wake.
Why do you drown?"*

They stop singing and watch me stumble forward. I drop to

Chapter 1

my knees a couple feet away from Canosa, my mouth open in admiration, my eyes teary, my troubles forgotten. All I can feel is a sense of calm emitted by their eyes, their voices, their bodies. It's not the comfortable calm of a clear, happy mind, but rather a chilling calm of violently suppressed pain. I don't care, as long as my pain is gone.

Canosa takes my hands into hers; they feel cold and slimy against my skin. Her breath washes over me in a thousand-year-old stink covered up by water-lily sweetness.

"Ailen Bright, silly girl, what took you so long? I've been waiting." She purses her lower lip and shakes her head.

I look at her, unable to comprehend that she's really talking to me, and her four sisters are nodding their heads behind her. There is Pisinoe, the youngest, clutching Canosa's left arm, peeking from behind her dark mane. Next to her is Teles, the perfect one, cupping her chubby cheeks with both of her hands, studying me. Raidne sits by Canosa's right side, braiding her own long, auburn, curly hair—the envy of my life. And behind her is Ligeia. I quickly look away so as not to see her breasts.

"How rude! Don't you know you're supposed to say 'Hi!' and 'How are you?' and 'I loved your song, it was so pretty'?" Canosa pushes me away and drops my hands.

I open my mouth to say something in my defense, but she's faster.

Her lips press into one hard line, her hands propped on her hips, her elbows stuck out like the wings of an angry bird. "I don't think I like you." At this, the other sirens begin to protest, but Canosa shushes them with a low hiss. They fall silent and peer at me. I feel uneasy, as if I'm food being studied for ripeness.

"You exist? I mean, I thought you were just a bronze fauc—"

"Fine, I forgive you. Let's start over." She dashes at me and grabs my hands. I nearly fall face down into the sand as she pulls me toward her. The other sirens circle us, their knees and hands in the sand, their hair falling into their faces. They lick their lips and, suddenly, I want to break free, yet I make no move.

"It's no fun to be dead. Booooring. Right, girls?" Canosa says, looking around for approval. The sirens nod, silent, their eyes not leaving me for a second, their circle tightening around me.

"Am I dead? What is this place, anyway?" I croak, suffocating from the overpowering stench of rotten fish that slides from their open mouths. I realize their skin, so clear and white from a distance, has a greenish tinge to it up close. Like a molding orange.

I tear my hands out of Canosa's. "It was very nice to meet you, thank you very much for the song, but I think I've changed my mind." They lunge at me. Ligeia grabs my feet. Canosa clasps my chin and raises my face up, her nose inches away from mine.

"Ailen Bright, I can give you something you want, if you give me something I want in return."

"What's that?" I ask.

"You're full of stupid questions, silly girl. You know what I mean." Her lips string into a hard line again.

"But—"

"Are you deaf?"

This is so bizarre, I don't know what to say.

"Listen to me. Hours upon hours of sitting in the bathtub, you asked a thousand times for help, telling me about a thousand tortures, all wishing you could hurt your father. Don't you remember any of it?"

I blink and feel my face turn red, betraying my desire to lie. I swallow and say nothing.

"All I need from *you* is your soul. Just a tiny, little thing. You don't need it anyway, do you?" The other sirens hiss at this, their eyes ablaze with hunger.

Hunter's words flash in my mind. *They find them dead in*

Chapter 1

the morning. They can't say what happened. It looks like their heart stopped. What's creepy, though, is that they're smiling. Dead, but smiling. Like they were their happiest just before they died.

"Are you saying you want to kill me?" As soon as it comes out of my mouth, I feel like I said something stupid.

"If we wanted to, we'd have already done that, don't you think?" Canosa cackles; they all cackle. Little hairs on my neck and arms stand up at the sound. "No, we want you to become one of us, right girls?" She turns to the other sirens without letting go of my chin. They nod their approval. Pisinoe begins clapping her hands like an excited toddler.

"Why?" is all I can say. A childish hope to belong grips me and suppresses all logical thoughts with a simple yearning. I don't care if they are dead or alive or real or not real. I've never belonged anywhere, always an outcast. Now to have five sisters tumbling over themselves to accept me? How can I explain how badly I've wanted this to happen my entire life? I can't believe that someone, at last, wants me. Someone else other than Hunter. My real friend, my only friend.

"I'm tired of repeating myself. Once again, stop asking stupid questions. Use your brain. Think, silly girl, think." She taps my forehead with her finger. "Your father hates women because they make him lose control, doesn't he? They are these beautiful things to him, to own. He doesn't know how else to love them. Am I right?" Canosa says.

"I think he's just an asshole."

"It's never as simple as that, and you know it. He must have been a very sweet little boy at one time in his life, don't you think? Large blue eyes, long eyelashes." She inches closer to me. "Someone must have hurt him, and hurt him badly. Maybe it was a woman, maybe it was his mother."

"I don't care. He's not a little boy anymore. He is beyond repair. There is only one thing I can do—hurt him back."

Canosa smiles as if that was what she was waiting for. She seems downright gleeful as she says, "How about you become a siren and torture his soul with your songs, almost kill him, hold him by the thread, near death, as long as you want to? Watch him squirm and plead, like a worm." As she says it, her entire body trembles, her eyes gloss over with a type of feeding-frenzy fever. "Hurt him, for hurting your mother. You want to badly, don't you?"

Hatred fills me to the brim of my being. My mother's face floats up in my memory, and stabs me with pain. Every single blow and insult I endured from my father's hand strikes me at once. Every joke and ridicule and mocking at school for being flat-chested, a recluse, a bookworm, stabs me under my ribs. I look at the sirens, all crouched on their fours, gazing at me, waiting for my answer. They want me to be their sister, girls who are much more beautiful and powerful than those stuck-up bitches at school, more powerful than my father. Unable to contain the urge anymore, I cry out.

"Yes! My answer is yes!"

Canosa shakes my hand, greedy.

"Good. I want you to come close, look at me, look me in the eyes and open—"

At this moment, a noise cracks across the sky as if something heavy has fallen. The shock sends big waves across the lake and I'm being pulled back into the water with one of them. The lake comes alive and I hear the sirens scream. I can only make out some of Canosa's words as water lily stems pull me under the surface, down into the murk: *Aurora Bridge. Your mother.* I reach complete darkness.

Warmth returns. My chest feels heavy and my muscles tighten. I raise my head to the light, blinded by its intensity. I feel as if I have been spit out by the lake—a foreign object that doesn't belong to it, not yet.

Chapter 1

I gasp for air.

The green water turns clear, and rolls off me. I sit up.

I'm back in my bathtub. The water is warm, yet I'm chilled to the bone as if covered with snow. I'm shaking and coughing up icy water, yet each breath is dry, fiery pain. As I cough, I look at the faucet. There she is, the Siren of Canosa, back to her faucety self.

I must have hallucinated her into a singing fiend from Hunter's story. It felt so real. *I just had a near-death experience, that's all. I'm alive, I'm okay.* A surge of happiness makes me jitter. I try to remember how many joints it took me for courage this morning. *Oh, Hunter, where the hell did you get this weed? I'm having a bad trip.* I see tiny specks of indigo dance in front of my eyes and remember I also dropped a tab of acid on top of it. Great.

I reach out and stroke Canosa's bronze hair, to make sure she's really made out of bronze, when a sudden silence makes me feel as if someone is watching me. I glance to my left and notice a layer of dust on the floor and a few scattered woodchips. I look farther out and see the bathroom door, its hinges still covered with plaster from having been torn out of the wall. My happiness vanishes in an instant, sucked away by the sheer terror of what I've done and what punishment is about to follow.

I turn toward the opening where the door used to stand.

My father steps on the door and walks toward me, his face set, his hands curled into fists.

"Papa?" I say and see his hand raised in the air, ready to strike.

Chapter 2

Bathroom Door

The wide expanse of the back of my father's hand nears me as if in slow motion. I can see his meticulously manicured nails, a few hairs at the bend of his wrist, his titanium Panerai watch showing a few minutes past seven in the morning—all peeking out from the cuff of his silken maroon pajamas. Kicked up from the floor by his handcrafted, Italian leather slippers, a million dust particles swirl and dance in the air, reflecting the early morning light and forming a tunnel of movement for his hand to follow. Aimed at me. Aimed at my face. Aimed at beating sense into me so I won't turn out like my mother.

Smack!

His hand strikes my cheek, and my head comes alive with livid fire. I convulse in a bout of coughing, sputtering water out of my lungs. My throat burns with the scorching sensation of abrasive pebbles rushing out. I try to stand. The bathroom doesn't just double-spin against me, it seems to turn inside out and fold into itself in consecutive waves. A pulsing rhythm

Chapter 2

matching my heartbeat.

"What the hell do you think you're doing?" Papa yells into my ear. "Answer me."

Perhaps there was a time when my head and my brain were one. Not anymore. My brain floats on its own in my skull. It sloshes to the side as I tilt my head in an attempt to hide from his yelling. Every syllable, every word that flies off my father's lips, threatens to pierce my sanity and explode my head into a million little pieces.

I don't need to listen to what he says. I'm sure it's the usual concoction. You just wait, one day you'll turn out just like your mother. Nothing will ever become of you. Would you look at what you did? You made me break *my* bathroom door. Do you know how much a door costs? How much it costs to replace the lock? To fill in holes in the wall and to paint it?

All I see is his mouth opening and closing, his thin lips stretching over his teeth in a dance of forceful monologue that's supposed to teach me, to do me good, to help raise me in such a way that I manage to survive in this world, as a woman. Because, in Papa's eyes, women are second class. Women are weak creatures who need to be controlled lest they decide to charm off men's pants and make them do stupid shit. They corrupt men's very spirits.

I'm really good at tuning things out—years of practice pay off. My focus shifts to the door. It lies on the tiled floor, its oak paneling covered with a layer of white particleboard dust. I feel sorry for my only refuge that can't be locked anymore. And I want out. Out of this room, out of this house. I want to run away and never come back, like Mom did on that rainy September morning.

"Did you hear what I said?" Papa's voice jerks me from my moment of contemplation.

"Yes, Papa," I say, shifting my gaze to Canosa, making sure

Bathroom Door

she doesn't move. I have a hard time suppressing the urge to jump out of the tub and look at the marble sirens, touch their marble faces to confirm that I haven't gone insane.

"Then, please, explain to me what this is doing in *my* bathroom?" Papa shoves his hand under my face.

I smell it before I see it and I know what he's found. Papa's upturned palm displays three joint stubs, twisted and stuck to the top of the crushed soda can that I didn't even care to dispose of because, by now, I was supposed to be dead. Every ounce of pain vanishes, swept away by the terror of being caught.

"It's not mine," I say, feeling my face turn red and hot, desperately trying to control the blood flow by gritting my teeth together. No use. It's as if I speed it up instead. Every single blood vessel in my face inflates with guilt. In some stubborn delirium, I insist, "I didn't do it. I swear. It's Hunter's." There, I just betrayed my only friend. Nice move, Ailen.

Another slap on my cheek makes me grab onto the tub's rims so that I don't slide under the water. This is slap number two, one more to go. I think I can taste blood.

Papa hovers over me, the collar of his silk pajamas hanging open and revealing his chest hair, his lips quivering. After an initial surge of anger, this is his typical remorse. "Don't you ever lie to me, Ailen. How dare you. Would you look at yourself, look who you're turning into. It's in your DNA. Your mother was a liar, too. It pains me to strike you, sweetie, but there is no other way for me to teach you. I care for you, I want you to have a better life than her. Do you understand?"

"I'm sorry I worried you, Papa, I'm fine. I'll be fine," I manage, talking through the pain, hoping against all hope that he won't make me look at him.

It's a futile hope, because he grabs my chin, as always, and lifts up my face. His huge eyes bulge out of his head in two menacing horror-balloons that have given me nightmares ever

Chapter 2

since I was little.

"Papa, let go, it hurts."

He doesn't hear me. He continues asking. He wants to know what I'm doing, fully dressed, in a tub full of water. Did I take any other drugs besides weed? How long have I been up? How will I go to school? He tells me he has no time to deal with it and I should've known better. I sense the ending to his tirade.

Here it comes. The pitch of his voice rises, balances on a precipice of that familiar place before tumbling into an abyss of rage. Bout number three, the grand finale. Three is my favorite number, because after three it's over. I stiffen.

Slap!

The back of his hand greets me hard, but to me, he caresses my cheek. I ignore the salt in my tears, pretending it's a taste of sea. My ears ring from the impact, but I imagine it's him telling me how to throw pebbles into a lake so that they skip along like frogs.

He reaches under my armpits and yanks me out of the tub, drags me several feet, and leans me against the wall. He begins mopping my face with a towel, like I'm five. Shaking violently from being wet and cold, I stare at Canosa, thinking back to our conversation, replaying her words in my mind. *How about you become a siren and torture his soul with your songs, never killing him, holding him by a thread on the precipice of dying, as long as you want to. Watch him squirm and plead, like a worm? Hurt him, for hurting your mother?*

I think about how my idea of hurting him, the only way I can, was stupid. Killing myself to make him feel sorry? Right. Throwing him deep into grief? Dream on, Ailen, dream on. Look at him, concentrated on drying me like his favorite doll that got dropped into the toilet by accident, with such a grimace of disgust on his face that can only be attributed to how much I stink. Canosa is right, he doesn't care. Never did, never will. He's broken beyond repair. There is only one way to hurt him.

"Yes," I tell her. "I want to."

"Who are you talking to?" Papa asks, attempting to trace my line of vision. I drop my gaze to the floor, stare at my bare feet, and watch small puddles form around them. Before he has a chance to say anything else, I remember something important.

"I'm sixteen today, Papa. You forgot," I whisper.

"I can't hear what you're saying, sweetie, speak up, please. How many times do I have to tell you?"

He doesn't hear me, of course. He never does. My bones scream in pain as he lifts my head again and looks me in the eyes.

"I asked you a question, I expect a response."

I look at the window, anywhere but at him.

"Would you look at those eyes darting left and right. You think you know better than me, don't you? You think you're so smart? Here, I'll give you a chance to prove it. Tell me what women were made for. Go on."

This is it, his favorite question to quiz me on. His way of making sure I remember it for the rest of my life. I'd prefer it if he was a religious freak who asked me to repeat a daily prayer. This is worse, a hundred times worse. His face fills the crack between my insanity and my freedom. His eyes bulge, his neck veins pushing against his skin. I open and close my mouth, twice, like a beached fish.

"Answer the damn question," he says slowly, as I slide against the wall, leaving a wet trace against it. He clamps the back of my hoodie in his left fist and pulls me back up. *Play limp, just play limp.*

"You forgot, didn't you? That's typical of you, another trait from your mother. Bad memory. Well, let me remind you."

His lips brush my ear, eager to share the big secret.

"Women were made to haul water, Ailen. Beat this into your pretty little head. I'm tired of repeating myself every day. Why

Chapter 2

else, tell me, would your mother make fun of me like this? Why else would she give me a daughter when she knew I wanted a son?"

I recoil, not fully comprehending what he said.

"She made fun of me, Ailen. That weak woman dared to mock me publicly. Imagine how that felt. She was crazy, crazy! I don't know what I saw in her. She twisted me around her finger, got pregnant, made me marry her. Then, she had her last laugh. You know what she did? She left me, to raise you all alone. You know how hard it is to be a single father?"

His words sink in. Ailen Bright, an unwanted child. *Good joke, Mom, I salute you.* I suppress a terrible urge to cry. If my own parents didn't want me, who will? I glance at Canosa again, willing her to wave or blink back. *The sirens. I belong with the sirens. How I wish they were real.*

Papa whispers in my ear. "I raised you my own way. I want to make sure you turn out different. It's in your voice already, those seductive notes. I can hear them when you talk. I'll root it out of you. You'll thank me later, I promise."

He finally lets go of me and wipes his hands on a towel. "She knows I hate getting wet," he mutters. There is a space of three feet between us. I look to my left. The gap where the door stood is wide open, like a passage into another world. This is how my mother must have felt on the morning she left. I think I understand her now, and I'm not as mad at her anymore. I see her face floating against the hole in the wall, smiling, beckoning me to follow.

"We'll talk more after school. I want you to be home by three." Papa smooths his hair and turns toward the sink to check himself in the mirror.

"I'm leaving," I say, set in my decision. I press myself into the wall, pushing my hands flat against it to hold my balance. I've never talked to my father like that in my life, not once.

Bathroom Door

"What?" He turns around; his bushy eyebrows fly up.

"I said, I'm leaving. I'm going to see Mom and you can eat shit." I lean away from the wall and stumble out of the bathroom, clutching the walls for support, with one clear goal in mind.

Get out. Get out. Get out.

"You're not going anywhere," I hear behind me. I shake my head and pull myself up against the rail, as my father's arm reaches for me. I let go and roll all the way down. The pain shakes me and a fresh shot of adrenaline gives me enough strength to stand up and reach for the front door handles. There are two. I blink. They're back to one.

My father, unable to comprehend what I'm doing, yells at me from the stairs above. His voice paralyzes me.

"Ailen, get back here, now."

It's now or never.

I focus on the door knob. *Take it, Ailen, just take it.* This doorknob was the source of my nightmares along with my father's bulging eyes. In fact, they would morph into each other. First his eyes would float toward me, out of his face, getting bigger and bigger, pressing me against the wall. Then they would merge into one and her face would appear. *Her* is the woman's head that serves as our front door knob. Our house is full of Italian relics of two types: women and fish. As much as I love my four marble sisters and one bronze one, I hate this one.

She let my mother out on that morning, the seventh of September. She didn't stop her. For that, I want to melt her in our fireplace and watch her face come off in a grimace of utter surprise. I hear Papa stepping down and force myself to grab the she-knob, my palm pressed against her round, bronze face, my fingers feeling every groove of her hair. Maybe she is Death herself and it's my turn to step through her door. As if I'm right, the knob feels freezing cold under my fingers as I turn it, gripping it

Chapter 2

hard so it won't slide in my sweaty hand.

Click.

The heavy front door opens slowly and rainy morning air gushes inside. I breathe it in and stop trembling for a second, forgetting I'm wet, forgetting I'm scared. I soak in the smell of damp asphalt, fallen leaves, fresh sorrows. Something cold traces my face. It takes me a second to realize what it is. We weep together, the sky and me.

"What do I do now?" I ask it.

It drips silence, full of gray clouds.

"Ailen, don't make me come out into the rain. You know I hate getting wet." I hear my father's steps behind me and, afraid to see his eyes, I run out onto the porch. Something makes me stop and raise my face to the sky. Maybe it's the unanswered question.

"Did my mother ask you the same thing six years ago? Did she ask you?"

The sky leaks more indifference, splashing my face with raindrops.

I curl my hands into fists and feel hot tears roll down my cheeks. The sky doesn't answer. I want to mash it with my fists beyond recognition, when I feel Papa grab me by the arm. I turn and twist out of his grip. He opens his mouth in shock, perhaps not expecting me to resist. His maroon silk pajamas soak up the rain. Before he composes himself, I run down our eleven painted porch steps and turn around, yelling at both the sky and my father.

"I hate you, I hate you, I hate you!"

"Ailen, I understand you're frustrated, but you can't go anywhere like this. Your clothes are wet. You're not wearing shoes, you'll get pneumonia."

"Like you care!" I yell, my teeth chattering.

His face goes dark. "I'm counting to three. On three, you

need to be back inside this house." He stands fuming at the edge of the porch, oblivious to getting wet, which is so unlike him. The only thing I see is his eyes, and I feel them pulling me back.

"One..."

I keep staring, swallowing tears and raindrops, not moving forward or backward, trembling from being wet and cold.

"Two..."

His gaze fills me with terror, all fifty-two years of his might against my feeble sixteen. *Fat chance, Ailen.* My shivering legs won't move. "Three."

He leans forward and I unfreeze. It's as if the sound of his steps breaks my stupor, tears off the lid from my suppressed feelings and they tumble out of me in one cry.

"Stop!" I yell. He pauses. "You forgot something." I back onto the concrete path, toward the white gate overgrown with vines.

"What's that?"

There are ten feet between us filled with my defiance. I grab the gate as an anchor and lift the latch with unbending fingers.

"It's my birthday today, remember? I'm sixteen. You didn't even wish me a happy birthday. Well, I won't bother you anymore, you can relax. I'm leaving and I'm not coming back."

"What makes you think I forgot?" He dashes toward me.

I fumble with the latch, jerk the gate open, and run down twenty mossy steps, my bare feet sliding against them, the gaps between my toes filling with dirt. At the very bottom I finally lose my balance and grab the fence post so I don't fall. My hands slide on the slick, painted wood. I let go of the fence and run out into the street. An oncoming car veers around me and honks. I flip its driver the finger and turn to look, my heart pounding hard and fast. Papa is a few feet behind me, dashing down the steps two at a time. One of his slippers flies off his foot and he falls on his bony ass, cursing loudly.

Chapter 2

For a second, we watch each other.

He hates getting wet, and his right hip gives out after a few minutes of running. He probably doesn't believe I'll go far. He's too meticulous to come out after me unprepared. I know what he'll do next. He'll dart back into the house, grab his keys and coat, step into expensive Italian shoes, run back down, and skid along the sidewalk to the front of our garage door that was built in 1909 for holding horse carriages. Next, he'll grab the metal handle that looks like a man's face, press the button on his keys, yank the garage door open, and get inside his Maserati—shiny, black, and, of course, Italian.

He pulls himself up and I bolt.

Chapter 3

Aurora Bridge

I run through the rain barefoot. I'm not ten anymore. I'm sixteen, wearing jeans and a hoodie instead of pajamas. And Papa is not catching me this time, not locking me up alone and leaving to search for my mother. It's my turn to look for her. A sudden memory from that morning nags at me. I hear echoes of the blows Father dealt to her delicate face from behind their bedroom door. I hear the swish of her nightgown against wallpaper. Somebody sings my name. Can it be her voice, calling me one last time before jumping off the bridge? All logic forgotten, mad hope sends me sprinting.

"Mom, wait for me, I'm coming!" I yell, out of breath. As soon as the words leave my lips, I think I've gone crazy. I make it to where Raye Street dead-ends into Mrs. Elliott's cookie-cutter house. I stop to sneeze three times, shaking all over.

Her poodle barks at me through the window, his front paws on the windowsill, as always. Mrs. Elliott sticks her head out, her ever-curious eyes taking in the scene for the latest neighborhood gossip. She looks like her poodle, with white curls framing

Chapter 3

her pasty round face. Her clothes are an indistinguishable pastel color. I firmly believe that she averted her eyes when my mother stopped by her front gate, perhaps uncertain of where to go. At least, that's what witnesses told police officers later. Mrs. Elliott claimed she was asleep that early in the morning. Which is bullshit, because she always takes out her stupid dog for a walk at seven in the morning sharp.

"Stop staring at me! And I hate your fucking dog!" I yell and wipe my nose, glaring.

"Oh!" She opens her mouth, covers it with her soft hand, pushes the dog back inside with her leg, and quickly shuts the door. I flip her the finger and mouth, *Fuck you!* as I turn and run down the mossy stairway, shaking from cold and anger.

Knowing this neighborhood so well gives me an advantage because I know my father has no way of driving onto the Aurora Bridge unless he goes south first, then finds a spot to turn around. And there aren't many. By the time he's done, I'll have gotten on to the bridge by foot.

Why the hell am I going there? To look for my mother? She's been dead for six years now. This is a ridiculous idea. Thoughts fly through my head as I pound down the forty concrete steps, clutching the railing on my right and inhaling a woodsy smell from the abundance of cypress trees.

I pause at the bottom of the stairs, looking left and right. The street is deserted at this hour. I jog across it, toward the Aurora Bridge. It rumbles under early morning traffic, a mix of commuter cars and huge delivery trucks.

I sprint to the point where the bridge begins to cross water. Another bout of sneezing makes me bend, placing my palms on my knees so that I don't lose my balance. My throat burns with irritation. I wipe my nose, stand, and glance around. Except for traffic racing to and fro, there's no one on the bridge but me. All 3,000 feet of its length, deserted. Somewhere on this side of the bridge, along its middle section that soars 167 feet above the water, my mother climbed over the railing and jumped.

Mom? What did I do wrong? Why did you do it? Why did you leave me?

I look along the bridge, hating its engineers. Hating its metal guts, its height, and the fact that it has become Seattle's most popular attraction for suicide jumpers.

I slam both fists against it and yelp in pain. Tears stream freely down my cheeks, mixing with rain. Steam rises from my mouth with every breath. Fury seems to have warmed me up a bit and I don't shake as much. Propelled by the need to do anything but stand in one place and freeze, I run toward the middle of the bridge, hoping for something, looking for something near a miracle. I want to see a white nightgown and my mother's long hair brushing the wavy pattern of its collar frills. I hope for a glimpse of some kind of answer—anything at all. And I get it. Three honks from the opposite lane, going north. I stifle a cry.

My father's Maserati slows down enough for me to see him gesticulate from behind the steering wheel, clearly with the intent of crossing the bridge, turning around, and picking me up from where I stand, even if he has to stop traffic. Three minutes left to either run all the way across the bridge and hide behind the Fremont Troll or even make it to Hunter's house on Linden Avenue.

Someone emerges from the stairs on the north side of the bridge and walks toward me with the familiar gait of a sailor. Except this is no sailor. It's Hunter, dressed in his favorite jeans and blue rain jacket, hood over his head, eyes set deeply in the shadows of his face. He waves, pauses as if observing my state, and breaks into a run.

"Hunter," I exhale, wondering why he is up so early. He's not a morning person; he always makes it to school at the last minute.

Chapter 3

"Ailen, hey!" he yells, waving.

At first, it fills me with glee to see him, making my heart beat faster; then my heart drops at the impending dread of getting him in trouble with my father. Because, for sure, he would think Hunter planned this escape with me, planned to meet me on the bridge. I don't care if I'm grounded, but I do care about not being able to see Hunter. My mind goes blank and my body takes over. I slump against the barrier and quietly slide to the ground, feeling defeated and sobbing.

Hunter runs up to me and takes my face into his warm hands. "Dude, what the hell are you doing out here in the rain, barefoot?" He tries pulling me up, but I don't budge.

"I don't know," I say through chattering teeth.

He feels my arms and legs. "Oh my God, you're soaking wet. You're freezing!"

Water from his jacket drips on my face. He peers at me for a moment, his eyes like two pools of indigo paint, pulsing in their splendor. Blue is my favorite color. It gives me an anchor to pull myself out of this state, a concrete fact to lean on, to shake off all these muddled emotions and turn to logic. Yet I can't move. I want to get lost in those pools of blue, all of me, skin and flesh and bones. I want to dive so deep inside his eyes that I'll never be found.

But Papa will be here any minute now, to lock me up at home. The hunt is on, and I need to keep running. My hands begin to shake and my breathing speeds up. I hyperventilate as I try to battle the oncoming panic.

"Oh, Ailen." Hunter brushes the hair out of my face. I feel the warmth of his breathing, see him lean in closer and then stop at the invisible line that we haven't crossed yet. Because we're just friends. I'm sure he's dying to kiss me, as much as I'm dying to kiss him. But I flinch and pull away, wanting it to be a special thing, afraid that he'll find me cold and slimy and disgusting. Perhaps he senses my thoughts, because he leans back a few inches. "Talk to me, please. What the hell happened?"

"I ran away from home," I say, forcing a smile. "And I don't want to go back, ever. Papa is coming any minute to get me though, so, I guess...fat chance." The end of the sentence comes out half chuckle, half cry.

He props me against the railing, unzips his jacket, and takes it off.

"No, it's okay. Don't. It won't do any good." I sneeze several times and yelp in pain. My throat is on fire and my toe pulses as if it's broken. "Hunter, I shouldn't have done it. I don't know why I did it. He'll be mad. What do I tell him? What do I do now?"

"You'll get sick, that's what. Let me give you my jacket and let's get you home first."

"I don't wanna go home!" I sob hysterically, pushing him away, pulling myself up.

"I'm sorry, it came out wrong. I meant some place dry!"

My breathing speeds up so rapidly I think I'll faint. My ears hear strange cricket noises, my eyes see dancing dots. I smell iron.

"Look at me!" Hunter grabs my chin and pulls my face up to his. "Ailen, look at me. Breathe. You have to slow down and breathe. You're just having a bad trip, that's all. We'll do it together, okay? I'll count to three."

That does it, that count-to-three phrase that my father has used on me for as long as I can remember. I flash cold, then warm, feeling sweat break out from every single pore. I heave, suffocating. There is not enough oxygen in the air.

"Listen to me! Breathe!" Hunter shakes me. My head rolls around as if it belongs on a rag doll.

"Come on, talk to me, Ailen."

I manage to suck in some air. "Remember what I asked you

Chapter 3

about yesterday?" I say.

"Yes?"

"I asked if you ever wanted to kill yourself."

"Yeah, I remember. It freaked me out, you know. And?"

"And, I tried to kill myself this morning."

At this moment, Papa's black Maserati slowly rolls up. I hear Papa yank up the handbrake, see orange emergency lights flash. A couple cars behind him honk, begin edging around him. One driver rolls down the window of his silver pickup truck and shouts his displeasure, waving his arm furiously and flipping the finger, his tanned face contorted in a grimace of hate.

Hunter turns around.

Papa steps out of the car, clad in his favorite Gucci, waterproof, leather half-booties, his black wool suit, and a black Armani trench coat on top of it. He leans deeply into the car for his umbrella. He pulls it out and opens it, holding it by the curved wooden handle, hand-crafted of course. He slams the driver's door shut and walks around the back of the car toward the sidewalk barrier.

"Hey, Hunter. Good to see you, son. How are you doing?" My father is always full of pleasantries when it comes to people outside of our family, so that you'd never guess his true nature. He stops at the waist-high barrier and sizes it up and down, probably deciding how to climb over it.

I note that he didn't bother to ask me how I was, or if I was okay. But, then again, those are mere details.

"Hello, Mr. Bright. I'm okay, but Ailen here…I think she's having a panic attack. I think, I'm not sure. She doesn't look so good though." It must be something in my father's face that makes Hunter abruptly stop talking. I don't need to look, I know it by heart—the menacing stare that's about to transform into a bout of uncontrollable rage, barely contained under the cover of his politeness. For now.

"Hunter, do you mind leaving me alone with my daughter, please?" He stretches his lips into what's supposed to resemble a smile.

"Sure." Hunter glances briefly at me.

"No, don't go! Don't leave me!" I hear my teeth chatter as I talk, my body shivering violently again. Both are symptoms of hypothermia. I don't care about getting sick, I just don't want Hunter to ever leave me.

Hunter spreads his hands wide, as if to say, *Dude, there's nothing I can do, he's your father.*

Papa presses his left hand onto the railing for support, and, with the umbrella still in his right hand, he lightly jumps over the barrier, landing softly on the sidewalk like a black panther getting ready to pounce.

"Strange to find you here, Hunter, so early in the morning. Going anywhere special?" My father walks up to me, and switches his umbrella to his left hand. I shrink instinctively to avoid a blow, but he simply places his right hand on my shoulder. It seems to weigh a ton. I'm lucky we're not at home.

"Oh, I was just...taking a walk, you know. Actually, I wanted to surprise Ailen with something on her birthday. I can't say what it is, though. It was supposed to be a surprise. I guess I'll do it at school then." He shrugs.

"Please." My father tilts his head. I can sense his impatience.

"Sure, sure. See ya, Ailen."

I want to say, *See ya,* but my lips won't move. I think this is the end of my life. I know what's coming and I know it will be ugly.

Hunter slowly walks away, turns to look back a couple of times, and keeps walking. I attempt to stand up, but Papa presses his hand into my shoulder and pins me down. I see a vein bulge on the side of his neck. I hold my breath, afraid to move.

"Get in the car," he says, barely opening his mouth. *It's now*

Chapter 3

or never, Ailen, now or never.

I nod as if in agreement, and begin to stand, carefully judging Papa's strength. After a few seconds, convinced I'm going to obey him, he loosens his grip and I duck from under his hand. Fueled by the last of my energy, I fling myself over the barrier. I hold on to the fence and face the water, like hundreds of suicide jumpers have before me, like my mother. I always wanted to feel what it was like for her to stand here, to think about taking her life, to let go.

For the first time in my life, I feel in control. I grin.

Papa rushes to me.

"Take another step and I jump," I say.

"Get back here. What do you think you're doing?"

"What does it look like I'm doing?"

I glance into the distance and see Hunter turn around. Passing cars slow down to a crawl.

"Ailen, sweetie, please get over onto this side. Let's talk about this. You don't really want to do this, do you?" Papa takes another step toward me, his hand outstretched.

"Stop right there!" I yell and edge away, passing my hands over the railing.

Hunter comes up behind my father.

"Ailen, what the fuck? Don't do this, please, don't do this."

Papa turns to Hunter, his rage about to burst.

"This is a family matter, young man. I asked you to leave. It's none of your business."

"But she's my friend."

"I'll make sure she won't be soon."

I try to understand what he means by that, when I hear someone sing my name. The sound comes from the lake. I look down.

"Ailen Bright, silly girl, we're waiting. Come join us. We already got interrupted once, I won't let it happen again. Come on." Canosa waves from 167 feet below, her tangled mass of silver hair bobbing in and out of the water.

"Ailen Bright, do it for your mother, remember? Hurt him. All I need is your soul. You have no use for it. Come on, jump. It's fun," she giggles, and the other sirens join in. Their laughter echoes across the water. I look up at Papa and Hunter to see if they heard. They're engaged in a conversation, their voices reaching me as if from the end of a tunnel.

"You swear? You swear you will do what you said?" I shout, looking down.

"Be one of us," Canosa sings back.

Nothing exists in my mind except the wish to join her. My clammy hands begin to slide. I imagine myself as one of the sirens, beautiful and fierce, my limbs strong, my body womanly, my voice enthralling. I curl my toes, gripping the concrete, and then relax them, ready to fly.

The height awes me. The water is blue. Blue is my favorite color. There is so much of it, and it's so beautiful, so calm.

"Mom, I understand now how you felt. I was wrong. This doesn't look scary at all. This looks like peace."

I hear cars honking, hear Papa shouting and Hunter calling my name; I hear police sirens whine, red and blue lights flashing in my peripheral vision. It's a boring drone against Canosa's ethereal voice, and I think, *What if she was here when my mother jumped? What if she will tell me why we never found her body? Was this the answer I was looking for?* This must be it.

I listen to my heart. It's calm like the lake. And I'm calm too, even happy. This is the best birthday ever, with the biggest present ever. And the best part? I don't have to share it with anyone else. It's all mine.

I turn to take one last look. Police officers, people who stepped out of their cars, they all blur into a wave of collective worry for me, one big canvas of open mouths and wild unbeliev-

Chapter 3

ing eyes. I keep searching for Hunter, but he's gone. My heart sinks. Then I see my father. He's moving toward me with his mouth open, his eyes bulging out, and his fists balled up. There are five feet between us and I'm done looking at him. I'm done trying to anticipate his every mood and shaping my life to his wishes, suppressing everything I feel. I want to burst free of his control, to be weightless, to experience flying. I glance across the road and see several yellow phone boxes that are supposed to help suicide jumpers change their mind. I know the instructions inside by heart, having imagined this moment a thousand times.

LIFT THE PHONE.

I turn toward the water, let go of the rail, and lift my arms.

PRESS RED BUTTON ONCE.

I imagine Papa's face, always full of anger and frustration. I balance, waiting for something, some sign that I need to live. But there is nothing. And I'm done waiting, done hoping.

SPEAK CLEARLY TO OPERATOR.

"Today, I'm sixteen," I say to the sky and look down. "Today is my birthday. And, like my mother, today, I'm going to die."

REPLACE PHONE WHEN FINISHED.

I jump.

Chapter 4

Lake Union

My name is Ailen Bright. I was born at 6:30 a.m. on September 7, 1993, two weeks early, weighing only five and a half pounds, sixteen inches long, head first, delivered by my father in our marble bathtub full of water, my mother giving birth naturally, without pain medication or any professional help. Exactly sixteen years later, I'm leaping to death, at seven in the morning, on September 7, weighing 107 pounds, five feet six inches tall, feet first, escaping my father into a huge basin of water called Lake Union, to meet my mother's fate, on a whim, having used acid and weed as pain medication after rejecting professional help.

And one more fact. Today is a Monday. Suicide rates are highest on Mondays. I'm about to become another number.

All of these thoughts take less than a fraction of a second. Air sucks me into a vortex of mad rush obliterating all thought. A floating sensation gets quickly replaced by sheer terror and an urge to grab on to something, anything, to keep from falling, but my fingers close on nothing. The wind sticks its cold hand

Chapter 4

into my open mouth and I can't make a sound. Funny how your life always starts with a scream, but doesn't always end with one. My arms thrash like the wings of an immature bird, legs climb invisible stairs, ears ring loudly. My heart leaps into my throat and threatens to burst me apart. I see everything and nothing, caught in a blur of sky, water, air, and tears.

Suddenly, I know that I just made the biggest mistake of my life. One minute of fantasy is better than nothing? Whatever gave me this stupid idea? I changed my mind. I want to turn back time, I want someone to save me at the last second, like in the movies. But this is real life, and in real life the surface of the lake rushes at me with inhuman speed.

All this gazing into water, wondering how my mother felt, every single image I conjured about it vanishes. Instead, a few intense questions overwhelm me. *What the hell am I doing? How the hell am I going to survive this? If I press my legs together and enter the water straight as a rod, feet first, will I have a better chance?*

Even that gets replaced by one internal cry: *FUCK THIS SHIT, I DON'T WANNA DIE!*

As if to answer my plea, an irritated voice rises from below. "You could've warned me you were jumping! You're falling right on my head, and I just did my hair. Absolutely no manners. Didn't your mother teach you? Oh that's right. She didn't."

I manage to lower my head against the rushing air and look down, unable to blink the tears away. All I see is five giggling sirens swimming away in a five-point star formation.

Then I hit water.

CRAAACK!

Everything I read about diving from dizzying heights turns out to be true. After sailing through air for only three seconds, I pierce the lake's surface with my body, feet first, at the speed of seventy miles per hour. It doesn't feel like plunging. It doesn't feel like pool diving. It feels like crashing into a rock, solid and hard. My science teacher told me that entering water feet first is the only way to survive a fall from a crazy height like that. Right. Try jumping off a sixteen-story building with the intent to break through concrete, and you'll know how it feels.

My leg bones break. The impact rips off my hoodie and T-shirt, turns out my jean pockets. Smell, sound, taste, sight, touch, all collapse underwater into a tight fist of abrasion that scrapes my skin, shatters my vertebrae, and collapses my lungs. Another line I'd read flashes through my mind. Most suicide jumpers don't die from drowning, they die from the impact. Only then, those who survive drown or die of hypothermia. The fact that I'm thinking this tells me that miraculously, I'm still alive, but not for long.

Water gurgles in my ears. Momentum carries me down, some concentrate of a girl, hard-packed with agony, hurled forty feet deep, to melt in her sorrow at the bottom of the lake and never come up. This is no marble bathtub. There are no rims to grab and pull myself out. This is the end.

Enveloped in white noise and excruciating pain, my mind is blank, an empty box that can't be filled because it stopped being real. Nothing is real, as if time and space ceased to exist, replaced by a strange void. I try pulling myself out of this nothingness, try focusing. Everything that needed to be fixed in my life doesn't need to be fixed anymore. It's perfect, it's absolutely fantastic. All of it. My books, my house, school, Hunter, even my father. Why did I ever think to escape it? I want to keep living, no matter how awful it is at times. But the freezing lake water presses on my eardrums, burns my sinuses, shoots terrible pain through my broken bones.

"Somebody get me out of here!" escapes from my mouth. The words make no noise, only bubbles trailing into murk. I cry out from the sharp pain in my chest. My body is balancing in that place of not moving down anymore and not moving up yet,

Chapter 4

a momentary pause. It's dark. I'm cold, but my skin is on fire, my muscles are mashed into one gigantic bruise. My head feels as if it's become a heavy bronze bell that tolls loudly, and its walls shudder to the rhythm of my still-beating heart.

I try kicking up and moving my arms, when darkness parts and a white figure swims toward me. It looms closer. I find myself face-to-face with Canosa. Her hair resembles a floating white blanket, her wide-set eyes dominate her face, her skin glows softly as if rubbed with a phosphorescent cream. I can't move, I feel paralyzed. She smiles, showing two rows of perfect teeth, too white for this darkness. It's not a happy smile, it's a type of final smile that's full of knowledge, and I choke on premonition. She licks her lips, cups my frozen face in her equally cold hands, and pulls me closer.

Our faces nearly touch. With one hand, she pinches my nose, and with the other, she clamps my mouth shut. As she does it, a little bit of liquid seeps in between my lips. It tastes like an old pond where fish go to die, to rot, to float belly up for birds to feast on.

She turns my face left and right, examining it.

"Jawbone too square, nose too small, all features out of balance. Short forehead, eyes set too close, but a nice blue color. I like that. Eyebrows okay. Small ears. Fine, that'll do. But why on earth did you have to chop off your hair!?"

I'm petrified. Partly because this is the last thing I expected her to say; partly because she told me everything I hate about myself as if it's me talking. And mostly because this is the first time I've heard anyone speak underwater. Momentary curiosity pushes my panic aside. I watch her lips and tongue move freely, with no air bubbles coming out. Every word is amplified, as if spoken into a microphone, yet garbled and slightly distorted. Sound travels four times faster through fluid medium than air. My mind escapes into facts again, but only for a fraction of a second. Lack of air, and an urge to inhale, yanks me back to reality.

I changed my mind, please, let me go. I scream in my head, but my body makes not a single movement of protest. I fall limp in Canosa's hold, mesmerized by her stare, fearing my chest will explode if I don't inhale soon.

She digs her fingers deeper into my skin, and scans my body. Her voice sends vibrations deep inside my ears.

"And no breasts. Fantastic. How do you expect to lure men without breasts? Explain to me, please?"

I want to cover up my pathetic chest, remembering that I'm naked from the waist up, but my arms won't move. Perhaps sensing this, Canosa's grip relaxes and she bites her lip.

"Oh, did I hurt your feelings? I'm sorry. I know how to make you feel better. Let's talk about your jump. That was one big leap, wouldn't you agree? You're a brave girl, I'm so proud of you. How did it make you feel? Was it fun?" She cocks her head to the side. *I wish I had never jumped*, I want to tell her. *If you take me to the surface, I'll never do it again, I swear. Just give me another chance. Please. I don't want to die.*

She's indifferent to my silent plea. She looks behind her and calls out to the other sirens.

"Girls, come over here. Look who I got. What do you think, she'll work out okay?"

I watch with a mix of horror and awe as the other sirens emerge from the depths of the lake and swim closer. At this point, the need to breathe makes me convulse; my brain feels like it is seeping out of my ears. Canosa leers. I'm a freshly caught fish to her, struggling to get off the hook. Oblivious to my thrashing, the sirens join hands and float in a circle akin to a pack of mocking kids at school, about to call me names and make fun of me. Newfound sisters, really? What was I thinking? How much more hopeful, naïve, and needy could I get? They're devious femme fatales who are about to kill me. Panic takes over

Chapter 4

and I let go of my bladder, feeling urine warm my thighs.

"I think she wants to tell us something," Canosa says. "What is it, silly girl? Go ahead, don't be shy, we're all friends. We're your sisters, remember? It's what you told us for years, didn't you? Isn't that what you wanted, to become one of us? Well then, this is what it feels like to be at the bottom of the sea. Get used to it." Her smile transforms into a sinister grin.

The other sirens call out to me and to each other. They clap, which underwater looks more like doing weird upper arm exercises.

"We're getting another sister!"

"I always wanted one."

"Shut up, Pisinoe. Who cares about what you want? She told me she wanted to be a siren 'cause she likes my breasts."

"Don't talk to me like that. She told me she likes my curly hair, that's why."

"No, she doesn't!"

"She does too!"

"Shut up, all of you, you're making my head hurt!" Canosa yells.

I watch the sirens shift up and laugh, pointing their fingers.

"She's almost ready," Canosa says. "Now, Ailen Bright, you'll give me your soul. I hope it tastes all right, I hope it tastes like..." She swallows.

Tastes like what?

"...but never mind."

Canosa lets go of my nose and mouth, and I gulp water involuntarily while someone grabs my feet and pulls me down. My feet touch the slimy bottom of the lake. At the same time, stinky water rushes into my lungs putrefying everything in its flow. Gray light begins seeping in shafts through the darkness. Someone pulls my head up. Two light bulbs blind me. No, it's not light bulbs, it's Canosa's eyes. Two gazing projectors—cold flickering fluorescents, with a bluish tint to them. She locks her gaze with mine and begins to sing.

> *"We live in the meadow,*
> *But you don't know it.*
> *Our grass is your sorrow,*
> *But you won't show it."*

It's the same song, but it feels as if she sings it with more force, directing it to some being trapped inside my chest. My soul. I want to turn myself inside out and scratch, to get rid of this impossible itch. I notice that I don't feel much of anything anymore, no pain from broken bones, no freezing water, no urge to breathe, no headache. I'm simply numb.

The other sirens float around me, glowing, grotesquely twisted in motion with their arms and legs stretched out, their eyes directed at me. Greedy. I'm fresh meat to them. In this darkness, I notice how everything about them is faintly glowing. I shudder.

> *"Give us your pain,*
> *Dip in our song.*
> *Notes afloat,*
> *Listen and love..."*

They huddle near me, reaching out, until Pisinoe, the youngest, touches my arm and then tears her hand away as if in fear. I frown. Pisinoe smiles widely and touches me again. As if that was a signal, the other sirens begin poking me, their hair floating, eyes glistening, fingers trembling in lust. Canosa keeps singing.

Perhaps emboldened by her indifference, the sirens pinch me, stroke me, squeeze me, and muss up my hair, as if I'm the

Chapter 4

most adorable baby doll they've ever seen. I gulp in horror because I still don't feel their touch. All this time Canosa floats directly in front of me, her gaze unbroken.

> *"We wade in the lake.*
> *Why do you frown?*
> *Our wish is your wake.*
> *Why do you drown?"*

Deciding that her sisters have had enough fun, Canosa snatches me away from them and holds me by the waist, peering deep inside my very core, willing my soul to come up. It beats against my clamped teeth, and I know that I won't be able to contain it much longer before it pushes my mouth open.

> *"Give us your soul,*
> *Breathe in our song.*
> *Words apart,*
> *Listen and love.*
> *Listen and love.*
> *Listen and love."*

I watch a stream of milky substance drift from my mouth and into Canosa's. Her face becomes immobile; her eyes turn blank like two silver spoons licked clean. All goes still. The other sirens stop moving and float quietly.

> *"We stir up your hope,*
> *Calm down and let go.*
> *Our love is your slope,*
> *Slide here, don't forego."*

Canosa raises her voice higher. It trails through the water, amplified by the lake, reminiscent of a thousand violins filling the space with mint that can calm a sore throat or a high fever. I want it to never end. I'm not scared anymore. The water clears up, and my soul trails through it like a tendril of smoke.

> *"Give us your life,*
> *End in our song.*
> *Because you*
> *Listen and love.*
> *Listen and love.*
> *Listen and love."*

I retch and watch the end of my soul escape into Canosa's mouth. She sneers and gulps it up, licks her lips, closes her eyes, then burps. Our gaze broken, I become emptiness, devoid of any thought or feeling. I hear a strange echo, my soul thrashing in a foreign ribcage. It sounds as gentle as rustling book pages, with undertones from my favorite songs and dripping water. It sounds...tart.

Canosa lets go of me, spreads her arms over her head, and hollers a guttural, painful, piercing cry. It leaves her mouth and enters mine, turning water to milk once again. Its terrible taste makes me want to throw up, yet it forces itself in, frosting my trachea, turning my chest to ice, and making my body feel heavy and swollen. This must be a part of her soul, given to mutate me, to turn me into a siren. Before I can think anything else, her voice fills me to a bursting point, as if someone turned the volume up, louder, louder. I can't stand the vibration, it's about to pop my ribcage, pulsing to the rhythm of my heart.

"Aaaaaah!" I cry out.

The skin behind my ears tears apart. Desire to get rid of the noise overpowers my physical pain and pours out into another yelp. Now the muscles behind my ears tear open. I wail, shaking

Chapter 4

the water around me. And then I realize that I just made a sound underwater without breathing and I promptly shut my mouth, astounded, processing what I'm feeling.

"Pity I can't have you for breakfast every morning, Ailen Bright. You taste pretty good, just like I expected. A sweet soul-cake of innocence, sprinkled with bits of hope, made from scratch. Delicious...and tart." Canosa burps again, covering her mouth. "Excuse me."

Everything she says sounds impossibly loud. I hear every vowel, every movement of her lips. The pressing and the rolling of her tongue. The gushing of water between her words. And my soul. It rustles softly inside her chest. I clasp my ears to shut it out, not feeling the freezing water anymore or my bones or my skin or my lungs, yet strangely suffocating.

"Go ahead, don't be shy. Inhale," Canosa says.

I try. Water cools my throat and exists behind my ears. I inhale more water, and it sort of chills me, spreading a pleasant calm through my chest and exiting through...gills? I raise my hand to touch them, two raw wounds that have been recently opened. Two smooth slits under my fingers, rhythmically opening and closing.

"All right, then, you're done. I think we need to make this a proper occasion. Wouldn't you agree, girls? Happy birthday, Ailen Bright. Welcome to our coveted siren family. Well, we welcome *you*, but *you* are not part of it yet." Canosa spreads her arms wide and attempts a bow, but floats upside down instead to the snickering of the other sirens. They swim up with the clear intent of touching me again.

"Give her space. Shoo," Canosa says.

The sirens float a little way away, unhappy yet obedient.

"Take a look at yourself, do you like what you see? Much better, I think. A far cry from that flat-chested, broken looking girl with unruly hair, I'd say."

I lift my arms. They're white. I wiggle my fingers, one by one, and try flexing my feet. Everything seems to be working as before, even better. I appear to be a faded self, just a few grades of saturation lost. The water feels lukewarm, which means I'm as cold as a fish. I reach again behind my ears, unable to believe that actual water is sprouting through my gills.

"This feels weird," I say and clasp my mouth, astounded at the power it emits. "I'm a siren. I'm a siren. I'm not dead. I'm a siren." I want to keep mumbling this over and over again, to believe it. "I can breathe underwater. I can talk underwater. I'm a siren. I'm not dead. And I've got breasts," I say, and swallow.

"What's the problem, you don't like them?" Canosa floats near me and peers into my eyes.

"I do, I do," I quickly respond, afraid she'll take them back. I wonder why I don't hear my soul anymore? It's as if she's absorbed it.

"Good. I thought you'd approve."

Just as I'm opening my mouth to ask her about my soul, a distant warble distracts me. It comes from above.

"Everything is so loud. What's that noise?" I say.

"It's food. People's souls. Hear it?"

I concentrate. There are car honks, rain patter, pumping hearts, breathing, and, above all, a multitude of noises full of things people do: music they listen to, things they say, the mechanical whirr of tools, a clinking of household items, an occasional swish of a paintbrush, a baby's cries, the smacking of a football, dog barks, and a million more. They mix into one breathing organism, fluctuating in its pitch, overlapping and creating a cacophony of impossible beauty—a pattern of human existence itself. Wishes, hopes, and dreams, orchestrated into a gentle concert that is both overwhelming and mouthwatering. I begin detecting flavors.

"Will I be able to taste them? Does every human soul have a

Chapter 4

taste?" I ask, instantly shrinking, remembering how I'm not supposed to ask stupid questions lest Canosa gets mad at me again.

"Babies are my favorite; their souls are so sweet, sweeter than candy," Canosa says, then grins.

"Babies?" I recoil. "Why would you eat a baby?"

"Why not? They'll grow up and die anyway. Would you rather live in pain for years and years or live happy for a few months and die without knowing what got you? Cause of death: lullaby. That's how I wanted to go." She looks through me, at something distant.

"So, if you converted me, then who converted—" I begin, when Pisinoe pinches my arm, hard. I hold down a yelp of pain and stare at her. She and the others glare at me, fingers to their lips.

"Anyway, we can't stay here for long," Canosa says, ignoring me. "Police are about to arrive to look for your lovely body. And I don't like their souls. They leave an oily aftertaste. Ugh."

At the word "taste," tightness spreads across my chest, nagging at me like a stomachache, except it's rather a yearning for fullness, a need for sound to fill an empty chamber.

"I think I'm hungry," I say, licking my lips and looking up.

Chapter 5

Lake's Bottom

An emergency flare drops into the water above. A tiny dot, it glows pink. I'm amazed I can see it sparkle and hear it fizz so clearly. Police use flares like this to mark the spot where a suicide jumper landed, so they can locate the body. That means they think I'm dead. They must've dropped it from the bridge, because Seattle Police Harbor Patrol arrives on the scene barely a minute later. The jittering whop-whop-whop of a boat's engine threatens to puncture my eardrums. I curse my heightened siren senses. Ailen Bright, reborn. It's what I wanted, right?

Deep inside, something sinister is grinning. That something tells me, *Try it out.* That something nags at me, *This is so cool. I bet you could do all kinds of stuff now. I bet you could crush bones between fingers, scream at a level that can shatter glass, swim anywhere you want, chase submarines, siphon entire oceans through your gills, charm people with your song, and kill, kill, kill. Just think what you could do to your father.*

I grit my teeth, ball up my hands in fists, and spread my legs

Chapter 5

wide, imitating a warrior stance. The sirens watch me silently; Pisinoe throws two thumbs up and Raidne winks at me, chewing on a curl of her hair. I wish there was a mirror. I wish Hunter could see me. His face would light up and split into that crooked grin that I love so much. He'd ask me how the hell I did it, and I'd tell him. I'd tell him all about it and we'd share a joint.

Two divers leap over the boat's side and plunge into the lake. They begin descending, trailing two streams of bubbles. Their souls are a racket of noises, amplified by water and my heightened hearing. One is a mix of baseball hits, beer bottle clinks, and what sounds like cracking crab shells, with a touch of ukulele on top. It sounds altogether...acidic. The other one emits something like a breaking of potted plants, gun shots, and a whizzing electric shaver, all on a base of bad shower singing. Rubbery. No, oily. Just like Canosa said. Forgetting everything, I crouch to push off toward the surface.

Canosa grabs my arm. "Hang on. Where do you think you're going?"

"Um, I don't know. I just..." I frown. "To eat?"

The sirens laugh; Canosa hushes them.

"Not so fast, silly girl, we're not done here. Not yet. If you want to be a part of our family, you've got to earn it," Canosa says. The sirens huddle away and whisper to each other, Ligeia slightly apart from them, in her own thoughts.

"But you said—" I begin.

"Hush!" She raises her right index finger. "I promised you *will* be one of us—a siren. But I didn't say you'd be part of our family."

"Sorry. I thought...well, if I wanted to be accepted into your family, how would I earn it then?"

"Wanted to? *Wanted to?*" Canosa stomps her foot and a small cloud of sand particles floats up. "Girls, did you hear that? She doesn't think we're good enough for her. After all these years, she's turned out to be a traitor."

"To hell with this, you know it's bullshit," Ligeia speaks up, her lips pressed into a line. She's taller than all of them, taller even than Canosa.

"Shut up!" Canosa shrieks.

I expect Ligeia to duck her head like the others, but she only shrugs and floats a short distance away.

Canosa is fuming. Her nostrils flare, water gushing in and out of them. "What is wrong with you? Aren't you grateful? I went through the trouble of giving you what you want, didn't I?" she shrieks, directly into my face.

"Yeah, you did," I manage.

"Good." As if someone flipped a switch, she's suddenly smiling. "I'm still not telling you my secret, until you prove worthy of it." She turns on her heels, rousing a little cloud of sand.

"Wait, where are you going? What secret?" I reach out to her, vaguely aware that the divers changed direction and are now swimming away. Bummer.

As if expecting my move, Canosa peeks over her shoulder and turns around. The sirens watch her. I get the feeling that they do this a lot. She's the star of the show and they're the audience. Any time one of them fails to play along, they fall victim to her anger. Lovely arrangement.

"Perhaps I know what happened to your mother."

I didn't think I'd ever feel frozen again in my life, yet here I float, frozen to my bones. In this instant, I decide to play along, to do anything she wants and pay any price to get her to tell me.

"You know what happened to my mother? What? Tell me, what? Please, I've been searching for an answer for six years. Oh, please, Canosa, tell me, I'll do anything you want."

"Really?" Her eyes flash with greed. "Hmmm, let me think." She taps a finger on her pressed lips.

"How about, for starters, you kill a siren hunter." She flashes

Chapter 5

me a row of teeth.

A helicopter flips its blades above us. The rickety noise is bearable; I seem to be adjusting.

"Where are your manners, girl, did you hear what I said?"

"Siren hunter. There is a siren hunter out there?"

"Oh, yes. And you're the perfect siren to kill him," Canosa hisses.

"Why?" I ask.

All sirens converge around me and begin swimming, singing out to me.

> *"Kill him.*
> *Kill him."*

Their calls become a chant.

> *"Kill the siren hunter.*
> *Sing his mind away.*
> *Watch his flayed skin shrivel.*
> *Leave his bones to rot in a pile.*
> *Bury him in the sweet siren meadow."*

They swirl and swirl. Their spinning makes me dizzy.

"How? Do I just eat his soul?" I ask.

"A siren hunter has no soul, stupid."

"We can't hear him because of it."

"It burned awaaay."

"He hunts us when we feed, spying on us, catching us when we're most vulnerable."

"He scares me."

"I think he's a pervert!"

I feel lightheaded at the amount of information. "If I have to kill a siren hunter, I'll do it. Just tell me what to do and how

I can find him."

Abruptly, the sirens stop spinning.

"Oh, that part is easy. It's your father," Canosa says.

"What?" My knees give out and I slowly float down to the bottom, sitting there with my mouth open. "My father is a siren hunter?"

"Duh! Stop asking stupid questions, silly girl. Will you ever learn to think before you talk?" Canosa swims up to me.

"But, my father. It's impossible. Why the hell would he do that?" I try to find an argument, but somehow all of this makes sense. His hatred for women, his favorite way to drill me about what women were made for, and his favorite answer to that question about them being only good for hauling water. His hatred of noises, and of all things wet. His constant yelling at me to shut up whenever I sang.

"Wait a second, did you turn my mother into a siren when she jumped off the bridge?"

"Will you kill him or not?" Canosa says, as if she didn't hear my question.

"Did you—" I begin, when she squeezes her fingers around my neck, choking me, and leans her face to my ear.

"If you want to play along with us, silly girl, do what I asked you to do. You kill your dear papa, and I'll tell you what happened to your mom. Do you understand?" She slips her fingers into my gills and a sharp pain sears through my body.

I nod.

Canosa lets me go. Staring up at them all, I'm torn. Here is my chance. I've never admitted my darkest secrets, my most gruesome ideas about what I'd do to my father, if only I could.

My hate collides with whatever is left of my childish love. I tether on the edge of indecision, hearing my heart beat like crazy, balling up handfuls of sand.

I love him. I hate him. But does he love me? Did he ever?

Chapter 5

Was there a moment maybe, when I was born, when he delivered me, or when I was a little baby?

As if sensing my doubts, Canosa asks, "Why are you doubting yourself, silly girl?"

Didn't you ever wonder where he goes on those long boat trips? Didn't you ever ask yourself why he goes all alone? Why he never took you with him?

"He hunts us; he wants to kill us all. Ailen Bright, not so bright. We're sirens and he's a siren hunter. We exist to kill each other. That's our game."

I look at Canosa's face, forever young. I know why killing myself would never have hurt him like I wanted. He doesn't love me. Never did, never will. He never loved my mother, either. He can't. *Of course he can't—he doesn't have a soul!* Another thought strikes me.

"So, you guys are saying that a siren hunter doesn't have a soul, which makes sense, because otherwise sirens could hear him. But how did he become a siren hunter?"

"Too many questions, silly girl. We'll talk after you do what I've asked you to do," Canosa says.

"So you know?"

"I'm tired of this." Canosa swims away from me. "See you."

The others follow closely behind her, leaving me swimming alone in the murk, unsure what to do next. I do know I'm starving. My chest grumbles with a rolling emptiness. It's tugging at my core, and I turn my attention upward.

"I have no idea how to feed!" I say to nobody and to myself at the same time. And she didn't tell me how I'm supposed to kill a siren hunter. If he doesn't have a soul, then how the hell am I supposed to sing it out? Does this mean that all this time my father had no soul? I shudder at the thought. But something tells me this is a test. I'm expected to figure this out on my own. And I suddenly do, I see it clearly. Either I kill him, or he kills me. My choice is obvious.

I propel myself upward with a single kick, amazed at my new power, then pause just below the surface. Where do I go now? I suppose Papa is still on the bridge, but if what Canosa says is true, I won't hear him because he has no soul. I wonder if Canosa turned my mother into a siren. Then, when Papa was looking for her, she turned him into a siren hunter. No, that doesn't make any sense. Why would a siren turn anyone into a siren hunter?

My thoughts get interrupted by the sound of a human soul, to the north, on the Fremont side of the shore. There are other sounds around it, but this one stands out. On impulse, I swim toward it. I hear the drizzle of the rain and the splashing of paddles. Someone is rowing out on a boat.

Curiosity wins, and I inch closer. It sounds delicious. A mix of homey sounds, the clanking of dishes at dinnertime, and the chirping of birds from behind a window, slippers shuffling across a parquet floor, a guitar, and some kind of rumble, a mechanical rumble. Delicious was the wrong word for this. I think this sounds sweet, sweet like a baby, like what Canosa said about babies' souls.

I run my tongue over my lips, and anticipation makes me shake. I'm very hungry now.

"I'll show you what women were made for, Papa. Just you wait. I'll feed first, and then I'll be after you. I bet you miss me, oh, I bet you're crying."

Fish swim past me, their souls ringing like bicycle bells. Jing-jing. I wonder if all animals have souls and if I can maybe eat them too.

The rowboat is closing in on me fast, as if the person in it knows exactly where I am. That creeps me out, but then I hear the soul's sound with new clarity, and forget everything I ever knew or wanted to know. No sound exists in the world except

Chapter 5

this.

It's familiar and warm, like home, like hands, like breakfast. A bit like Vivaldi's "Summer" concerto. Everything I hear coming from this soul feels sweet and warm like a freshly baked homemade apple pie, like comfort food. I decide I don't care who it is, I have to try it.

The boat is ten feet away. A few seconds, and it will be upon me. The soul bursts into such a sweet melody that it wipes every thought from my mind but one: *I want to feed.*

I tense and close my eyes, to concentrate.

One. Two. Three.

The boat slides directly above me, its hull nearly touching my face.

I don't know how a siren is supposed to feed! The thought enters my brain a second too late. It all happens on some newfound instinct. I'm not human anymore. I'm a newborn siren. I strike.

Chapter 6

Brights' Boat

I tense and kick, leaping into the air with inhuman speed, shrieking mid-jump to scare and arrest my target. But the second my head pierces the lake's surface, noise, smells, light, all hit me with unexpected intensity and I promptly shut up. The sky is too bright, the air is too warm. Raindrops are too sharp, and the sounds are too many. There is screeching, talking, whirring, honking. I cross my arms over my face for protection. With my eyes closed, scared to see who it is I'm about to kill, I hang midair for a split second, and fall. I land within inches of someone warm.

It's a he—I don't know how I know, I simply do. As if done waiting for an opportune moment, the melody of his soul hits me full force, a beautiful harmony broken up by a hinge of pain. I can taste emotions in its vibrations. Surprise. Fear. Awe? Is this how it's supposed to be, some kind of killer admiration?

Perched like a bird, and holding the sides of the rowboat for balance, the first few verses of "We Can't Be Apart" by my favorite band, Siren Suicides, rings from my lips. I don't know how I

Chapter 6

decided to sing exactly this, but I always listen to it when I miss Hunter; it makes me ache and feel comfortable at the same time.

"There you are,
Without me you cry.
I surround you,
Love me or I die..."

I feel human warmth roll over me in waves of breath; it makes me hungry. All logic squandered, my new primitive side drives to push for more, but something is blocked. There is no flow. I don't know what flow there is supposed to be, but the process seems to have gone wrong. Whoever it is I decided to feed on is trying to say something. I don't want to hear it or I'll lose control.

"I adore you.
See me or I fly.
I dream of you.
Dream with me, don't lie..."

His soul reverberates to my rhythm, tunes in and morphs into a submissive harmony. I imagine it happening. I imagine bending it, telling it to shed its host, pulse to my beat, slink inside of me. I imagine the warmth filling my chest, unclenching an agony of hunger, replacing my void with fresh soul. What's really happening is... nothing. Nothing happens. Something is wrong, I'm doing something wrong. Still, perhaps out of sheer stubbornness, the siren in me urges me to keep trying.

"Can you hold my hand,
Can you hold my heart?
Can you hold my soul,

I can't be apart..."

A warm hand touches mine and I choke on the last note, nearly shrieking, hunger piercing me with a jolt. I open my eyes. Light sears my retinas with excruciating clarity. Visions filter through a kaleidoscope of colors and shapes. I blink through tears. My song dies.

"Hunter?"

Because it's Hunter's hand that's touching mine, Hunter's face that's blinking inches away from mine, Hunter's breath that warms me. I'm both horrified and ecstatic to see him.

"*Fuck!* I thought you were some random guy, I almost killed you," I say.

Hunter grins his crooked smile, with that familiar dimple in his right cheek. He looks nonchalant, as if we just met up on the Aurora Bridge and decided to go for a boat ride to observe rain from the open lake on a cloudy Monday morning. A fancy new way to skip school.

"What the hell are you doing here, in..." I notice the finely polished paddles, the maroon paint of the bench Hunter is sitting on. "...my father's boat?"

"Um...being snuffed out by a siren?" He swallows hard.

I realize both my T-shirt and my hoodie are missing, having been torn off on violent contact with the water. The only item of clothing I have on are my favorite skin-tight, faded jeans, soaked against my skin. Which means that I'm naked from the waist up.

"Oh my God, I forgot. Stop staring!" I hug myself, covering my chest with my arms.

"I wasn't looking, I swear." He gulps and focuses intently on his rain jacket zipper. In one swift motion, he unzips it, takes it off, and throws it to me, pulling the hood of the cotton sweatshirt under it up. Raindrops quickly stitch dark dots on his shoulders.

Chapter 6

"But what about you?"

"I'll be fine."

"No, you won't. You'll catch a cold or something."

"Ailen, we live in Seattle. I'm pretty sure I can handle a little rain. Put on the jacket already. We're running a risk of being spotted."

"Oh," I say. I've been so preoccupied with Hunter and my own new existence, that I completely forgot about the possibility of witnesses staring down at us from the bridge. Not to mention the Seattle Police Department Harbor Patrol and their motor launch, gently bobbing about twenty yards away, or their divers.

I quickly ball up the jacket and press it against my chest. "Turn away or close your eyes. I'll tell you when you can look."

"All right, all right." Hunter raises his hands and theatrically puts them over his eyes. "See, I'm not looking."

"Don't peek!"

"Put the damn jacket on!"

I thrust my arms inside the sleeves, run the zipper all the way to the top, and stick my hands into the pockets.

"I'm done." By now we're south of the Aurora Bridge, having drifted off past the marina and out of earshot of the commotion. Red and blue lights flash on top of the bridge, and a couple of officers peer down from the side where I jumped. If they look from the other side, they will undoubtedly see us. Further north, a Harbor Patrol boat floats idle. I seem to be taking in noises better, as well as colors and smells. Out of the depth of my sluggish memory, a question surfaces.

"Wait a second, how did you know I'm a siren?" I turn and look Hunter in the eyes; he quickly glances up as if to check out the rain, then looks at me, steady.

"Who else could you be, to survive a drop like that?"

His answer comes too fast, without any doubt or surprise on his face, as if he expected me to ask.

"You say it like you knew it ahead of time."

"No, no, not at all. Are you kidding, how could I know? I mean, there I was, strolling along the bridge this fine morning..."

"Yeah, what exactly were you doing on the bridge? It's not like it's a new way to walk to school, is it?"

"I tell you what, let's get out of here and talk on the way, I'll explain everything. Cool?" He grabs the paddles and plunges them rhythmically on either side of the boat, heading east and deeper into Lake Union.

I open my mouth, swarmed with a sudden urge to ask a million questions, but not knowing where to begin. I'm shaking from the sinking understanding that I am, indeed, alive—and a siren at that. I'm tempted to jump into the water and test how fast I can swim. At the same time, hunger raises its ugly head again and I try to push it down, because Hunter's soul sounds too tempting. I take a deep breath. So my lungs work on land, and the gills work underwater. Nice.

"First, where exactly are we going?"

"I don't know, we'll figure it out. Let's dock the boat somewhere and catch a bus to my place. The brakes on my truck have gone bye-bye, so—"

"Fine, that works."

"Do you have any shoes?"

"No, I'll be okay barefoot. Don't you change the subject! Did my father give you his boat, to look for me? Is that how you got it? Did he tell you where to find me?" As I talk, I think back to what Canosa said about my father. He is a siren hunter. He must have known that if my body wasn't found, I've probably turned.

"No, I sorta...borrowed it."

"Borrowed it?" I repeat.

"I'll return it, I swear."

"Bullshit. And," I say, before he has a chance to come up

Chapter 6

with a lie, "somehow, you knew exactly where to find me, as if you knew I was being turned into a siren. And yesterday you were telling me all those stories about sirens—girls next door and other shit like that. I thought you were stoned out of your mind! Yet, here we are. I'm a real siren now, and you're helping me run away. How do you explain this?"

"Well, let's see here." He lets go of the paddles for a minute and scratches his head. With my new senses I can almost see steam rising from his worked-up muscles, warm under his cotton hoodie, now an unidentifiable shade of wet rug. "For one, you don't strike me as the Fremont Troll's wife..."

"Stop it. It's not funny, okay? I'm being serious. I could've killed you." Talking is easier now, I'm adjusting. My ears have stopped hurting and objects have stopped looking as if they were traced with a neon marker.

"That would've been a pity. I'd feel so sorry for myself. Poor Hunter Crossby, snuffed out by a siren."

He gasps for air and rubs his forehead, then, miraculously, he breaks into a grin. "Dude, that was awesome. Totally worth wetting my pants. Hey, I got something for you."

"What do you mean?"

He starts fishing in his jeans pocket and pulling out a crumpled envelope made of blue recycled paper. He places it on his right knee and attempts to flatten the creases with the palm of his hand, which proves to be a futile effort because the paper gets wet in the rain.

Hunter pushes the envelope at me. "Happy birthday, Ailen." He peeks up at my face. "Is that a smile I see?"

"Go away." I press my lips together, still trying to be mad, but unable to. My heart's racing, and one thought pounds in my head: *He didn't forget. He got me a birthday present!*

I hear my fingers touch the envelope, hear the slightest movement of skin against paper fiber. Over this gentle rustle, I hear Hunter's soul, the impossible sound of happiness wrapped in that homey, comfortable feeling. And in the background, I hear the rolling waves, the drizzle of rain, boat and car traffic, and, above it all, the buzz of human souls, each amplified by the open sky over the lake.

"Are you gonna keep guessing or will you rip it open already?" Hunter says, tapping his foot.

"Stop it! It's not that." I cradle the envelope to my belly, trying to think of how to explain. "It's just hard. I'm hungry. And you're..." I fall silent,

"...so sweet and delicious?"

"How the hell did you know?" The racket of the patrol boat's motor echoes off the lake's surface, moving toward us. Another noise joins it, a mechanical purr that I know all too well, though my father never took me on any of his trips. His boat. I strain to see where the noise is coming from, and it seems as though they're speeding along the shore just behind the Gas Works Park's half-island. That means, in another couple of minutes, they will pass it, turn the corner, and see us.

We look at each other.

"That's my father's motor boat, hear it?"

"Yeah, and the Harbor Patrol." Hunter grabs the paddles. "We are so toast."

Chapter 7

Blake Island

I look at Hunter but I don't see him. A brilliant image of my father's face flashes through my mind, asking me his favorite question, *Tell me what women were made for, go on.* My legs seem to fill with lead, my stomach flips up and down. A familiar fear makes me want to die rather than face him again. For as long as I can remember, he would ask me this question, and I'd always stumble, not knowing what to say, not understanding what he meant. He'd wait until I was filled with humiliation, and then offer his answer, *To carry water on their backs.* If I asked why, he'd slap me, and say, *Because back in time, if you had weakness in your character, you were forced to deliver water. And women are weak. I want you to fight it, to grow strong, to do better in life than that, do you understand?* And I'd nod, afraid to anger him any further. *I want you to stop being servile, to learn to protest.* But I'd always just shrink further, which would anger him more, until his hand would hurt and he'd leave me be, silently crying.

"They'll be here in a couple of minutes. Three minutes, tops," Hunter says, breathing heavily from rowing. I look at him, not remembering who he is, or where we are, or what's happening.

"Huh?" I say, blinking. Reality rushes at me and I realize I'm clutching the blue envelope Hunter gave me, still unopened, as if it's a rope thrown to me overboard a ship and I'll die if I let go. I quickly stuff it into the rain jacket pocket and try to act normal. "Three minutes, you said?" While I say it, I try to remember who *they* are and why I should be worried. Then I hear the engines and the world rights itself. Panic replaces my wonder, but before it has time to flourish, a strange tranquility calms me. I remember I'm not a weak girl anymore. I'm a siren, and I can do wicked things. *You just wait, Papa, I'll show you what women were made for.*

"More like two, now," Hunter says.

"Don't worry, I think I can handle them. At least I'd like to try and see what I can do, but I have a feeling this is going to be good. This is going to be fun," I say and flash Hunter a forced smile.

"Fun? You're going to take on a Harbor Patrol boat full of cops and have fun?" He chuckles, raising his eyebrows and questioning me with his eyes.

"What, you don't believe I can?"

"You just tried, unsuccessfully, taking on a kid sitting alone in a rowboat, so I'm sure this will be easy." He waves dismissively toward the approaching boats. "Take your time, go ahead." He continues rowing, shaking from adrenaline, his heart pounding like crazy. His grin fades, his eyes focus on me, and his arms move in one fluid motion. We're advancing at a turtle's pace compared to the motorized boats approaching.

My heart falls. This is Hunter's favorite trick to talk me out of doing something stupid. Paint a picture of a gruesome outcome and then nudge me on, knowing that I'll start doubting myself and eventually agree with him.

"I hate you, because you're right." I bite my lip.

Chapter 7

I can hear them. Both boats have sailed past the peninsula and are clearly on their way to get us. They're closing in fast, perhaps twenty yards away or so. An incomprehensible headache pounds a spike into my head. Great. I'm supposed to kill my father so that Canosa will tell me what happened to my mom, yet here I am, fleeing.

"Fine, you win," I say, and drop my eyes.

What a coward, always running, never daring to face my fears. I promise myself that, one day, I will.

Harbor Patrol is advancing on us, my father's boat just behind it. My father's boat is three times bigger, a sleek Pershing 64 made by Ferretti—Italian, of course. It's more like a stylish bullet than a boat; a pleasure for the eye, with a maroon inscription on it that reads: *Talia*. My mother's name. He bought the boat when they met, and named it after her. Then they got married, and honeymooned in Italy for Christmas.

Hunter is talking but I can't make out what he is saying. I look at him and through him, hear him and don't hear him.

"Ailen?" He snaps fingers in front of my face; I don't move.

"Come on, Ailen!" he shouts. I don't blink, mesmerized by the advancing boat, like a deer caught in headlights, paralyzed, understanding that I'll never be a part of my previous life again, that I'm dead.

"Ailen, we're not gonna make it if you sit like this, do you hear me? Ailen! *Ailen!*" he yells in my face.

Ailen. It's a boy's name. My father picked it out, because in Old English it means "made of oak." It meant strength to him, only I was a surprise. He wanted a son.

I feel a tear silently roll down my cheek. Hunter pauses, takes a deep breath, wipes the tear off my cheek, and holds up my face. A wave of hunger sweeps me.

"Hey, you okay? Listen, we've got to get in the water and swim to the shore, do you hear me? You're a siren, for Christ's sake, stop acting like you're freaking stupefied!"

I force myself to focus on Hunter, terrified by my desire to drink his soul. All of this is too much. The sounds, Hunter's touch, the hunger. All I want is to get away from here, as far away as possible, to somewhere colorless, tasteless, and quiet. To hide under a rock. Disappear.

"Shit!" Beads of sweat roll off Hunter's forehead as he leans over me. I don't remember how I slid to the bottom. "Don't you pass out on me now, breathe! In and out, in and out." I breathe, and hear the boat engines. Someone is shouting into a loudspeaker off the patrol boat to our left, announcing themselves and asking us if we're okay. To our right my father's boat levels with us. I can't see him, but I can hear him take quick steps out of the cockpit, through the saloon, and onto the deck. He leans over the rail and I see his face, set in a strange mix of pain and anger, dark against the milky sky. Our eyes lock. I gasp for air, trembling, shaking my head *No!*

"I'm not coming home, Papa," I say. "I don't want to go back there. And you can't make me, I'm a siren now."

My breaths come out in sharp draws, fast, faster.

Then I see father raise his hand, and, like a signal, my body seems to take over. The siren in me, she drives me. I touch the lake's surface, ignoring Hunter's swearing, Papa's repeated shouting, and a police officer's voice through his loudspeaker. Except for the lulling sound of water, all noise vanishes into a long tunnel, far away.

My fingers are wet, then my hands, wrists, and arms up to my elbows. I feel the cool water. It calms me. I dive deep into its rhythm, letting my arms hang and lightly bob on the waves, my eyes gazing into the deep blue liquid. I listen to the lake's vibration; it hums to my bloodstream, reaches my heart, answers its beats. And I answer back, humming.

I begin with a low drone, deep from within my chest, blend-

Chapter 7

ing with the gentle rush of the wind and the chirping of morning birds. It grows stronger, fueled by pain, with wings like a swan, and lands into the lake's sorrow. It understands me; we speak the same language. I feel like it nods. I nod in return. And then it hums back. Together, with the lake, I create motion.

Perhaps mesmerized by this, the rain stops.

The rowboat begins to slide forward, between the Harbor Patrol and my father's yacht. I take a breath and hum more. No words are needed. The lake hums with me, and I feel a stream of energy passing through us. The water's surface becomes a corridor of speed and the rowboat happily glides down it. Foam sprays my face in a shower of droplets. Going from a speed of three knots to twenty in a few seconds, it feels like flying.

"Whoa! This is fucking awesome! We've lost them, look!" I hear Hunter yell to me from behind, over the noise of rushing wind. "How the hell are you doing this?"

His question interrupts my flow and I abruptly stop humming. Still, it takes me a moment to get back to reality and focus on what he asked. The rowboat instantly slows down and we pass through a shadow from the Ballard Bridge that's blocking the sky above us. I lift my upper body, twist, and sit up facing Hunter.

"I don't know. It just sort of came out on its own. But you interrupted it."

"Shit, I'm sorry. I didn't mean to." Hunter works at righting his hair, but it only bunches up on top of his head.

Another two and a half miles and we'll make it to Shilshole Bay. After that, I'll find us somewhere to land and we'll have to escape on foot, somehow.

I take time to breathe. The sky clears from behind patches of clouds. The wind picks up and small waves break against the boat's body, swaying it gently.

"Would you be able to do it again?" Hunter asks.

"I think I can talk to the water. I'm not sure how though, I just kinda feel it..." I trail off, searching for some kind of answer.

"Awesome. Can you talk to it right now? Like, tell it to get us out of here? *Now*?" Hunter hugs himself, shuddering. His cotton hoodie is wet and sticks to his chest, his jeans soaked from the water's spray.

"Oh my God, you're wet!" I want to reach out to him, but stop myself. I realize that the closer I am to him, the better I can feel the warmth of his breath, which has the effect of a freshly prepared meal wafting off its aroma toward a hungry person. I drop my hands into my lap.

"I'm fine. Do you think you can keep us moving?"

"Where?"

"I don't care where, anywhere!"

"Wait, why are you so eager to get away?"

"I was rescuing you," he says.

"Then why didn't you simply hand me over to police or to my father?" I ask, while carefully monitoring my hunger.

"Huh," he chuckles. "Like I had a choice? You started your humming thing, and..." He grins, and I see a flash of mischief deep in his eyes, maybe for a split second. "Can you hear them at all?"

I focus intently for a couple of seconds. "I can't hear them, but that doesn't mean they're not close," I say finally. "Hold on, I'll get us moving." I tense to turn into position, then look at Hunter again. "Wait...you have absolutely no idea *where* you want to go?"

"Well, I was thinking...we could go to the Ballard Locks and hide there," he says with hope.

"That's not very far."

"Yeah, I know. At least it'll give us a break and we'll have some time to think about what to do next, right?"

Trembling, I turn and lay down on my stomach to become

Chapter 7

one with the boat, its sides pressed into my armpits, my head positioned over its nose.

I touch the water and try to concentrate. The lake responds like it was waiting for my command, obedient, happy to oblige. It feels like touching the strings of a well-tuned guitar that's waiting to be played, still warm from the previous song. Instantly, it vibrates to the rhythm of my breath. It grabs my desire to connect and, as soon as I hum the first note, it hums back. Relieved, I inhale and hum more. It's as if the connection was so strong that it wasn't fully broken, its presence waiting to be picked up again, eager even.

I feel its particles gather in an urgent uproar, beginning from the bottom, forming a current, picking up speed, and catching the hull of the boat in its wake. In one powerful lurch, we propel forward.

"Whoa!" comes from behind. "Holy shit, Ailen! Not so fast, I almost fell out!"

I grin and hum some more, partially happy to show off my power, to get another *Whoa!* I'm humming like mad, feeling the vibration of water atoms resonate to my rhythm, talking to me, singing with me, and making motion together.

Seattle's usual clouds hang in a thick layer of weight over the lake. More and more cars come to life and make their way onto the roads, but there are no morning joggers or dog walkers yet. It's still too early.

We keep gliding, perhaps at a speed of eight knots and no more. I slow the boat down, afraid to attract too much attention.

It's raining, and it makes me happy again. I watch the drops plummet through the sky and, on impulse, stick out my tongue to catch them, still humming but now sort of half-singing.

"Look up,
The sky is gray.

Blake Island

Can you see?"

In this moment, I'm back to being six or seven, with the sense of wonder and tranquility I had when my mother was with me, and, I mean, when she was truly with me and not spacing out in her daydreams or one of her songs. I don't remember much of my childhood, and every time I do, it's a treat. Elated, oblivious to everything else, taking a chance on the danger we're in, I let the memory carry me away for just a moment.

I'm lost in my reverie, laughing with my mother, jumping in the puddles, and each time I jump, the ground shakes. No, it's not the ground.

It's Hunter. He's sitting across from me in the rowboat. His eyes are bulging and he plants his unbending fingers into my shoulders again like I'm his last resort in a matter of life or death.

"Shit, Ailen, snap out of it already! Wake up! Wake up, *damn it!* Look! We're headed out to the middle of the sound!"

"What?" I croak and turn my head left, then right, straining to stay upright in the swaying boat. I realize that I've brought us to Blake Island, and I know why. The island is covered with acres of almost virgin woods, where we can hide. My mother took me here once, just me and her, and ever since she died, even though it would take me three buses and a boat ride to get here, it's where I'd go when skipping school. I'd wander along hiking trails, eat wild berries, and then sit alone on driftwood, pretending it was the benches of an outdoor amphitheater, pretending like I was watching a live performance of my favorite songs by Siren Suicides, as I smoked the afternoon away thinking of my mother.

We reach the island's north shore.

The boat's bottom scrapes against gravel and we stop. I purse my lips and climb out of the boat, examining the pebbles with my bare feet. I can feel the roundness or sharpness of each stone,

Chapter 7

yet the familiar pain you'd expect from having them dig into your soles doesn't register. I take a few steps, pretending to feel for pebbles, but I realize with horror that my whole body is dialed in on Hunter's warm breathing and longs for it, hungrily.

"Let's get this baby out of sight," I say, glancing back over the waters, watching for our pursuers, and casually registering the distance between me and Hunter. A few feet. I feel like I can control this. I scan the horizon. It's clear, only punctured here and there by the shaking masts of parked boats along the shore.

"Sure, boss. Yes, boss." Hunter pushes against the end of the boat to help move it forward. I tug at the front, and accidentally tear it out of his hands. In one move, I manage to drag the boat out of the water and propel it a few yards toward the woods. It slides across the beach, throwing sand up.

"Holy shit," I say, staring at my hands, still not fully comprehending my new strength.

"Nice throw," Hunter says behind me. I hear him lift himself up and brush off his jeans. I want to turn to look at him, to say sorry, but I can't tear my eyes away from one of the trees that's standing a few feet away, my hunger forgotten.

It's a tall Douglas fir, nothing special about it.

"Uh-huh," I say, distracted by the fir's greenery, studying its every needle. Because it's not just green like I remember, like it should be. It's emerald, pulsing with shades of chartreuse on one end of the color spectrum and malachite on another, with every possible shade of green in between.

I hear the wet slosh-slosh of Hunter's sneakers behind me, and take off, intending to put a greater distance between us. Sure enough, my hunger diminishes as I run across the trail and to the blackberry bushes that grow at the beginning of the forest line. I catch my breath. Every tree and bush and every blade of grass looks magnificent. I try to take in as much of this beauty as I can—the colors, the smells, the feel when touched. It's as if my senses have been dialed up a turn of a volume knob, to the max. Water is brilliant blue, trees are brilliant green. I hear movement whisper to me from across the entire park—muskrats, beavers, river otters, turtles, owls, eagles, woodpeckers. Their souls form a cacophony of life, punctured by the souls of rare hikers. It all adds up to a divine concert that makes my empty chest rumble with hunger. I'm ready to hunt. An idea crosses my mind. I gently pull a blackberry off the nearby bush and place it in my mouth, bite on it, expecting a familiar taste.

Instead, I shriek and spit it out as soon as it bursts between my teeth, wiping my tongue with both hands like mad, tears breaking out in my eyes.

"What? What is it?" Hunter runs up to me from behind. "Ailen, what's wrong?" I immediately feel his warmth and hear the melody of his soul; they overpower the rest of the noises. A soul so sweet, I want to gobble it up right there. I close my eyes and squint to suppress the urge. A series of coughs has me bending over.

I can't talk, pointing to my tongue. The palms of my hands are purple.

"What did you do, eat a blackberry?"

I nod, breathing hard with my tongue stuck out, blinking tears out of my eyes.

Hunter begins laughing. I pick up and we laugh together. The burning sensation on my tongue slowly fades away and I swallow. My insides feel as if they've been scalded by acid, yet it's bearable. I cough again.

"Did it sting you or something?" he asks, and slightly brushes my cheek with his right hand, quickly drawing it away again. Both ravenous and terrified, I flinch at the warmth in his fingers.

"It burned me. It was like ten times the sourness and the sweetness and the tartness. I think I won't ever be able to eat human food again. It's too much. Too strong."

Chapter 7

He is still, looking down and hugging himself, clearly struggling not to show me that he's cold. I'm afraid to reach out, afraid to feel the hunger again. I think I detect a flicker of pain and then it's gone.

Not knowing what else to say, I inhale the smell of pine, pungent after the recent rain. I can focus on the sound of a single droplet of water splashing to the ground, or I can choose to hear it all in one loud stream. His warm breath, that comes at me in waves, touches something deep and cold inside me and makes me hungry. His touch is worse.

And then Hunter cups my face, his palms on fire. His breath is like summer filled with bird whistles, laughter, and all things home, and I give in to it, to this feeling, unable to care about anything anymore. "Forget about your dad for a second. Look at me. I'm not your enemy. I'm just trying to make you feel better, okay? Why did you jump off that bridge? Give me the real reason."

"Right now?"

"Right now."

I blink and try to look away.

He exhales. "It's okay. I get it. Listen, I'm happy that I found you, that's all. I thought I never would. I thought you drowned." His soul emits such a heavenly melody, that I think, *I don't deserve such beauty.*

"I did drown, if you haven't noticed. I'm dead, Hunter. *Dead.*"

"No, you're not."

His eyes lock with mine.

"See this?" I crane my neck. "Those are gills." I place his hand on them and wince at the heat. "Feel them. I'm not human anymore. The human Ailen is gone. Gone! I'm a siren now, understand? S-I-R-E-N. A soulless killing machine, slimy and clammy and rotten and—"

"You're not rotten."

"You're so stubborn sometimes, I hate you."

Before I can say anything else, Hunter pulls me into a kiss. The melody of his soul overwhelms me. It's right there, at the edge, and I almost inhale it, feeling almost alive. I try to resist, pulling away, horrified at the sudden urge to fall apart and cry. *What are you doing, Hunter, you're going to get yourself killed!* And then holding it, holding it, holding it. And then losing it completely and letting go, unable to keep on the lid. Melting. I'm a thief, I have no right to take this, but I draw on it like a thirsty fiend. More. More. I want more. I want this to never end. Hunter's lips and tongue burn mine with living heat, making my skin tingle. It's pine. He smells of pine, Linden flowers, and sugar. The taste of that first Linden blossom fills my mouth, like an edible flower dipped in stolen honey and set on fire.

We've kissed and made out before, when stoned. Everyone does. But this is different. It's not tainted by being high or drunk, it's real and it's wonderful. And I'm bitter. Bitter that I can't be one or the other, neither girl nor siren, neither dead or alive.

Hunter breaks away. "What's wrong?"

"You're not helping, what with the siren, soulless, killing machine part." I flinch away.

"I don't care." He cradles my face.

"Dude, let's be real here. I'm dead already. Well, almost. Maybe it'd be better if I finished the job. You'd be...safe."

Our noses touch. "Ailen, why are you saying these things? What's wrong?" he asks again, and that does it.

"Why do you keep repeating the same stupid question? What do you mean, *what's wrong*? You're...I'm..." I stumble, bewildered at his idiocy and at my inability to communicate clearly. "I just explained everything to you!" Then I jump up again and stick my hands under his nose. "See this? Feel it." I push them into his chest. "What do they feel like?"

Chapter 7

"Um, like your hands…"

"Jeez, Hunter, I hate it when you act like an idiot. You know what I mean. How do my hands feel to you, temperature-wise?"

"Cold."

I grab his hand with both of mine and press it against my chest, right in the middle.

"How about here?"

He blinks.

"Answer me. Do you feel my heart?"

"Yeah, sure." He blinks again as if unsure where this is going.

"You know what it pumps?"

"Not really," he stammers.

And somehow, though Canosa never told me, I know. "It pumps water. Cold, dark water. It's not even blood, it's some dead liquid, get it? Dead!" I must look scary, because he takes a step back.

"I get it. Honest." His hands rise in a self-protecting gesture.

"I'm dead, Hunter. D-E-A-D. Dead. This," I tap my face, touch my gills, spread out my fingers, "is fake, okay? It's not real, it can't live. It exists by stealing. Stealing life from others, temporarily, while it lasts."

"You," he says under his breath, his eyes open wide, his face vulnerable somehow.

He just stands there, looking helpless, wringing his hands as if he's unsure of what to do next. It makes me even more furious.

"What do you want, Hunter, tell me, what? You want to be in love with a siren, is that it? Is that what you want? For me to constantly fight the urge to snuff you out, for you to walk every day in danger of potentially dying from my song? I want to murder you! I want to murder you right now and feed on you, do you understand?"

"Sorry, I can't help it. I just…love you." His mouth slightly open, he stares at me like a child who's discovered the biggest piece of candy on the planet. Unable to believe in its existence, he's dumbstruck and euphoric, fingering his empty pockets, knowing he can't afford it.

"Why?" I nearly shriek. "Why do you love me?"

"Because, I just do. You're...awesome." He stares at me with such naïveté, I begin to tremble all over with fury.

"That's a stupid reason. I don't believe you. I'm not worth it. I'm a monster. You can't...love...a monster," I say in a loud whisper and recognize my father's voice in mine, the tones of a barely hidden anger that's about to break loose.

"Yeah, you can," he says.

A curtain of blind desire clouds my vision and all I want to do is strike. Hunter stops being Hunter. He is food.

"Step...back," I hiss, now visibly trembling, drowning in his soul's melody.

"Try me," he says, endless admiration in his eyes.

"No!" I say, but this is it. Something snaps and the siren in me takes over, greedy and happy to finally have her most coveted meal. I charge at Hunter, ravenous, reeling with blind determination, my mind pulsing with one single thought.

Food.

I jump forward, locking my eyes with his. I ignite his soul. I begin to sing "We Can't Be Apart" again, the song I tried to kill him with before, appropriately from the Siren Suicides' *Fatal* album. Everything that's been bottled up in me erupts into one powerful gush, pouring out into first verses, sounding less like singing and more like wounded, animalistic howls.

> *"There you are.*
> *Without me you cry.*
> *I surround you.*
> *Love me or I die."*

Chapter 7

Hunter falls to his knees a few feet away from me, opens his arms wide, and lets his soul escape, a thin ribbon of his precious sixteen years; a silky strand of his essence. A thin puff of smoke at first, it trails through the air between us and lands into my open mouth, thickening as it goes. I taste it on the tip of my tongue and my hunger intensifies, ringing through my empty chest. *Forget smoking weed, this is the best junk ever.* I inhale his soul with a whoosh, wolfing it down.

> *"I adore you,*
> *See me or I fly.*
> *I dream of you,*
> *Dream with me, don't lie."*

I'm high. I can't stop. It feels so good, like a first drag after a week of abstinence. No, like a shot of heroin, the way they describe it in movies, because I've never tried it myself. It feels like a double dose, right in the vein.

> *"Can you hold my hand?*
> *Can you hold my heart?*
> *Can you hold my soul?*
> *I can't be apart."*

I want more. I realize I won't be able to stop until he's all mine. Never mind me wanting to dive inside his eyes—reserve that for stupid romantics. He'll be swimming in my ribcage soon, around and around, for real. This is so much better. I watch his soul string between us in a ribbon of smoke, linger, like the herbal smell of marijuana. Pungent.

It gives me power. I inhale and holler more.

> *"Here I am,*

Without you I fall.
You astound me,
I'm a crumbling wall.
You let go of me,
I'm a broken doll.
You dream of me,
I'm your waking call."

The trees shake, the ground shifts. A storm begins to roll in with dark clouds. I feel the water from the shore splash and creep, creep toward me. I command it with my voice, command it to come. Lightning flashes, and in those few seconds, when darkness is complete, Hunter's soul illuminates the air between us. Fog rolls off my skin like a cascade, obscuring everything around us.

And before descending into an ache of falling that's sweet and final for both of us, the last feeling I register of this world is the peculiar sensation of being watched.

I ignore it.

I focus on Hunter, ready to finish him.

"Can I hold your hand?
Can I hold your heart?
Can I hold your soul?
We can't be apart."

The last of his soul wisps up in a barely visible plume and I swallow it. His eyes well up and shed tears, his face goes gray, and he loses his balance. He falls and rolls to his side.

He's dying.

And I know what I did. I let it happen, fear pierces me and I gag. I retch and retch and part of Hunter's soul oozes back into his mouth, greedy to reconnect with its rightful owner. I make

Chapter 7

myself heave and vomit more, until all of it is out, snaking in a faint trail of clouds back into his mouth. He gasps and arches in a spasm, then groans and rolls onto his other side, laying still.

I fall down on my knees next to him, exhausted and momentarily sober, my hunger gone in a flash.

"Hunter! Hunter, are you okay? Oh my God, I'm sorry. I'm so sorry. What did I do? Oh, shit, I almost killed you. Will you ever forgive me? Please, please, please..." I continue yammering excuses.

Before I can say anything more, Hunter pulls on my sleeve. I hover and peel hair off his forehead, clammy and sweaty.

"Are you all right?"

He moves his lips, dry and cracked. "Wow, that was way better than when—"

"Say what?" I stick my ear right over his lips.

"Man, that was...awesome. Can we do it again?" he gulps.

So this is how a hungry siren feels.

I look at Hunter, understanding that I will have to tear myself away from him, in order not to kill him.

Chapter 8

Stern Trawler

I can feel her with my skin before I see her. Canosa seems to materialize out of nowhere. She props her head close to our ears to deliver her message, grinning, whispering with her usual condescending drawl, "Ailen Bright, my favorite food kisser, I asked you to kill the siren hunter, didn't I? Then I practically delivered your first meal into your hands. Was it so hard to do?"

We turn our heads, startled, but there is no time to react, and I'm slow, still entangled in Hunter's soul.

"You should have snuffed him out at the lake; he would've been less trouble to deal with now," she says, looking down at Hunter with pity. Then she looks at me, suddenly serious. "You know, you won't be able to stop next time. Once you've tasted a soul, you can't let it go." Deep inside, somehow, I know she's right. I look at Hunter, terrified. "So, would you like to finish him off now or later? Because we need to go. Your old man seems to be very impatient, which won't end in a good way. I'd bet my life on that." She grabs the back of my hair, curls her fingers around my neck, and adds, "We were going to be sisters. But

Chapter 8

no, you made me follow you for miles! All because you weren't killing the siren hunter. All because of some *boy!*"

And then Canosa shrieks. Every single sound dampens. I cover my ears, and when I look up, I see she's dragging Hunter to the water as he flails uselessly. She swims out with him and I dive after her, searching the murk until I find them, Hunter entwined in Canosa's hold, her arms and legs resembling the long white tentacles of an octopus. I almost expect her to expulse ink to make it harder for me to see. No need, the water is dark on its own, dark and thick like plasma. Hunter's face opens into an inaudible scream through the murk. Canosa's hands circle his neck, her fingers closing under his chin to suffocate him. She sports a strange smile, her mad hair flowing around her shiny body in the crazy halo of a sea monster. I kick toward them and, this time, I know exactly what to do to make her let him go.

She doesn't flinch away; she expects my attack. She's confident in her invincibility, as if this is a game for her, to see how I will react, or even, to *make* me react. I'm now ten feet away from them, now five, now I'm upon them, twisting my body to position myself directly behind her, away from Hunter's eyes lest he distracts me and causes me to do something stupid.

Canosa spins to face me, but I spin behind her. For a second or two, we spiral into a downward whirlpool, until I sense the perfect moment, her hair trailing around her in a silky helix and exposing her neck. It flashes directly in front of my eyes. I pull the sleeves of Hunter's rain jacket over my hands so that the sharp edges of the Velcro closures sit on top of my forefingers, then I raise my arms and stick both fingers into Canosa's gill openings, pressing hard, turning once, feeling the edges of her frayed skin rip.

She utters a high-pitched shriek that pierces me with its agony and travels for miles, scaring ocean life into crevices to hide. I yank my fingers out just in time. She lets go of Hunter, lifting her arms and covering her gills as she bends forward and doubles down. I swim up and push her away by kicking my feet into her temple, ending up inches in front of Hunter's deathly pale face; his eyes bulge out of their sockets, and bursts of air bubbles are coming out of his nose and mouth.

I press my hand over his mouth and pinch his nostrils. He gets the message and stops exhaling, nodding to me.

"Hold on!" I yell. He does, immediately reaching and digging his trembling hands into my shoulders. I seize him under his armpits and throw my legs into a speedy scissor kick, creating a powerful stream of water that propels us upward. We're not very deep, perhaps forty feet at best. A few seconds and we surface, gasping for air.

Well, I don't exactly gasp for air. But out of habit, I act the same way Hunter does and mimic his panic, gulping in short inhales and shivering all over.

"She nearly killed me! She…" His teeth chatter. "Man, she's strong." His lips are quivering, two purple lines across his ashen face. His dancing fingers stop shaking and clamp onto me like iron grips. "How the hell did she find us?"

"That bitch," I say through pressed lips and turn my head around to look for Canosa. She's nowhere in sight. Instead, the annoying clickety-clack of a diesel engine looms over my back. I twist in time to see a trawler advance upon us. Its many outriggers stick out this way and that like legs of a giant insect that's gone belly up, holding its prey in a tangle of nets wrapped around the gallows on the deck. A scary-looking metallic creature. It rocks forward, bobbing on the surface, closing in on us, barely twenty feet away.

"What the fuck is that?" Hunter mutters through dancing teeth, jabbing his fingers deeper into my shoulders.

And then I know. I couldn't have defeated Canosa that easily. It was a setup.

Chapter 8

I can distinguish three human souls onboard, surprised by the distinctions, though they're mostly salty like seawater, and reek of a fishy taste. One must be the captain, standing behind the wheel in the pilothouse. Another one crouches on the deck, and the third one is on the nautical bridge, hiding behind the railing like an inexperienced troublemaker. I only have time to see his orange bib peek out as he rises and throws his right arm full out, a toothy grin spreading between his beard and his knit beanie, his gloved hand holding a plastic loudspeaker aimed at me. Only it's not a speaker, I find out too late. It must be some kind of a sonic weapon designed specifically to kill sirens, to blast us into oblivion. I open my mouth in surprise when a shot rings through me.

Crack!

A powerful sonic blast hits my right side, the one conveniently turned toward the trawler. I go limp and begin losing my hold on Hunter's waist, but not before registering how the man who shot me throws both his arms up and jumps with glee, shouting, "I got it, I got it!"

"Ailen! Ailen, oh my God, are you okay?" Hunter shouts in my ear.

"Where the hell did you get that thing? Who gave you a sonic gun, you asshole?" Hunter yells at the guy on the trawler.

How does he—my thoughts are arrested, turning inward.

A searing pain traces my throat, and my eyeballs threaten to pop, my eyelids drooping over them for protection. Hunter's still holding on to me, shouting something in my ear, but it comes in as ringing noise. I move my legs weakly, struggling to stay afloat. I dip my head backward, pivoting my body into a horizontal position, hoping to relax and make myself buoyant, yet feeling the weight of Hunter's body pin me down and push me under.

One second I inhale air, the next I'm under the surface, my gills beginning their steady pumping job, the clacking of the

Stern Trawler

trawler engine subsiding into an annoying echo. My grip loosens completely and Hunter drifts out of my arms. I splash in a tangle of surprise and fear, too slow, too chaotic to move me in any direction.

I can only hear distorted noises through the thicket of the sea—some distant grinding and revolving and metallic crunching, first to my right and then above me. A feeling of dread takes hold of my mind and I attempt to move. It's dark and I appear to be drifting directly under the trawler's belly. There's a pattern of some sort hanging in the water making it appear checkered. It takes me several blinks to will my vision into focus.

A net. It's a fishing net. I'm inside a net!

I grope around and feel a stretch of rope, multiple ropes, rough to the touch yet slippery, covered with a layer of mold and some other oily grime. The net looks like a cone, with me slowly drifting into its narrow end. The checkered pattern shrinks rapidly and envelops me like a gigantic cheesecloth.

The noise intensifies and the net digs into my flesh, pushing something toward my back. I'm unable to move around to look, but I can hear a barely detectable echo of his soul through the thin fabric of my rain jacket. It's Hunter.

We're inside a trawl net being pulled up like the catch of the day, together with a few fish trapped by accident, flipping their silvery bodies around me, desperate to escape. Another second, and we're lifted out of the water. The racket of the machinery erupts and intensifies. I want to cover my ears but I can't move; my arms are pressed to my sides. My legs are bent with my face jammed into one of the square openings of the net, its ropes cutting across my forehead and over my lips, and another two tracing vertical lines on my cheeks, with my nose sticking out right in the middle.

What worries me most right now is not how I feel, but what I feel behind me. There is no talking, no movement at all, only

Chapter 8

a limp body. I can't even detect breathing, only his remaining warmth. I don't know how long it will last, hoping Hunter can stay alive. I struggle to move but fail, so I open my mouth to sing, emitting a sad, low quaver.

A crane arm creaks, slowly lifting us up. From the corner of my eye, I see a drum turn winding on one end of the net, tightening it. There are shouts underneath. The two men in orange bibs are directing the guy in the pilothouse where to move the net. I smell machinery and this tangy electric stink coming from some sort of exhaust, straining under the load. I decide to make another attempt at singing, to move the water. I clear my throat, take in a deep inhale, and—

Boom!

Another shot passes through my ribs. Blackness is absolute and soothing.

The net must be swaying. I feel its gentle motion from side to side, an easy rocking. Perhaps I'm small again—I'm a baby and my mother is rocking me in an old-fashioned crib, and she's singing me a lullaby. I hear it and I don't, drifting into that twilight between wakefulness and sleep.

I must have blacked out only for a few seconds. My body is still on top of Hunter's, firmly pressed together inside the latticework of ropes. The light assaults my eyes with its brightness and I squint to make it bearable. A migraine hits me, prompted by a combination of the blinding glare, the saw-blade noise of the net drum, the whine of the wind, the shrieking of the seagulls, and the shouting from the trawler's deck below.

The crane's arm positions us directly over the deck, all the while producing a racket that pierces my eardrums with its intensity, adding to the strain and the creaking of the gallows, suspending us for our execution. The bright orange flotation work suits of the fishermen reek of mildew. The rough twines cut into my face. I ignore the discomfort, peering down, suddenly famished. My only hope to gain any strength is the sound of those three souls below. I don't care if they taste salty or fishy. They're food, and that's all that matters at the moment.

The crane stops abruptly and lowers us. We jerk forward and swing back on inertia, dangling from the hook, moving down until we're about five feet over the deck. Another lurch and we stop, swaying in rhythm with the rocking motion of the trawler.

Two of the three men onboard, looking rather funny in their clunky headphones over their tight beanies, peer at me through the ocean mist with their sharp and sinister features. I sense a lurking fear in their bones; hear their souls afire with trepidation. I grin with immediate satisfaction.

They're afraid of me, and they know that I know it. I'm a beast they've been instructed to catch. I don't want to think about who instructed them, and chase the thought away.

The squat man points the sonic gun at me, holding it with both hands as if it were made of steel. The other one, the tall, haggard forty-something-year-old man with irregular stubble on his chin, points a flashlight at me. Blinded, I scowl. My elbows dig into Hunter's stomach and he groans. Good, he is conscious then. I let out a sigh of relief.

I manage to twist my hand, find his neck, and feel for his skin. It's cold. He's suffering from hypothermia. I need to get us out of here and warm him up before it's too late.

Somewhere, a heavy chain begins rolling with a terribly loud drone.

Questions swirl in my head like a pile of restless maggots. That's a good thing, I suppose. I'm gaining some degree of sanity, finally. When all else fails, facts are my crutch. Let's see, if I were to divorce myself from my emotions and apply logic…the logical thing to conclude would be that there are other siren hunters besides my father. In theory, there could be, right? I mean, what if there are other places with—wait, does this mean there are other

Chapter 8

sirens out there? Perhaps not one or two, but hundreds, or even thousands? It strikes me that the ocean is vast and I have no idea how many there might be. But it makes sense, yeah?

I curl my fingers around the ropes of the net, stretching my neck to listen through the racket. There are three human souls—an auditory version of mixing different colors of paint into one ghastly brown mess. The one on the bridge, the skipper, promises to taste like stale fish. I stifle my gag reflex, wondering if they seem so rotten on purpose, like a protective measure from a siren. That would be clever; even cleverer would be if, once you swallow the soul of a fellow like that, then it poisons you from the inside out. I shake my head to concentrate on the task at hand.

Keep counting, Ailen, keep counting.

Three souls, and that's all. I hear nobody else. Could there be a siren hunter on board, one I don't know and can't hear?

I realize the tall man is staring at me, about six feet away, our eyes perfectly level, him standing on the swaying deck of the trawler, and me hanging in the swaying net.

He whistles, clearly astounded. I grin back, trying to look sinister. It works. He blinks several times and takes a step back.

"Are you out of your *fucking* mind, Jimmy? You never whistle on a boat, it's bad luck!" the squat man shouts at the tall one, sending one of Jimmy's headphones askew with a slap from his meaty hand. The short, beefy guy is still firmly holding the sonic weapon in his other hand and pointing it at me. I'm sure this was done in an effort to make Jimmy hear what he just said. It seems like the tall guy is an amateur.

"Sweet Jesus, mother Mary, the blessed virgin, save me," Jimmy says. "Would you look at that..." His soul jumps in fear as he points in our direction. "It's just a couple of kids! It's just...I didn't sign up for this, no way." His long face turns gray. He gapes at me, and scratches his stubble with the pallid resin of his glove.

The squat man pulls down his own headphones, letting them sit on his thick neck, and jerks Jimmy's headphones off his beanie completely, sending them flying across the deck. He tiptoes to lift himself up and yells into his ear.

"You heard what the man said, he wants them alive. We get the cash and wash our hands. So quit your whining and stop being a sissy. Let's be done with it." He grins an unpleasant smile that cuts through the middle of his round face, scathed by ocean winds into the red muzzle of a beer drinker.

Jimmy glances around, and then sticks his hands in his pockets. "He didn't say they'd be kids, did he? If I woulda known... He said—"

"Never mind what he said!" the squat man cuts him off. "You want to repair the roof of your house or not? How many years has it been now?"

Jimmy mutters under his breath, takes out one hand and folds fingers into his palm, mouthing the numbers. "Three, I reckon. That sounds about right, three years."

"Hey, Glen, what's the holdup?" The third fisherman leans over the railing of the pilothouse, shouting and waving his arm for the guys below to hurry up. That means Jimmy is not important. I get the hierarchy. Whoever is paying these guys is the boss.

"Just a minute, Stevie! Getting her situated here," the squat man, Glen, shouts back.

"All right, you're worried about them, Jimmy? How about this. How about we ask them to quiet your mind, eh?"

He looks up at me, points the sonic gun again, and opens his mouth so wide I can see yellowing teeth framing his purplish tongue. I try not to think about what his breath might smell like.

"Hey, kids, you all right?" he shouts. I try to pull myself up from Hunter, but my muscles give out, and all I can do is curl

Chapter 8

my fingers into fists of weak hatred.

"There. See, they're fine." Glen slaps Jimmy on the back with his free hand and waves to the skipper, Stevie.

"But they didn't—" Jimmy begins.

"I said, they're *fine*," Glen says with finality.

We descend several feet, jerking, and now hover over the floor, nearly touching it.

"Unzip her," Glen commands with a wave of the gun.

Jimmy nervously steps closer, grabs the rope from somewhere underneath me, pulling on it, and then stops.

"Glen, I'm not sure about this."

"I can't hear you, you idiot." He taps on his headphones which he managed to put back on, then shouts into Jimmy's face. "You want your pay, you keep your mouth shut. Haul them in and be done. Let her loose!" By *her,* I suppose he means the net; must be some affectionate fishermen term.

Jimmy glances at us again. With a heavy sigh, he yanks at the rope. It unravels beneath Hunter like the loose thread of a sweater, loop by loop. Another jerk and we fall out of the net and onto the slimy deck with a sickening crunch and the sound of slapping on bare skin. Hunter moans when I land on top of him, then the floor begins moving. No, it's not the floor. It's the white plastic side of a chute of some sort, an opening on the deck that I didn't see. And it's not moving, the trawler is moving, causing us to slip into a square opening the size of a large manhole, cold and stinky. For a beat, we hang folded over its rim. It reminds me of the polished rim of my bathtub. Then, with an unceremonious rain boot shoved in my ass, Glen sends us both flying down.

Down the rabbit hole, crosses my mind. *Down the rabbit hole I go.*

Chapter 9

Fish Factory

Hunter grunts and groans with every twist of the shaft. I don't have a chance to look at him, to make sure he's okay, as my head bangs against metal walls, unable to stop the work of gravity. As abruptly as our fall started, we stop moving, slamming into a flat surface. I land on top of Hunter again and he cries out involuntarily. I test my voice. It's feeble at first, and then after coughing up salt water, shaky but clear for the most part. Good, at least I have my weapon back.

A soft gray light emanates from the low ceiling painted a dirty beige, jammed full of pipes, aluminum chutes, and bundles of wires, with a few flickering fluorescent lamps in between. We're both lying flat on what appears to be a three-foot-wide conveyor belt used to sort and process fish. Or sirens. Who knows what these guys are catching here.

Hunter's body twitches underneath me, his head face down and propped against the low metallic lip that prevented us from sliding another three feet to the floor. My legs are still up in the chute's opening behind me. I hold on to the slippery belt-rim,

Chapter 9

wiggle, and roll off to the left, scrambling to all fours and leaning to look.

"Hunter?" I try. It comes out warbled. I clear my throat, feeling weak all over. "Hunter, you all right?" I shake his shoulder, the wet cotton of his sweatshirt clammy under my palm. My arm gives out from the effort.

"Huh...Wha...I...Sssss..." he mutters.

"Talk to me, please. Are you—"

Before I have a chance to finish, a low whine of a motor comes to life and the belt jerks to the right, its rubbery surface squeaking. I fall over, and by the time I gain balance and scramble on all fours again, the belt falls out from under us and we get dumped onto the floor, roll forward another few feet, and end up hitting a freezing wall. It's covered with frost and crunches lightly as my forehead rams into it.

I manage to sit; trembling from the strain to stay upright, I rub my face and eyes, gagging from the stink of what smells like spoiled herring, on top of an oozing, condensed coldness.

"Oh my God," I say involuntarily. Because my hunch was right, this does look like a freezer. Worse. What's directly in front of me resembles cells, sort of like cooling compartments for fish except they appear too large for that purpose. They remind me of tiny rooms, the likes of which you see in prison, complete with black iron grate doors that can be locked, judging from the heavy locks hanging by their knob handles.

Four, no, five units about six feet high and four feet wide line the wall; or, rather, they are *dug* into the wall, if you were to dig out cells in a mountain of ice. Underneath the ice there are places where paint is visible, white perhaps years and years ago, but now it's dirty and peeling, reeking of iron. Rusty, eroded, tarnished.

A heavy thump from above yanks me from my horror.

"Hunter!" I yelp.

Fish Factory

He is curled up on the floor, shivering.

"Hey, look at me." I lean in and cradle his face in my hands, when another thump shakes the ceiling and causes the lights to flicker out briefly.

"Hey, how are you feeling?" His breath warms my palm in short, raspy gasps.

"Can you talk? Are you cold? Darn it, of course you are. It's freezing here, and you're wet all over. I wonder if I can..." I don't finish, perking up at the noise coming from above. Hunter's face slides from my grip back onto the floor.

It's Glen—I can hear his soul. It's a mix of loud chewing, fire crackers, and some annoying, mechanical whine on top of it, all promising to taste of raw fish and iron. He walks across the deck away from the chute hole where the net was unzipped. I tilt my head up for a moment, listening. Ragged breathing comes in. It's Jimmy. His soul has a simple melody to it—the shuffling of hard paper, perhaps playing cards, and a tinkering with metal-sounding tools or bells. He appears to be leaning in to check, to make sure we got swallowed properly into the depth of the trawler, yet still uncertain, muttering under his breath.

Then...

Bang!

...the lid over the opening slams shut, and all the lights go out at once.

"Hey!" I yell.

I feel around for Hunter, calling his name frantically several times. My words sound hollow in the hushed silence amidst these walls—probably soundproof because every word I speak dies with barely a chance to escape my lips. Slowly, my skin begins to glow, faintly. It's enough to make out shapes that are close.

"Hunter! Hunter, you all right? Where are you?"

"Never felt better, thanks for asking." This comes out weak,

Chapter 9

but with his usual sarcasm. It tells me that he feels awful, but is fighting it by trying to appear cool. "What about you, you okay?" he groans; his breath rolls over me in a wave of warmth. My eyes are adjusting. His face is barely visible, a gray ghost in the darkness.

"Yeah, I'm fine. Are you hurt?"

Now a stream of his soul hits me square in the ribcage, especially pronounced. It has a strange smoky aroma that I never noticed before. I have an urge to circle my hands around his neck and suffocate him. It takes an enormous effort, and a deep exhale, for me to suppress it. How much longer will I be able to withstand the urge?

"I was so worried, I thought you got hypothermia," I break the silence, touching his cheek. Then I trace the smooth bridge of his nose, my hands shaking.

"Nah, it'd take more than Canosa to nuke me." His usual bravado comes out. It's a good sign. "I'm surprised she managed to find us. I wonder how it works, actually. Can you hear her if she's miles away?"

At that, we dive into small talk, pretending as if everything is normal, in an effort to avoid our weakness, terrified of the impending danger.

"Nope. At least, I haven't yet. I mean, I could feel her just before she jumped out, but that's about it," I say, wondering if I could detect her presence on purpose, to try and tune in to her as if she were a radio station. "I could try?"

"Hmmm...interesting." Hunter appears to be thinking, and then quickly changes the subject. "Man, it's cold in here..." He shifts and rubs his hands, and before I can ask him if I can warm him somehow, he launches into another attempt to fill the silence. "Hey, did you see the gun? They used a sonic gun on you. The guy with the beard, the short one..." Hunter falls quiet, perhaps realizing that of course I saw the gun, felt it, too. His pause leads me to believe he's as afraid as I am to breach the subject on why he seems to know more than he's told me.

My fingers trace his lower lip, and he nips on them lightly. "And the headphones?" I add. "Did you see them? Must be against my voice, right?"

"Maybe, maybe not. I think fishermen use them all the time. You know, chains and engines and stuff." His hands feel my shoulders through the thin fabric of the rain jacket, and I want to crumble into his embrace. "What is this place, did you get a chance to see when the light was on?"

I follow the folds of his ears, from the outer edges to the inner cartilage, letting my fingers travel across their smooth landscapes. Hunter lets me, I can even detect him moving a bit closer and holding very still.

"They said some guy hired them, did you hear that? I wonder who. I wonder if...there might be other siren hunters out there?" There, I said it. I fall quiet, scared of Hunter's reaction.

"Who knows," is all he manages, clearly not tuned in to the conversation, his hands slowly traveling down to my waist and under my jacket.

"That *bitch* Canosa." I relish the word *bitch*, thinking that this use is absolutely appropriate, after what she had done. I perk up even. "Can you believe it? I thought I could trust her. I still don't get it how..." I feel Hunter's breath grow faster and shallower, blowing hot air against my cheek. "...she found us. By my voice, I suppose. I need to try it myself. I bet I can do it, too—don't you think?"

"Yeah. I think...this is all so surreal...it's also kinda awesome," Hunter mumbles, his fingers counting my ribs, moving higher, my heart ramming against my chest.

"Jeez, you're freezing!" I get my own hands under his sweatshirt. "I wish I could warm you up somehow. God, I hate that I'm cold-blooded." I grit my teeth and begin rubbing his belly

Chapter 9

unceremoniously, exerting myself too much but not caring. As cold as Hunter is, my hands must be colder, because he abruptly yanks his arms from under my jacket and grabs my hands to stop me.

"Don't."

"Why?" I ask, taken aback, knowing that he must have meant to say, *Your hands are cold*, and then thinking that he would hurt me with it.

"You're not helping, Ailen. Relax and enjoy the scenery, all right?" He's nervous and exhausted, his voice trembles, and I think my eyes have adjusted enough to see the faint outline of his profile. He turns his head toward the freezing cells, no doubt wondering what the hell they are, yet not being able to clearly see them.

A momentary pause is all it takes. Our magic is sapped clean from the air, leaving only teenage awkwardness behind. I sigh, sad to feel it go; my hands are still in Hunter's, held tightly, but with no affection. Only with a desire to hold on to something, in the middle of exploding chaos.

And then it hits me. "Hunter?"

"Yeah?"

"How did you know Canosa's name?"

"Shit. You caught that, didn't you? I guess I owe you an apology." He hesitates for a moment. "I started working for your father, Ailen. I was going to tell you. I...I'm a siren hunter."

"A *what*?"

"Well, I *was* a siren hunter in training. That's how I know about the sonic guns and all the siren stuff. I did it for my mom. There are so many medical bills, and your father pays well. It sounded easy enough—cool even—killing some undead creatures at the push of a button. Poof! Exploding them into nothing. I never imagined that you...well..."

"I what?"

"You know how siren hunters become siren hunters, right?"

"No." I grit my teeth.

"*Then they put it back. Burning and smoldering.*"

I get it, and I don't believe my ears. "Is this a joke?"

"No joke. A siren hunter's soul has been ignited and given back. Until it burns away."

A million questions swirl in my head, but I'm too angry to ask them. I hear him explain how Canosa turned my father into a siren hunter, and how he is really sorry he didn't tell me before, how he was desperate. But all I can think of is how Hunter's soul is burning now, and it will eventually burn up. I can hear it burning and I'm not angry anymore, only sad.

He stops talking. I lean my head on his shoulder, and he doesn't push me away. For that, I'm grateful. I'm scrambling for anything I can get, to gain an ounce of my strength back.

I think back to every single time we fooled around in the past, each lovely occurrence transpiring while being high on weed and not feeling much at all. Neither of us was brave enough to try anything when fully awake and alert, making feeble passes at each other and never going past kissing and some affectionate squeezing on the couch or pressing stomach-to-stomach against the bathroom door.

"I'm sorry—" I begin, into his sweatshirt, and then pause, not knowing what it is I'm apologizing for.

"Huh?" Hunter seems deep in thought, shivering.

"Wait, listen—" What dawned on me briefly before, blooms into full knowledge. "Do you hear it?"

"Hear what?"

"Listen," I say and lift my head. "La-la-la..." I sort of attempt to sing, but my voice comes out dull. The usual sharpness and thrill gets sucked out of it the second it leaves my lips.

"It's soundproof! This place is soundproof. Holy shit!" I say.

"Of course it is," Hunter says.

Chapter 9

"What do you mean, *of course*? How would you know?" I retort, wanting to yank my hands out of his, but curbing the urge, conserving my energy. I don't know when I'll have another opportunity for an intimate moment like this, bizarre as it is. We've both narrowly escaped death, told our truths, and now we're freezing our asses off, locked up in an enormous ice maker.

"I dunno, just guessing. But it's one hell of a siren hunter's boat, I tell ya." He glances at the cells and I think I see his lips crack into a grin, though it's hard to tell for sure in this darkness. "Your father's thing is a toy compared to this baby. This is how the big guys play. Yeah."

There is a tone of admiration in his voice, badly covered up with deliberate sarcasm. On some deep level his comment pokes me in the wrong place, and I feel like defending my father's boat and his hunting legacy. Plus, he bought it for my mom, which has a special meaning to me. I'm mad at both thoughts. They immediately make me angry and form the words before I can arrest them.

"I think my father hired these guys. There, I said it. Isn't *that* what you were thinking?" I wait for his answer.

"How would you know for sure?" Hunter counters.

I must be right.

"Who else would be smart enough to do this? Perhaps this trawler was his all along, and he simply never told me." I notice a tone of pride in my voice.

Hunter must notice it too, lashing out at me. "Smart enough? You mean, you actually have to have a brain to hunt a siren? Look at you, Papa's girl all over again, aren't you?" Badly covered contempt seeps through his remark. It feels like he pumped himself up to be angry on purpose. That's as far as my logic goes. Suddenly, fury pounds in my skull with blazing intensity.

"What, we're animals to you, is that it?" I throw at him.

"That's not what I said!" he raises his voice.

"Well, it's not what I said either," I hiss. "What I said has nothing to do with my father. I hate him, and you know it!"

"Awesome. Point taken. Agreed." He exhales loudly. "Hey, I don't know about you, but I don't feel like arguing anymore. I feel like a nice long joint on my favorite couch under a warm fuzzy blanket, okay? So unless you object, I vote we try to find our way outta here." He scoots away, scraping the floor with his wet jeans. It must drain a lot out of him, because he stops after a short while, panting.

"Oh, yeah? So *you're* the smart one here? Okay. Explain to me how exactly you're planning to escape. I'm all ears." I cross my arms and wait. I can't believe I was actually kissing this guy not too long ago.

"I don't know. *Just out!*" He bangs his fist on a wall in a childish move of frustration, and yelps in pain. "We'll figure it out when we get there." Despite the pain, he continues hitting it again and again, sending snowflakes flying toward me. They stick to my face without melting like they normally would if I were still a warm-blooded girl.

"When we get *where*? Let me see if I understand. We're somehow going to manage to pry open the metal belly of this beast, quickly, too, before those guys are back. Then, we'll swim out and fly off into the night sky, on magic wings, and we'll land on some paradise island with a loud splat. Am I right?" It's not the time to be sarcastic, but I can't help it. "Is that what you have in mind? That my siren magic will save the day? Is that what you're counting on?"

"What do *you* suggest?" Hunter says angrily, and then sneezes loudly, several times. I can hear him wipe off the snot with his sleeve.

"See, you're already sick. If it was just me—I can survive swimming in the cold water, even in freezing water. But you

Chapter 9

can't, don't you get it? Look at you, you're shaking." Not that I can see him, but I feel his vibrations come at me through the air.

"What do *you* care?" His voice catches at the end. I immediately feel awful.

"Why are you so bitter all of a sudden? Everything was fine just an hour ago." It comes out wrong, of course. I grope for him in the dark, but Hunter scoots farther away. "What's wrong? What did I say wrong?"

Heavy breathing.

"Nothing."

I wait. Sometimes silence is the best answer. Sometimes knowing when to shut up is better than knowing what to say. Sure enough, it works.

"I'm just scared is all." Hunter deflates, sniffs, shuffles his sneakers on the floor.

"Scared of what? If it's my father who's manning this boat, he'll welcome you with open arms, I'm sure. He'll give you a personal ride home, you can count on it."

"It's not that..." He trails off.

"Then what?"

"We're stuck here. I can barely move, everything hurts, even breathing hurts." I hear tears in his voice. "And I don't know what will happen to us, what those people will do..." He pauses. "...to you." Another pause. "You're like a magnet. I can't tear myself away from you. Here I am, a siren hunter, sitting and talking, doing anything I can to *keep* talking, to *keep* hearing your voice, when any other normal guy would pound on the door and cry for help." He catches his breath.

I can't breathe. I seem to have forgotten how to. I want to say, *Ditto*, but I don't dare, don't dare to tell him that snatching a moment of being together is more important to me than escaping my fate. Unbelievable as it is, touching him gives me comfort, makes me feel less fatigued. I sense that it gives both of us solace, not to the point where we can give up past conflicts and our yearning to kill each other for good, and not to the point of gaining strength to try and climb back up, to kick off the lid, or at least to go search for some door and try to open it. No. Not yet, but we're getting close.

"I'm scared…of losing you, again," he says.

Thick silence hangs between us, broken only by the steady pounding of the trawler's engine, rolling ocean noise echoing from far above, and Hunter's occasional sniffling.

I don't know what to say. And I don't need to, because before I can say anything, a voice comes alive from behind us—no, two voices, in the corner of the lab.

About thirty feet away, deep in velvety darkness, a lock turns, and then the door bursts open with a sharp metallic clang.

Chapter 10

Wet Lab

Jimmy and Glen materialize on either side of the doorframe, their soul melodies assaulting my hearing and making me hungry. Good, maybe it'll give me some much needed strength. Repulsive, but edible. My chest agrees with a growl of famished void, ready to make me pounce. They must be afraid of me. The thought gives me pleasure and I hiss involuntarily, pumping myself up for a fight.

It's show time, Ailen. You can do it. It's what you were made for, isn't it? Admit it, you love it. Get back at them; get back at your father for all of the pain he's inflicted upon you. He doesn't deserve to live, nor do they. Suck out their lives, you can do it! Sing to make them lose their minds, bend their sorry wills with your voice, gut those babies, make their every bone pop and break.

I know, I know, I want to answer myself, but I'm terrified that I can't do it at will, that I need a powerful emotion to kick myself into gear. This drives me insane, mad at my own constant self-doubt and the fear of accepting myself as I am.

Hunter glances at me. I press a finger to my lips, telling

him to be quiet. He nods his head, eyes expectant, miraculously trusting me this time.

Ailen Bright, I tell myself, *you're a siren.* So, *act like one!*

There is muttering by the door, phrases exchanged in a hushed whisper, and then Glen, the squat bearded guy, takes a few tentative steps into the corridor.

"Hey, kids, easy now. Easy..."

Emboldened by our unresponsiveness, he crosses the rest of the distance, his resin boots squeaking on the floor. A sonic gun in one hand pointed at me, he reaches for Hunter with the other. That's my cue.

"Uncle Glen, here, to take you kids upstairs. I have me a gun, you hear? Let's not—"

I shriek, lunging forward and pushing Hunter aside. I grab Glen's orange suspenders that hug his beer belly. Surprised, he loses his footing, kneeling forward like a sack of potatoes with a dull thud. That must hurt his knees. Good. Before he gets control of his upper body, I straight-arm his chest and he folds back, falling flat onto the floor, his head smacking it with a juicy crack. He screeches. I hop on top of him, pinning his right wrist to the floor until his fingers uncurl and he loses his grip on the plastic weapon. The trawler rocks and the gun rolls away into the darkness. Hunter catches it and scoots into the shadows, out of sight.

I hug Glen with my thighs and squeeze hard, not allowing him to move. I press his other wrist to the floor and lower my face within inches of his nose.

"Hi there, fatty. Nice beer belly," I say into his face, seized by a mad desire to scare him.

He gapes at me, speechless.

Hunter shouts behind me at the tall guy, Jimmy.

"What the fuck are you looking at? Get your sorry ass out of here while you can, you stupid dickhead!" he shouts. It's his way of attacking, yelling obscenities before he gets scared or before

Chapter 10

his opponent realizes his fear. I smile. This is the Hunter I know. I also realize I love him so much it hurts.

"Hey, don't point that thing at me, son, you hear me? Put it down, put it down!" Jimmy's voice yelps back.

It feels disgusting sitting on Glen's belly, sensing his gas and intestine movements, like I'm on top of a water-filled pillow that constantly shifts and sloshes underneath me.

"Please, please," is all he manages to say, his assaulting courage gone, replaced with pathetic mumbling. His eyes droop deeply into their sockets, a thin sliver of saliva making its way down his beard.

"You're a piece of crap, you know that?" I say.

"Please...I didn't do nothing. Please, let me go...I only..."

His muttering annoys me. Without thinking, I tilt my head back and hit him hard with my forehead, knocking him out and making him shut up. He promptly goes limp and lets his bladder loose.

"Shit!" I exclaim, sensing the warmth. I quickly jump off him. "He peed himself!" I announce and turn around, looking for Hunter.

The place where he was a few seconds ago is vacant now, and I see him charge forward, a dark shadow in the gloom of the corridor, legs spread wide against the rocking of the trawler, left hand threading the wall for balance, right hand firmly clasping the sonic gun pointed at Jimmy.

"Who hired you? Who the *fuck* hired you?" Hunter yells.

Jimmy, on the other hand, seems to be frozen to the spot, clutching the door frame. He stares at me, though, not at Hunter, that much is obvious. Then, it dawns on me. I forget that I'm glowing, that my skin is glowing in the dark. I must be a freaky sight.

The boat lurches. We plunge with it, and I lose my footing. I grab on to the grille of one of the cell doors to my right.

Simultaneously, Hunter fires the sonic gun.

Crack!

The echo of the blast reverberates in a stream of hollow popping sounds, finally reaching me all the way in the back. Deafened, bending in pain, I curl my fingers around the iron latticework so I don't fall. I emit an involuntary moan, feeling my feet slide apart on the wet floor.

Hunter, I want to cry. *Why did you fire, you stupid-head? That thing doesn't work on people. Does it?*

A bout of nausea passes and I raise my head, when another blast throws me off balance again. Its echo erupts around the room, bouncing off the soundproof walls once and hushing. Like the previous blast, this one was not directed at me, yet its ambiance seems to be enough to weaken me. I tighten every muscle in my body to power through the vibration of pain, feeling as though a hot metal spike has been rammed through my eardrums and turned. Once, twice, three times. It drives its sharp end deeper, piercing my brain in a thousand places at once.

I swallow a cry.

Another blast.

Bam!

What the hell is going on? I want to shout. Agony threatens to break my skull and shatter every bone. It seems intolerable, as if my teeth are being drilled without anesthesia, past their roots, all the way into my jawbone. I retch into my hands, sort of half-hanging, half-standing, clutching the iron bars for dear life.

Distant shouting erupts from the corridor. Without looking up, I have a pretty good idea about what's happening. The tall guy, Jimmy, seems to be fleeing with a wail, his boots paddling the floor and squeaking. Hunter shouts something after him. Both sounds come at me warbled, as if I'm at the end of a tunnel, perhaps a yard long. I cough.

Hunter, you all right? I want to shout, but wince as I open

Chapter 10

my mouth. It hurts. Everything hurts. The sonic boom aftershock buzzes with its hundred flies around my head, nagging and constant. A metallic-tasting bile fills my throat, and I force it down. After a couple of breaths, I manage to raise my head long enough to look in the direction of the door. There, framed by daylight and facing me, stands Hunter. His face is gray in the dim light, stretched into a mask of surprise and horror. He yells something to me, something that has my name, and waves his arms. But my ears refuse to do their duty at discerning speech patterns and my head falls back down.

A series of squeaky steps, and both his hands on my face later, I can hear him clearly from this close.

"Ailen! Ailen, dude, I'm sorry, I'm so sorry. Shit, I didn't think it would have this effect on you, I was aiming at the guy, I—" He looks into my face, and I glance back at him through the slits of my eyes, letting my head lean into his hands for support, my fingers still curled tightly around the bar, afraid I'll tumble if I let go.

"Hey, I know what you need." Hunter smiles and points to Glen's body on the floor, whose belly rhythmically moves up and down. He's breathing, he's alive.

I manage to nod.

"Okay, hold on to me. I'll help you get over. Here, take my hand." Hunter unclenches my fingers one by one, takes my hands in his, and leans me on his shoulder. I take one tentative step, then another, knees shaking and swaying, until he gently lowers me next to Glen's face. I suppress a gag at the stink of urine, plopping onto the floor. Hunter sits next to me and embraces me. I lean my head on his shoulder, terrified that if I attempt to shift any more, I'll fall face first into Glen's breathing stomach.

"There. You need to feed," Hunter says.

This shocks me into opening my eyes wide.

"Are you out of your mind?" I say, but it comes out more like, "Ah...ou...offa...mannn..."

"You'll need all the strength you can get to fight these guys, baby."

I hold my breath. Hunter never called me *baby* before, it was always *brat* or *turkey*, or *dude* thrown in with my name. I want to freeze time. No, I want to rewind it and hear him say it again. And again. And again.

"You can't even stand on your own. It won't do. I should've..." He sighs, unaware of my inner turmoil. "Come on, someone is getting ready to run back here right this minute. That Jimmy dude is probably bitching about us right now, so..." He points to Glen's face and pulls open his eyelids. "This is how it works, right? You've got to establish eye contact?"

I nod, speechless. A siren hunter helping a siren to feed?

"You realize what you're doing?" It comes out more or less distinctly.

"Yes, yes, here you go." He lets go of my shoulder, raises his arm, and slaps Glen several times on the face, to which the guy groans. His eyes turn from glazed into some semblance of comprehension. He coughs. The sound of his soul does the rest.

I don't care how revolting it will taste. Hunger overwhelms me. I lean over his face, plop my arms on either side to support me, shaking. Hunter holds my waist. I root my stare directly into Glen's pulsing irises, then deeper into his pupils. It seems to be enough. They stop flexing. He fixates his stare at me, until his irises stop pulsing as well, shimmering with an eerie light of ignition. His mouth cracks open and a faint puff of smoke trails into the air. That's it, I ignited his soul. Now on to feeding.

"Come *on*, Ailen, we don't have much time!" Hunter rubs his fingers on my waist. Half-hanging in his embrace, I nod and produce a feeble first note. It sounds sad and weak. I cough, take a deep breath and sing another note, bolder, stronger.

Chapter 10

This time it works. Glen's reddish eyelashes flutter. His pupils slowly widen, fully dilating. His gaze turns drowsy, then blank. The sound of his soul overwhelms me with its ugliness. In fact, it's so repulsive, I don't know if I can eat it; it tastes of rotten fish. Perhaps this is why he was able to shoot me, perhaps he's a special kind of a man, one of those woman haters who has been hating us for so long their souls have rotted out without having to be burned, without having to fall in love with a siren. Perhaps not being able to fall in love at all.

It's the last thought that crosses my mind. I wince and make myself eat, digging with my song deep into his slime, knowing that I need this for survival, if only to hear Hunter call me *baby* again. Maybe it'll give me the will to continue to live. Maybe, just maybe.

"I live in the meadow,
But you don't know it."

I link my first few notes with the melody of his soul, no matter how ghastly it sounds. They become one in tone and merge, in the way two different chorus voices merge, ringing into harmony, becoming a slur of life itself. There it comes, another rivulet of steam slipping through Glen's open lips. I gulp it. My arms stop shaking and my skin begins oozing its usual fog, nearing my temperature to that of the freezing room we're in. I continue singing, letting it flow.

"Why do you frown?"

There is a faint snap, an audible popping, and a thick soul vapor shimmers between us in the surrounding darkness, pumping from Glen's mouth to mine in a fast-flowing river. In that instant, his face softens with a childish glow. His wrinkles smooth out, his lips stretching into a smile, showing off his yellowing teeth framed by a reddish beard. And his eyes...his eyes glow with wonder and admiration.

"Calm down and let go."

As I sing, I remember what Hunter said in the bathroom at my house, about a siren's victims. *What's creepy is that you're smiling. Dead, but smiling. Like you were your happiest just before you died.*

It crosses my mind that sirens are most vulnerable while feeding, because of the necessary eye contact and time it takes to sing out a soul. I brush the thought aside, feeling Hunter's hands on my waist. I'm safe. My chest rumbles with hunger, wanting more. Glen's soul wavers, the rest of it hinges on his lips, its hazy presence tender like spring breath—no longer revolting. This is the very end of his life, all of it, all of his bells and whistles and drunken tunes.

Overcome by the moment, I can't help myself and break the song.

"I'm sorry, Glen," I say, looking into his eyes. Dazed, he doesn't see me.

"I will kill you now. But before that, I will make you happy. I promise. Because one minute of happiness is better than nothing. I owe you that much." I inhale and force my voice into the last string of notes, making them to come out loud and clear despite the soundproof walls that threaten to hush them into nothing.

"Give me your life,
End in my song.
Because you
Listen and love.

Chapter 10

Listen and love.
Listen and love."

The word *love* dies in the air, and my song ends. So does Glen's life, with a swift whoosh. I lick up the rest of it and burp. His life explodes in my chest, trickles its essence into my limbs, my head.

"You all right on your own now?" Hunter asks, unclenching his fingers.

Overwhelmed and gorged, I nod, attempting to stand up. I promptly go limp, falling with my face directly onto Glen's beer belly. Too much food, too fast. Great, just what I was trying to avoid. The smell of his sweat mixed with the stench of years of fishing and spoiling his gut with beer drinking, making me gag and roll over to get off of him.

"Ugh!" I exclaim, sitting up and brushing my face with my hands, sputtering. I yank on my jacket, attempting to get rid of the rotten stink. "God, I hope I can keep it down. It was so disgusting, you have no idea. It was like…you know Pike Place Fish Market? You know how those guys throw the fish away, the spoiled stuff…"

I begin brushing my pants and stop, noticing an ominous silence. I turn my head to look at Hunter and see him staring with his mouth open toward the door, his right hand groping for mine, finding it, squeezing it.

I squeeze it back and follow his gaze. On some level, deep inside, I always knew. I think Hunter did too.

"Papa."

My father's figure is dark against the hazy morning light, as if traced with a black marker. He's dressed in the same orange overalls and jacket as the other fishermen, but somehow his suit smells new, of resin and synthetic lining and protective waterproof coating, as if he snagged it from the factory's floor while still warm. I gag, doused in the chemical odor. Even his rain boots emit the scent of rubber latex. That's not the worst of it. The worst is what's left of his smoldering soul, breaking through the ocean drone in bursts of crackle, incomprehensible in its beauty. It simply can't belong to a man like that. The distant trickle of a flute? The flapping of butterfly wings? Really?

I let out a big exhale, close to a moan. I gulp up air in an equally big inhale, sensing that his soul would taste burned and tart if I were to eat it.

"I'm so sorry to disappoint you, sweetie. I admit, I was hoping for something...more than this. Oh well," he says in his usual calm manner, as he steps into the corridor.

His boots make a whiny sound, like he's rubbing a tightly inflated balloon. His face stretches into a knowing smile.

"We're fucked," Hunter whispers to my left, standing.

I squeeze his hand a couple of times to reassure him and myself. Of what? I don't know exactly. Somehow that faint echo of his soul makes me hope for the best, that somehow we can awaken whatever in him that's good. There must be some left. I believe it, I can feel it.

"Hello, Mr. Bright. Nice boat you have here," Hunter says.

"That's my girl. Good work." My father ignores the greeting and points at Glen. "I was going to fire him anyway, though his kind is hard to find lately, I give you that. It makes me, in some way, very disappointed."

He takes another few steps in, holding his right arm behind his back. I know for sure that he has a sonic weapon in his grasp, his fingers curled tightly around it.

Focus on the facts, Ailen, focus. He talked about Glen, so ask him about Glen.

"What kind would that be?" I ask and flex, casually, as if to suggest that my legs have become numb and I need to stretch them. I notice with a strange glee that my father seems to be

Chapter 10

talking to me only, completely ignoring Hunter. There's no usual *son,* or even a *hello*. This is wrong to think—very, *very* wrong—but the little girl in me, that needy creature, is aglow with pride.

"We will save this discussion for later, if you please," he says. We're about ten feet apart.

"No, we won't. I want to know right now. Whose trawler is this, anyway?" I ask, and cringe. My question comes out like the demand of a toddler. All I'm missing is to stomp my feet and the impression would be complete. I need to be smarter than this. Sure enough, he ignores me, employing his usual treatment as an indication of I-won't-answer-your-stupid-demands. The music of his soul, as burned and broken as it is, gives me hope.

"Ailen..." He levels his eyes with mine, pronouncing my name as if he struggles with each letter.

There is something different in how he says it. Something... human, in a way he hasn't been able to say my name before. As if there is a trace of affection in it. I trust my intuition, letting go of the capricious little girl commanding my thoughts, trusting the siren within me; I know that no matter what he does to me, I'm stronger.

"Unless you want to bore your lover boy here, I suggest you save your breath. Don't talk, just listen. What I'm saying is, I'm glad to see you, despite the fact that you abandoned me in your haste. It was very inconsiderate of you."

He takes another step. I don't move, don't flinch. This is not defiance; no, this is a dare to myself, to finally face what I must. Right here, right now, without my usual squirming. I look my father in the eyes, my heart open.

His right hand trembles slightly behind his back. His smile, even in this darkness, is all-accommodating and fake-welcoming. Yet he's nervous, stinking of fear and sick wonder.

Instead of being scared, I'm happy, happy that my fears can be put to rest. I know he's horrible, but he's the only parent I have. My only true family by blood. There must still be a chance...and I'm willing to take it.

"We'll talk when we get home." On the word *home* I know I guessed right.

"Sure, Papa," I say and pause. "Take me home." I spread my arms wide.

"What the hell, Ailen, wh—" Hunter begins.

My father takes his hand from behind his back and aims the wide muzzle of a huge sonic gun at me.

BOOM!

Chapter 11

Dry Lab

It feels like my body is burning at the stake, my spine nailed to its post, my misery its fire. The darkness is overwhelming. I can smell my hair singed from heat, hear my skin crack as it starts to blacken and curl and split. What's happening? Is this some sort of siren hell and I'm stuck in its hottest room as punishment? It's certainly *not* siren heaven. Perhaps I'm balanced in that divine fold between life and death, the one that rips open as soon as you enter. The afterlife. One of the three destinations where Canosa is supposed to bring those who pass.

The only thing I know for sure is I'm hot. Before my vocal cords dissolve in this brilliant blaze, I want to utter one final cry. It promptly dies on the back of my tongue, stifled by a wall. I'm gagged.

My whole body shakes in a burst of dry coughing. I'm certain that if I was dead for real, coughing would be the last thing on my body's agenda. My throat constricts in another spasm and I make funny whooping sounds through a bundle of cloth stuffed into the cavity of my mouth. My lips sting, stretched out to the biggest O shape they can make; the gag pulls the skin tight all around my jaw, unhinged to near breaking. There is tape over my mouth, and the odor of its glue tickles my nostrils.

I groan, breathing through my nose. It feels like I'm passing fire as each inhale and exhale burns with blistering air. My chest is aflame and my gills feel cracked and dry.

I'm laying on my back, on the floor of a room. My eyes hurt from being dry, so I close them, take another hot breath, and look again, determined to find out exactly where I am.

On my second try, I understand a simple truth that chills me to the bones. It's not just any room I'm in, it's padded. There are a series of square pillows covering walls the color of washed-out sand, reeking of synthetic leather. I concentrate on one thing at a time. I have to focus on the facts.

The room. It's the size of a typical bathroom, or a prison cell, depending on how you look at it. At least it's not dark. On the ceiling, a single round fluorescent light shines through a net of protective wires. The light it emits is soft, as if filtered through a cloud. Everything about this room is soft—the foam on the walls, the floor under my back, even the sound. Rather, the lack of it. Each of my coughs comes out hushed and disappears into the dead silence.

This room, no, this *cell,* is soundproof, perhaps specifically designed for locking up sirens. Yell all you want, nobody will hear. Not like I can test this theory, thanks to the gag.

I wheeze.

The floor shifts and I sway. Does this mean I'm still on the boat? I suck in air through my nose and cringe at the stench of fake leather. Breathing rapidly, I turn my attention to my fingers. They're stuck tight against my elbows in a cup hold, yet I don't feel like I'm holding them. I try to move one, then another, and can't; they all feel numb. My whole body is numb, as if it's not there. Shifting my gaze down doesn't help either, my eyeballs

Chapter 11

burn like they're about to turn to lava and I can't see anything beyond the faint outline of my nose and jaw. There, in the distance, blurry, are my feet that I can't feel. The length of my body is shrouded in the semblance of a cotton sheet, several cotton sheets, layer upon layer.

Great, I'm the first siren pupa.

Off-white cotton, perhaps the same material that fills my mouth, holds me in a cocoon. I flex my hands again, finger by finger, like I'm playing a piano. Imagining who did this, how long it took them to wrap me up like this, and whether or not I'm naked underneath, makes me want to puke.

My father...his face was the last I saw...where?

"Let's see here," I mumble into cloth, but it comes out more like, "Uhuhuheee." I keep talking, to feel sane.

"My name is Ailen Bright, and I'm a sixteen-year-old siren." That much I remember. "I'm a siren and that's all that matters. I have *awesome*—as Hunter would say—powers, and I can get myself out of this mess." Pause. "My father is a siren hunter and he wants to kill me. We were on a fishing trawler wh—" Hunter? What happened to him? *Later. I'll think about this later.*

The floor tilts lightly and I arch and contract. The boat bumps on the wave and I flop face down.

My nose hits the padded floor and I retch into the gag, overtaken with hunger and revulsion at the smell. I strain my neck and turn my head left so that I can breathe, or at least avoid inhaling this synthetic rot.

It takes an eternity for me to repeat the roll. Again. And again. The padded cell revolves around me like a kaleidoscope. I'm in the land of "I don't know why the fuck I'm here and maybe I don't want to know."

I'm mad, lying on my back again, staring at the ceiling. Being mad doesn't help me get out of this situation. However, I can't help it. I'm fuming and my mind's blank, no thoughts in it, only fury at my helplessness.

A minute goes by, but it feels like an hour.

Breathing through my nose is getting harder. My gills are dry to the point of lacerating. One more flex, just one more. I need to get out of here somehow, I need to!

Facts, Ailen, facts, focus on facts.

I glance around. Where is the door? Somehow, they must have gotten me in here. The wall on my right is within my reach, only a couple feet away. The floor shifts once more, and I roll flush with the wall, using it for support to lean away a little, my back about a foot away. I bend my knees as much as the cocoon allows, and hit the wall with my feet. Once, twice, three times. I pause to breathe, noticing the feeble trickle of my energy seep away. But my legs moved, and it gives me hope.

I grunt in anger and hit again. Nothing. No sound, no movement. Not even the tiniest vibration. The smooth cotton on my feet slides over the equally smooth fake leather and doesn't give me any traction. I curse under my breath. How many layers of foam are there?

The constant rocking of the floor intensifies, making me dizzy. It appears the weather outside is as mad as I am. I try reaching out to the clouds, but without my voice, I'm nothing. Maybe that's why we're both frustrated.

I want to break out. I bite into the gag and hit the wall again, pause to rest. Repeat. I ignore the ringing in my ears and the rainbow circles of my blurry vision; closing my eyes, I concentrate every ounce of will on making a noise, at least letting them know I'm here, I'm still alive, and I'm kicking.

A storm. We hit a storm. Its soughing wind walks across my skin in a march of goose bumps. I can feel it even through these walls.

Queasiness bears its sticky fingers into my stomach and I lose it in a series of empty puking spasms. Time turns elastic and

Chapter 11

I forget where it started, don't know if it will end. Maybe it's an unbroken circle. Another hour goes by like this, or two? What was it that needed to be done here?

The wall. Hit the wall, and maybe try your voice again.

But my throat sears with fire when I attempt to sing. So I bend and stomp on the wall one more time with as much force as I can muster.

Something gives.

The temperature inside my cell falls a few degrees. A foreign noise breaks through the matted silence. I don't dare breathe as I concentrate on the noise.

An echo of...it's metallic, like keys on a ring.

A turn of the lock, a click, and several revolutions of what sounds like the hand wheel you see on bank safes in movies. It's large and heavy. One more gentle, metallic din, and I see a vertical line grow from a shadow to a slit to a door opening inside.

I was hitting the wall on the wrong side. Directly across from me, six feet away, a door opens.

There is no immediate soul melody, and the burned tang of butterfly wings on a flute solo enters my hearing. It's off-key. It floods me in a wash of memories, drowning me in images of being caught, the trawler in the ocean, Hunter's kiss, Canosa, the net, and the terrible drum rolling us out of the water and onto the deck. I see the image of Jimmy, the tall fisherman, followed by Glen. Papa. And then me, letting him blast me with his sonic gun, willing to see how far he intended to go.

There is hurt in him, I hear it. An old patina of pain. That means he still feels. It's what I wanted to see for myself before giving in to my overwhelming desire to rid this world of the siren I've become, before I turn out like Canosa—hateful, bitter, grim, unable to stop killing.

A waft of cold air rushes in; I nearly choke on it as I greedily take it in through my nostrils. The door opening widens and I raise my head to look my father in the face, straight in the eyes, bright blue against the dimness behind him.

Hello, Papa, you came to check in on me, I transmit with my eyes. *What a treat. You'd be surprised to find out that, on some level, I have missed you.*

A mask of indifference planted firmly over his features, he holds my gaze, carefully steps inside, and shuts the door behind him with a clank. This is the first time I can't see what he's wearing, don't notice the style of his hair or the smell of his cologne. They don't matter anymore, not even his grimaces that I usually try reading, to know how to behave to avoid his anger.

I'm so afraid of you, Papa. I've been afraid of you my entire life. You're worse than my most horrible nightmares, because nightmares fade away in the morning. But you're real—flesh and bones—and you always seem to find me, no matter how far away I run.

Perhaps he detects what I'm trying to say, because he pauses with his hand still on the door that has no knob, now flush with the wall and invisible. I don't exactly see his hand there, I kind of feel it, a skill I acquired from years of being slapped and hit, to know exactly where his hands are without looking.

His two dark pupils burrow into my consciousness with vivid hate. This time, it's unmasked, borne from a deep place inside, perhaps one that's beyond mending and that was torn out a long time ago, maybe when he was a child. A horrible, empty hole that he didn't know how to fill with love, so he filled it with hate, because keeping it empty hurt more than filling it with anything at all. To survive. Yet there is something, something that still kindles, and I latch on to it, holding his gaze, talking to him in my own silent way.

You know what? There is something I never considered in my constant terror. It never even occurred to me until I died and was reborn as a siren. But I know it now for a fact. He still studies me, unmoving, as if waiting for the punch line. And I deliver.

Chapter 11

As much as I'm afraid of you, you're afraid of me, too.

At this, I exhale, feeling like I've just practiced a speech that maybe one day I'll be able to make in real life.

My father keeps digging deep into my eyes with regard.

Three seconds, that's as long as I last. I can't stand looking into his eyes anymore and avert my gaze. He wins, for now. The air in the room shifts with both of our certainty on this account.

Grief floods me. To my horror, tears of understanding cascade down the side my face.

He's afraid of me, but he has a lifetime of experience turning his fear into violence. No, it's not just me; siren or not, it doesn't matter. It's women, *all* women. He's terrified of women.

Oh, Papa, I wish I could heal you somehow.

That thing that's gone, that place that's been torn out of him, I know what it is. I've known it all along. It's his soul, even before it was stolen by Canosa. It was mostly gone before she ignited it. She simply put the last nail into his coffin. His mother... his own mother must have damaged him before that, the woman he never mentions, the grandmother I never knew. What level of betrayal must a son feel when it comes from his own mother? What kind of hurt would that inflict on his ego, and how permanently would that screw him up? For life.

In this moment, I realize something else...the futility of my attempts. There is no use dying in front of him. It won't work. He doesn't care and would rather see me dead, when he gathers his courage to actually do it. Because I represent his fear and, perhaps, I also look a little bit like my grandma. There is only one thing I can do—keep singing to him, and hope to rekindle more of his soul.

I need to keep singing, despite my fear that he'll never hear, afraid that he's permanently deaf to me. It's not that he doesn't want to. It's that he can't, on his own. He needs help. There is no apparatus that can receive my signal and transmit it into an intelligible wavelength that his brain can then transpose into a jolt of his heart so that he can, in turn, interpret it as a feeling. Into the one, and only, feeling that's worth living for.

    Love.

Chapter 12

Padded Cell

I have to keep trying, even if it means dying in the process. I will know that I did everything I could and will pass in peace. He lets go of the wall and takes a step toward me. His eyes are empty. Finally, I know why. *Papa, I won't give up on you, I swear. I know everyone has in the past, and I'm sorry. I give you my word. I'll fight you, just to make you see that I mean it for real, okay?* I don't know if he got my message or not, as he closes in on me. There is only one way to fight his emptiness: by reflecting his emotions.

He squats next to me and raises his hand.

I recoil on instinct but arrest it before closing my eyes, relaxing my facial muscles as much as the gag allows. I'm glad I do because, instead of slapping me, he gently traces the rivulet of tears on my left cheek, from the bridge of my nose to the wetness on the floor. This unnerves me even more than being slapped.

"There, there. Quiet now. So nice to have you back." His voice comes across as soothing, his face blocking the lamp.

I shrink out of habit.

"You all right?" he asks.

Like you care. Stop this game, for once, and tell me how you really feel. Come on.

His face wavers with a hint of fear, and then it's gone. I smile, if you can call stretching cheek muscles on an already ripping mouth, burning behind tape, smiling.

He leans a bit closer, mouth tight.

"Sorry, I couldn't quite hear you. What was that you said?" His hand is curled over his ear, his favorite way of intimidating me, by asking me to repeat something that is obvious and making me feel like a fool. It doesn't work this time; I ignore it.

He looks out into the distance, through the wall, focusing on something miles away from the cell we're in.

"My dear Ailen, I need to tell you something important, and I apologize it has to happen in this…fashion." He glances at me, indicating my position on the floor.

"It seems as if my other attempts to explain why I'm doing this have not worked, which is a pity. What you don't understand is that your future is at stake. And, because we're a family, my future is tied to yours. I'd like to make sure that you get the message."

I glean the bottom of his shoe, made of the finest Italian leather, as he kicks right into my gills, swift and precise.

Smack!

I hear the sound of impact, like ripping paper, and yelp into the cotton. It hurts like hell. No, worse. It hurts like cutting open a wound that just started healing, over and over and over again.

I pant hard, snorting in effort, and manage to contain my agony without screaming, reveling in my mastery of suppressing the pain.

My father just stands and looks. Cold and calculating.

There is sickness in this, twisted and disgusting, yet I'm en-

Chapter 12

joying myself very much, perhaps rising to a level of masochism that can only match my father's.

Mirror his feelings, Ailen, mirror them. It's exactly what I do, turning my head to look, to show him that he can kick me all he wants, that perhaps I'm enjoying it as much as he does, curious to see what it will do to his psyche.

I see the sole of his shoe one more time.

Whack!

Stars explode in my field of vision and a rod of hot metal pierces me from neck to toes and back up, making me excrete whatever leftover water I have in my system through the skin in a layer of sticky moisture.

It'll take more than that, Papa, you know that. Go ahead, do your best. I attempt to smile, seeing my message reflected across his face. Good.

If he's disturbed by my defiance, he doesn't show it. Still looking into the distance, he drones, "What you don't understand is that life is hard. It's not all clear water, sand castles, and sun, none of these beautiful things, unfortunately. It's a mirage. The second you dip your foot in, you sink into a swamp." He pauses. "What I want you to learn is that good things come to those who wade all the way through, to the other side."

He looks down. Another kick. I hardly feel it this time. He can see it, because a muscle twitches slightly on his left cheek, freshly shaven, as always.

"Oh, did that hurt? Tell me how you feel." He squats and strokes my right gill with one long and gnarled finger. I tense to stop shuddering so that he cannot feel a single vibration.

I look straight into his eyes when something extraordinary happens—something snaps inside of me and is gone. I don't waver in an effort to withstand his scrutiny as I usually do; for the first time, I'm able to sink past this decade-long habit.

Have you ever looked your own terror in the eyes? There

is doom there beyond imagination. But once you've stepped past the place where death is a scary thing, it's possible to hold that gaze, unflinching and calm, knowing that if you look long enough, that's all there is to it, really.

Papa's pupils widen for a fraction of a second. Unperplexed, he continues. "What I want you to learn is that discipline is the answer. You need to learn to suppress the pain, learn to carry on *even* when you feel like you want to die."

The kicks are over. With a grimace of repulsion, he stands and swiftly steps on my neck with his left foot. I notice a flash of his silk maroon sock, framed by the hem of his pant leg. I can't breathe. Water swells in my vessels, fills my eyes, pulses in my ears. My gills open and close like the gaping mouth of a fish thrown on the sand. I will myself to be still and manage to suppress the pain, mentally departing from my body to observe it from the outside.

I push the pain deeper still. There is a victorious glee that's spreading on my face, and I have no doubt my father can see it.

He presses down harder. A minute goes by, maybe two. The sharp-soled edges of his brand-new shoes cut into my jaw and collarbone. I don't flinch, don't make a single sound, and I never look away.

At last, he lets go, removing his foot.

"Good, Ailen, very good. I'm impressed. Continue pushing your pain down. Practice silence."

I take in a sharp breath. My nostrils flare.

Do you want to play another round, Papa? I guess I won this one, wouldn't you say?

His face contorts and he steps away from me as if I'm road kill that stinks.

"Listen to me, Ailen. Silence makes you think." He taps on his temple. "Noise is chaos. It distracts you. Without discipline, you're nothing, just a piece of sweet meat. Think about it. Think

Chapter 12

about your life, about what you want to do. Think about your future."

I want to sing! I wish I could yell it out loud. I reminisce his words, the ones with which he hoped to teach me, to toughen me up, to raise me in such a way that I'd survive in this world as a woman. *Women are weak. Women were made to haul water.*

No, we're not, Papa, you are. You're the one who is weak, because you've forgotten how to love, how to care, I say with my eyes.

He continues, perfectly latching on to the meaning of my glare.

"Contrary to what you think, I care for you. Deeply. That's why I'm being so hard on you. I want to help you...help you carve out a place in this world. You've proven to me, Ailen, that perhaps...you're worth more than just hauling water."

I hold my breath involuntarily. Did that really just come out of my father's mouth?

"Perhaps. I intend to test my theory." He always takes his time to deliver the punch line, holding me in suspense, relishing my terror. Not this time.

"When we cut your vocal cords, sweetie, you'll become useful to me, I think. Yes. You'll help me with an important task... killing other sirens. As payment, I will let you live."

Before I can react or utter a moan, he pounds on the door with his fist. No, not on the door, it's a viewing window.

A small rectangular sheet of glass glistens, reflecting fluorescent light.

Synthetic leather on synthetic leather, the door slowly opens with a soft swoosh and then comes to a stop, barely an inch ajar.

I try to gasp, wishing someone would pierce my eardrums for good so that I could not hear. Not now, not this.

I'd be better off dead.

Hunter takes small steps inside, looking beaten and haggard in his dirty jeans and sweatshirt, matted hair hanging over his pale face. His head is down, lips pressed together. He holds on to the door as if he was a drunk trying to steady himself.

"Come in, come in," my father urges him. Hunter doesn't move. His left hand stays on the door, the right one kneads the pocket of his jeans. There's a brief moment of awkward silence, and I know it's about to erupt.

"Don't just stand there, pick her up!" Papa raises his voice, and then lowers it again. "Please." At this, he throws his hands in the air and rubs his temples. An angry fit is about to begin. It'll only go downhill from here.

"Mr. Bright..." Hunter bites his lower lip and looks up, still avoiding me. "Do we *really* have to do this? I mean, isn't there another way? She ca—"

"I said, pick, her, *up*." This comes through pressed lips, and I know inside my father is boiling.

"But you could simply send her away without—"

"*Pick her up!*" A vein pulses in the hollow of my father's temple, his hands curling into fists.

"Yes, Mr. Bright." Hunter's lips barely move.

"I don't want to talk about this anymore, is that understood? We've discussed everything there was to discuss already, end of story." He turns his back on me and makes for the door.

End of my story, you mean? Will you really go this far, Papa? It's a final test for you, to see if you can do this to your own kind, to eradicate your nightmare. And I'm the one who represents it for you, aren't I? I understand, but you know what? You're no more than a stinking coward, making someone else do the dirty work for you. You're weak, with all of your false bravado.

Hunter takes a small step, and then stops.

My eyes dart to his face, searching. *Oh, Hunter, what did he do to you, what did he tell you to make you do this?*

Hunter avoids looking at me directly as he takes a few tentative steps and bends over me.

Chapter 12

He rolls me onto my back, sits on his haunches, slides his right arm under my shoulders and his left under my knees, and then heaves me up with a grunt. Hunter's heart beats over a hundred times per minute; his muscles shake in effort; a faint odor of sweat mixes with his natural smell of pine, linden flowers, and sugar. I melt into his body, strangely happy and calm.

I pretend I'm a swaddled baby, hungry and distraught, needing care; to be held by someone I love, someone who loves me back. One second stretches into an eternity. My head plops on his shoulder, and I close my eyes and glow.

There is, perhaps, an understanding that travels through our skin, touching through layers of fabric. On purpose, I'm certain, Hunter barely makes a step toward the door before following a lurch of the boat too perfectly and losing balance. His arms let go and he drops me on the soft floor, and then falls down on his butt, hanging his head in theatric humiliation.

"Shit!" he says too fast, his tone a little too convincing. "Sorry, Mr. Bright. Man, I don't think I can do this, she's just too heavy for me." He raises his head expectantly, and I know what he's fishing for.

Nice try, dude.

"What's the matter, son? I'm sure you've fantasized about carrying her over the threshold, haven't you? Here's your chance to practice, go ahead. Or is she too much of a burden for you?"

"No, no, that's not what I mean. Man, you got it all wrong," Hunter nearly stutters. He never minces words, so this tells me he's scared out of his mind. "I mean sh—"

"Do me a favor, stop talking and do what you're told. Now. Unless you want to break our agreement?" I don't need to see him to know that Papa's eyebrows fly up in question. *What agreement?* I immediately know what it is. He bought Hunter's help in exchange for keeping me alive, I'm sure of it.

"'Course not. I'll try again here in a minute. Just...stretching my legs is all," Hunter lies again, leaning over to hoist me up, his face a tight mask of strain.

Hunter, don't believe him, he's bluffing! I mumble into the gag. *Don't do this, please. He won't dare kill me, trust me, he's too weak! He's a coward underneath all of this yelling and anger and...* only a hushed mutter comes out. I growl, frustrated.

"Don't talk, Ailen, please." Papa appears over both of us and promptly puts his shoe on my neck. I choke. Hunter raises his arm and lets it fall, resigned.

"It's better this way. Learn to be quiet," Papa says, looking at me with a strange sadness. "Carry on, son." Although the last remark is directed at Hunter, I no longer feel jealous at the word *son*. I only feel pity.

Beads of sweat prickle Hunter's forehead. He squats, spreads his legs apart for added balance, and, with a strained groan, heaves me off the floor. I squirm, a siren pupa. A quick blow to the back of my head makes me hang still. My father delivers it with his usual quiet precision, and that is my last thought before I black out.

When I come to, a cold waft of chlorine hits my nose. Bright light blinds me as if it was a thousand suns. My eyes water, making everything blurry and causing me to squint. It takes a moment to stop seeing the floating blotches of glow. When my vision finally adjusts, I wish my eyes were gagged instead of my mouth.

I'm stark naked, chained inside a tub, in a chamber about fifteen by twenty feet in size. It looks like a hybrid between an old-fashioned lavatory, a surgery room, and a communal shower. Its walls are gray painted on top of metal, most likely steel; a round pipe opens directly over my head, the end of its opening roughly three inches in diameter.

I gulp the moisture from the water through my skin, not

Chapter 12

exactly inhaling it, but absorbing it the way a sponge does. At the same time, I strain to expand, to snap off the chains, to bend open their links and make them fall apart. Hunter's words come back to me...*You know what I mean. Not the mythical kind. No. I'm talking about a real siren. The killer kind.* I realize, in retrospect, it was me he was talking about. He meant me, my stubbornness and my ability to move forward on sheer will, when other girls would've given up. I am the killer kind, and it's time to show it.

I'm not a little girl anymore, Papa. You can't do the things you did to me when I was little. You can't just take my voice away by force. It belongs to me and me alone. I'm my own being, capable of living without your constant control, and I'm not a thing to play with. I have a name. My name is Ailen Bright, and I'm a siren. And I'll show you what that means.

I begin humming, directing my power upward and into the atmosphere. This is the beauty of sound—it can penetrate the walls. There, in the expanse of velvety darkness, first a few feet and then miles away, droplet to droplet, rain carries my hum all the way into the clouds. Slowly, I begin pulling moisture from miles around into one spot, hanging heavy over the trawler. There is a rumble of electricity and a crack of lighting, caused by the force of my voice. I feel like the conductor of a giant orchestra.

I hum more, adding intensity.

Something ruptures from above. Water gushes down in one focused stream. As an overturned shooting geyser, it falls on the roof of the pilothouse first, then slides down and breaks through several feet of deck material, denting it and forcing its steel panels apart, like it's no more than sand.

I no longer hear Hunter or Papa. I'm humming *"Rain"* by Siren Suicides. I pull and nag and coax every single water drop in my vicinity to move, calling on the ocean itself. Now even the rascal glow of the emergency light flickers, the boat careening dangerously to the left. The tub must be bolted to the floor, because it doesn't move. But the chains slacken from the force of me jerking around, and I hear the links begin to give.

The light pulses with the sputtering of a failing electrical circuit. It goes dead and in the darkness the wail of the alarm breaks into abrupt silence.

I feel pressure on the boat's hull, from all sides, as if it's about to be squished between two mighty Greek mythological monsters, Scylla and Charybdis. I imagine their evil faces from the books I've read, opening their toothless mouths, wanting to swallow the trawler in an almighty whirlpool, sucking it to the bottom of the sea. There is a loud rumble and fizz, followed by the cracking and groaning of wood and metal before bolts begin shooting out of the walls and the ceiling, landing on top of me like empty bullet shells. Dust from the ceiling's splintering wood covers me in a thin layer of powder. After a few seconds, the trawler seems unable to withstand the enormous force of water pressure. It starts to collapse and I win.

Water spurts through every crevice it finds and begins flooding the room. I hear it rising quickly, with a deafening determination. I twist around in my chains and manage to break my feet free; I pound them against the tub's end, hoping the friction will let me free the rest of my body. I want to call out Hunter's name but I'm afraid to break my humming, wanting to cause as much damage to the vessel as I can, holding on to the hope that I will have enough time to get out of here, find him, and flee together.

I work my fingers, clenching and unclenching them, and then finding the loop-hooks and breaking them one by one. They're holding me suspended like a floating bridge, about ten inches from the bottom of the tub. I undo every chain hook along my body, starting from my shoulders and getting all the way to my knees, my clumsy fingers slipping and my body sag-

Chapter 12

ging into the tub as I go. After unhooking each chain, I yank it, along with its fastening bolt, out of the tub, unceremoniously throwing them on the floor, one by one, until at last I'm free.

A loud crack traces the floor above me and water begins falling down in freezing sheets. The first pangs of panic begin to rise and my humming stops at once.

I rip the tape off my face, together with a few hairs tearing from the back of my head. It takes three tries to get off every single layer, until I reach the ball of cotton, now soaked through with my saliva. I grasp it with unbending fingers and pull it out, coughing. I take another few seconds to bend my head down over my knees and retch, buried in a sudden wash of nausea.

I quickly touch my throat, as if to confirm it's still there.

"Hunter!" I croak, coughing and sputtering water out as I sit up in the tub. "Hunter, where are you? Answer me."

Shaking, still weak, I awkwardly climb over the side of the tub. My foot hits something soft and warm. Jimmy lays unconscious, slumped against the tub platform. I consider sucking out his soul quickly and decide against it. Maybe he helped Hunter. Maybe he helped Papa. There isn't time. I have to find Hunter and get him off this sinking ship before it's too late. And my father...what will I do with him? Leave him to sink? Rescue him too, hauling them both on my back? It's impossible.

I'm momentarily perplexed, remembering the promise I made to myself to find the good in him, to try and revive him all the way. Yet, somehow, I can't find the motivation after what just transpired.

There is, however, one more thing I need to do. I squat next to Jimmy, dipping my hands into several feet of freezing water on the floor, and feel for his jacket and pants, swaying together with the rocking trawler. I try to find a zipper or button of some kind. It seems to take an eternity, but I finally manage to pull both rain boots off of his soggy feet, strip him of his orange overalls and jacket, and drag them over myself. The ensemble is huge on my petite frame and sticks to me with its rubbery coating inside, but I don't mind. It's a thousand times better than being naked.

The boat lurches again and I fly to the other end of the lab, hitting my head hard on one of the protruding hooks, yelping. Jimmy moans as his body slams into the wall next to me. Though his head stays above the water, he won't be able to keep afloat and will soon drown.

With a sigh, I lean over and stick my hands under his stinky armpits, pulling him in front of me and carefully stepping backward and up, because, at this point, the trawler stopped lurching from side to side and is steadily careening in one direction.

"Hunter!" I yell, making my way to what I hope is the door. "Hunter, answer me!"

The door is open, and I can feel the rush of water and air with my back. At the speed it's rising, I think I have ten, maybe twenty minutes before the trawler sinks.

"Hunter!" I try again.

A motor whirrs to life somewhere above—must be some sort of an emergency generator. At the same time, the red emergency light turns on.

"Hunt—" I begin and bump into someone with my back. I turn around and gawk, "Papa?" I hate myself for uttering this involuntary greeting.

No matter what he does to me, no matter what I decide the night or day before, in the most critical moments—when I think I've lost him—my inner child comes out. For a split second, I'm happy to see him alive. My father's wet face grins in the sinister blood-red glow of the emergency light. He's standing in my path, blocking the doorway and holding on to the frame with his right hand. Hunter is slumped against Papa's left shoulder, half-standing and half-hanging in his one-armed embrace.

Chapter 12

We lock eyes and he smiles.

"I thought I might find you here," he says.

"You. What..." I breathe, suppressing the urge to cradle Hunter's face, to call out his name, to ask him if he's okay. This is when I need my siren self to take over.

"Let go of him. Now," I say, squatting, ready to attack.

My father holds something in his right hand—something that was hidden behind the doorframe.

It's a gun.

He points it at Hunter's head. It's not the plastic sonic weapon he uses on sirens. No, this is real.

"One more step and your boyfriend dies," he says in a level voice, though I still detect a hint of fear behind it. He knows that time is not to his advantage.

"You wouldn't dare," I whisper, curling my fingers into fists.

"Who are you to tell me what I would or wouldn't dare?" A childish note creeps into his voice, and I have a feeling it's not me he's talking to.

"How dare you talk to your own father like this? How dare you to doubt me." There's an echo of his soul that mixes into the conversation, and I feel it waver. It's uncertain; he doesn't want to do this. I want to reach out to it and hold it, but I don't get the chance.

"What you don't understand is that men and women were made differently. *I* was made differently." I notice how he switches from his usual generalization of men to talking about himself. I must have cut deeply into his wound.

"*I* don't hesitate. *I* control my emotions, I control *things*. I *do* things. You must learn from me if you want to live. Move."

Fast as lightning, he straightens out his arm and shoves me to the left, causing me to stumble and lose my hold on Jimmy. He slides out of my grasp and my father shoots him in the head.

"Jimmy!" I lean over him, ignoring the ringing in my ears.

Padded Cell

When did I decide that saving his life was my responsibility? I don't know, but I failed. "You shot him!"

They say your whole life flashes in front of your eyes, in a split-second, right before you die. A lucid dream composed of moments of love, if you had any.

What they don't say is what happens when you watch someone else die a senseless death. It flashes before your eyes in just the same way, only double. Everything held in your memory spills out in a myriad of pictures, silly snapshots of life, making you wonder what it would feel like to be in this person's place. I killed Glen, yes, for food. This is different. What my father just did is mindless murder.

I sense the sound of Jimmy's soul moving up and out, toward me. Involuntarily, still bent over, I suck it in, letting the much needed strength course through my chest, to my heart, and throughout my body. I raise my head, wondering if my father knew this soul would feed my strength.

Papa continues to point the gun at Hunter's head. "Do we have an agreement?" he asks, coldly.

"Yes. Yes, please..." I say, sticking out my hands in a protective gesture. My defiance evaporates in an instant. "I'll do whatever you say, just *please,* don't...don't kill him."

The floor shifts and slides out from under our feet.

I fall forward, on top of my father, and we crash into the corridor, slipping on the wet floor and sliding toward the narrow stepladder—the only way out of this metal beast before it's consumed by the ocean.

Chapter 13

Lifeboat

Thoughts course through my head as we fly with incredible speed toward the ladder, bumping into pipes sticking out here and there, and then come to an abrupt stop, draping over the steel bottom rung like three heavy sacks filled with sand, one on top of another. Darkness throbs in the red flickering light. The boat's tilt must be close to a thirty-degree angle now. I remember reading somewhere that once it careens past forty-five degrees, sinking is inevitable and happens within minutes.

I find my face pressed into my father's chest, hearing his beating heart, his warmth touching my forehead.

"No!" I weep into his shirt, soaked and smelling faintly of fabric softener. Why has Jimmy's death hit me so hard? I don't even know the guy. Why it makes me weep from grief I can't comprehend.

My father jerks up, attempting to sit.

"Off! Get off me! Get—" he yells over the rumble of the creaking trawler that's about to give up. He pushes his free hand into my left shoulder and shoves me away, like I'm the most disgusting creature that's ever touched him. This is as close as we've ever gotten to a hug, and I wish he would drop his gun and drape his arms around me, letting me sob into his shoulder. I need him to tell me that we all will be okay, and everything that's happened in the past will be forgotten. We'll start new, and it will be always sunny, warm, and loving. Only life doesn't work this way, and neither does Papa.

Life has a way of reminding you of its fragile balance, just when the future looks rosy. It sends me that reminder as it dunks the trawler another foot down, digging sharp fingers of panic into me, siren or not.

"Hunter!" I yelp over the rushing water, reaching for him. My father intercepts me and pushes my arm away, yelling in response.

"We don't have time for this. Get him up. There is a lifeboat on the deck. Move!"

I glance at him. Impulse makes me want to circle my hands around his neck and choke him, choke him to his natural death. It's like a cruel joke, a joke on this whole siren hunting thing; we are forever destined to torture each other, both armed with unlikely weapons—sirens with their voice, siren hunters with a sonic boom.

Hunter's body is slumped against the ladder, hugging its very bottom like a torn rag doll. Half of his face floats in and out of the water.

"I said, move it! Get him up, now!" Papa yells, pressing the gun into my left shoulder. "You want to keep your boyfriend alive, don't you, sweetie?"

Papa's manner of mixing a cute name that indicates affection, into a furious tirade, hits me with its ugliness. I only manage to nod.

"One arm on the ladder, one arm on the waist. Here—" My

Chapter 13

father points to direct me, grabbing the ladder with his free hand and pressing his back against it to stabilize himself; the ladder is nearly vertical, so Papa leans against it as if it were a wall, while the trawler continues tilting.

He shoves me toward Hunter. I fall to my knees and lift Hunter's face. He moves his lips, coughing. There is a dangerous cracking noise above.

"Move it!" my father directs me. He doesn't like to dirty his hands, always finding someone else to carry out his commands. This time, it's me. It's my job to carry Hunter to safety, and I'm glad to do it. So I hold my mouth shut. I pull Hunter up. He moans and his knees buckle, so I rely on my strength alone. My father watches me struggle, his gun at the ready.

For the next several minutes, I fight the flood and haul myself up with one arm, holding Hunter with the other, carefully stepping up with my bare feet, curling my toes around the metal bars. I leap up to grab the next rung, and the next, until I make it to the upper level and pull us both onto the floor, covered with fishy-smelling litter, metal trays, bags of melted ice, and other debris that got washed down. One more level and we'll make it to the deck.

I turn and see my father emerge from the hole as well, first clamping his hand with the gun over the edge, then the other one, yanking himself out with an agility I didn't think he possessed, and sitting on the edge a little sideways, his legs dangling down.

"There. Go!" He points at the opening, propped on all fours for balance.

"Now!" he barks, and I move. The water gurgles above in splashing waves, and there is another tug down and a dangerous-sounding metallic moan of the boat's hull. In my haste, halfway up the second ladder, I don't notice how Hunter's head lolls to the side and hits one of the protruding pipes on the wall with a wet smack. He shudders in pain and yelps loudly, suddenly fighting my hold.

I let go from surprise and hear him collapse several feet down, with a crack of the back of his head against steel.

There is a moan and a kick.

"Fucking klutz. Get up!" Another kick.

My helpless rage is close to driving me insane. Surely, in this chaos, I can easily snatch Hunter away—right from under my father's nose—and escape with him. But the risk of having him killed in the process is too much to bear, so I slowly make myself go down to help both of them.

I ignore my father's insults in an attempt to get me moving, and I try to block out Hunter's moaning. I touch the floor, lean, and scoop up Hunter. Methodically, I make my way back up, step by step, hearing the resin of my new overalls squeak, gripping the rungs with my toes, and my arm firmly around Hunter's waist. I hear him mumble something into my shoulder, but concentrate on making it to the deck.

I grab the edge of the hatch; someone, thankfully, must have left it open. I tense and leap out, landing on top of the open cover, Hunter firmly in my lap. The wind slaps my face and whistles through the gaps of my fisherman's suit. Heavy-laden clouds hang low over the horizon. It must be the dawn of day two since I jumped from the bridge.

Lightning strikes, briefly illuminating the storm's angry rain. The rolling thunder deafens me with an earsplitting accord. This might be the last day I'll see Papa and Hunter alive. I feel a push in the small of my back and turn, watching my father struggle to stand on the leaning deck without sliding, holding on to the railing, wrongly clothed for this weather. Curling his shaky fingers around it, he aims his gun at Hunter and urges me to get him up and into the lifeboat.

I nod, indicating that we're still good with our agreement,

Chapter 13

lifting and draping Hunter over my shoulder and carrying him like a baby to the aft part of the deck where the orange capsule of the lifeboat gleams in the gray of the early morning. Suspended from ropes attached to one of the galleys, it careens at a dangerous angle, about to snap and fall. The other half of the deck is fully submerged in the water now, and as far as I can hear, there are no other living human souls on the sinking trawler. Hadn't there been another crewman?

Our predicament, its terrible beauty, arrests me for a moment. A colorless background of dull water meets the dull sky, and I'm precariously balanced on its edge, with only a drop of orange acting as my salvation. It occurs to me that I can leave them both, Hunter and father, right here, right now; I can leap into the waves, swim away, and never come back. But my feet won't move, and my limbs won't listen. I can't run away anymore.

I grab on to the ropes that are stretched in a pulley mechanism designed to lower the lifeboat, and with a powerful yank, I tear at them, breaking the elaborate on-loading system. I watch as the lifeboat drops on the deck, screeches, and slides across its remaining twenty feet and into the water. The lifeboat has an orange waterproof cover, hatches in its roof, and a series of circular windows adorning its front, each large enough for one person to peek through.

The trawler growls and tilts, rapidly reaching the forty-five-degree incline. Yelling into Hunter's ear to hold his breath, hoping he'll come to his senses and hear me, I let him slide to face me, hugging him tightly. I dive from the trawler's deck, emerging a second later; I hear his breathing to my satisfaction, and circle about the bobbing lifeboat. Leaping into the air with Hunter firmly pressed to my chest, I plop right into the middle between both of its hatches on the roof. Feeling it shift to the side, I have time to rip off one of the hatch's lids and push

Hunter into the opening, feet first.

He moans and grabs hold of my ankles, but I have no time to explain what is going on.

There is a deafening explosion of gunfire, my father no doubt thinking that I broke our agreement and decided to take off with Hunter alone. And I could, right? But I won't. I'm simply unable to leave my father stranded, letting him die of hypothermia or exhaustion, or both. I hate myself for feeling this way, but I can't help it. Deep inside, under protective layers of loathing and revulsion and teenage defiance, I still love him. I love him the way every little girl loves her father, idolizing and adoring him no matter what.

"Get in there and wait for me!" I say into Hunter's ear, shoving him into the hole and diving back into the ocean.

I land in a froth of turbulent bubbles, white foam on the ocean's surface created by the sinking trawler. A few life preservers float around, the only things left to indicate that, only seconds ago, a fifty-foot trawler was here. The whole thing is simply gone.

About twenty feet away I spot a bobbing head.

I swim across the whirlpool, held back by the clumsy fisherman's suit that's catching on the water and not letting me move fast enough. Diving under, I emerge directly beneath my father, grabbing his shifting torso and surfacing with him in my hold, willing myself deaf to his threats and shouts and two more gun shots in the air, which is just a pointless waste of ammunition. I repeat my trick of leaping out of the water and landing on top of the lifeboat, managing to turn midair to hit it with my back, protecting Papa like I did Hunter from the fall. The impact makes the boat rock dangerously and we begin sliding. I reach out and hold on to the protruding contraption that was secured to a hook before I yanked the lifeboat down from its hold.

My father is shouting and motioning me in, shaking from

Chapter 13

the cold. I'm in a daze of suppressed rage, moving automatically and focusing on the task at hand so that I don't lose it. Crawling on top and worming inside, my father urges me in. I descend into what looks like a small bathroom with a low ceiling and tiny circular windows. No, it looks more like a sauna with those shelf-like seats stacked on either side of the boat's interior, four in total, strapping belts hanging loose across them and contrasting their orange color against the walls' white. My bare feet touch the smooth surface of the floor. Papa hops down next to me and pushes me into a seat to the left, positioning himself in the top seat to the right, the one next to all kinds of controls and knobs and a couple of sticks.

Hunter is slumped into a seat below me, his eyes open, studying me, clearly uncomprehending and dazed. He is mouthing something, shivering and wet, his arms crossed over his pulled-up legs.

I open my mouth to talk when, incredibly, the first thing I hear in the relative quiet of the lifeboat is my father's voice, complaining—not about losing his trawler, no—about his outfit.

"Do you know how much I paid for this suit?" he mutters. "Finest Italian wool. Look at it now, it's ruined."

An incredible thought passes through my mind. Is he embarrassed by having to accept my help? Because that's what it sounds like. I've never seen my father embarrassed before, so I can only guess. He lifts his eyes and there is stunned wonder there, a question in them. I know what it is, without him having to say it aloud. He's wondering why I didn't leave him, why I saved him when I know that he will make it hell for Hunter and me.

"Thank you," he says, gun in his lap. Then clears his throat and repeats again, explaining. "Thank you for sticking to our agreement. I admire the fact that you held to your word and did as promised." But I know by his face that the first thanks was not meant for this. The first one was an important one that slipped off his tongue before he could catch it. He thanked me for not leaving him out there all alone, and I smile, returning the favor.

"You're welcome." I lean in with the urge to...I don't know what. To touch his hand? To hug him? A second later, I'm sorry I did.

A contortion of repugnance crosses my father's face, wrinkling his forehead. He points his real gun at me, simultaneously groping behind him and yanking a sonic weapon off the wall with his left hand and pointing that at me, too. How considerate, now I know that this was indeed his siren hunting trawler after all, stocked with the necessary supplies to do the job. He even had them stored in the lifeboat.

"Stay back!" my father shrieks.

I freeze, studying his eyes. Rain softly patters on the floor, falling inside through the open hatch, breaking up the white noise of relative silence.

He's still afraid of me. After a second or two, I slowly lean back against the smooth wall, feeling my legs dangle over the seat and my feet catching on warm drifts of Hunter's breath below. I suppress my anger by turning it inward, and now it's eating me inside. It's tearing me apart—one part of me loving him, the other hating him, both not being able to peacefully coexist.

Chapter 14

Allen Bank

The worst part of hating your parent is looking in the mirror and seeing that parent in your face. In my case, my father's big blue eyes are the eyes I inherited, so are his pointed nose, angular cheekbones, and lanky limbs on a lithe body. I wish it didn't go farther than looks, but it does. I was raised by him; I soaked up his atmosphere, his way of living, his teachings, his mannerisms, his way of talking and walking and even thinking. His fears are my fears, his fury is my fury, and his memories are my memories. We are one, yet we are two, like the vast sky and endless ocean, separated by a horizon line. Therein lies our constant struggle to split apart. Yet we can't, forever bound as father and daughter.

"Stay where you are and don't move," my father says to me, lowering the sonic weapon to rest on his knees, its conical end pointing directly at my chest. His upper torso sways slightly to the movement of the waves.

I raise my arms to push myself deeper into the seat.

"I said, don't move!" He raises the gun again, his voice mechanical, his words minimal on purpose. I can tell he's covering up his unrest. The thought, nevertheless, gives me pleasure. And sadness.

I realize he's weaker than me, and it's me who must make the first step, to show him that it's possible to heal, possible to extract his pain no matter how encrusted with age. I feel like his equal, if not his superior, and I know that he senses it.

"You don't need to threaten me, Papa," I say, looking him directly in the eyes. "I won't hurt you, I promise." I want to add something else, but he jabs the muzzle of the gun in the air with renewed force. I don't flinch, knowing he won't shoot me.

"Don't you dare talk to me like that!" His breathing comes out in sharp wheezes, blotches of red blooming on his cheeks.

"Look what you did!" Here comes his usual attempt to make me feel guilty. "My trawler. It's gone now! Do you have any idea how much it costs? Do you—" He's visibly shaken. "You," he says, jabbing the sonic weapon at me. "You keep destroying my property. You…" At first, he searches for words, and then he proceeds to explain how much it really cost him to get it and have it all equipped, but I'm not listening anymore. What fascinates me is the fact that he's sharing this information, deeming me worthy of knowing it, which he has never done before.

"…over, you hear me? Your diddle-daddle outside of the house is over. Now, listen to me. Here is what will happen. We will go home and you…"

I tune in and out, taken by his eyes that seem to cast me into an acidic bog of misery and elation at once. He's talking to me, actually talking to me, for real, like an adult. Does this mean I have proven something that makes me worthy of his bother? His face grimaces, spelling out each word that I don't hear. He lost his jacket and his pink shirt sleeves are carefully rolled up and wet, forming two elaborate rolls around his bulging triceps, smeared with dark lines of machine oil or some other dirt. His

Chapter 14

fingers curl around the two guns, his knuckles white from strain.

I don't know if it's the rocking of the lifeboat, the soothing patter of the rain combined with the ocean grumble, or the fact that my adrenaline—if sirens have adrenaline—is retreating, but I enter the zone of aftershock. Whichever it is, it's causing me to imagine myself as a swaddled baby, in need of a change. The sticky, moist fisherman's suit adds to the illusion.

This is my lucid dream, my one minute of fantasy that's better than nothing, worth every second, paid for with suicide.

I'm in a crib, in a soothingly swaying crib. Papa is coming to change my clothes, to swaddle me up, to sing me to sleep with a private solo, for me alone.

He keeps talking and moving his arm about, forgetting to aim the weapon at me and pointing it at the boat controls instead. I imagine him lifting me and putting me on the changing table with a soft smile, stroking my face, telling me what a bad girl I am to wet myself from head to toe. The lifeboat bobs on a wave and I hit my head on the low overhang, but I think it's Papa throwing me into air so high that I brush the ceiling with the top of my head. He points with the gun at the buckle straps and then at me, explaining that, siren or not, I need to buckle up. I daydream that he's about to give me a warm bath, gently shampoo my hair, hug me in a towel, help me with my pajamas, and tuck me in to bed, kissing my forehead good night. Something my mother used to do, but something that he never did, not once, in his life.

"...again, do not open your mouth unless I ask you a question or tell you that you can. Do you understand?"

Does he feel the effect of my voice on him? I wonder and nod, feeling the poison of self-hate seep back into my veins. "Excellent," my father says, lowering both guns to his lap again, glancing down. He hangs his head, knowing he has no choice but to believe me, and I can almost feel his hysterical outburst leave him, yield to a sense of being lost.

At this point, the nausea caused by my father's barely audible soul, and my sudden hunger, overwhelms me. I draw a deep breath and convulse in a series of coughs, each threatening to tear me apart.

Any noise I make irritates Papa to no end and makes him yell at me to be quiet. He yells at me to stop and slaps his knee in frustration, but it doesn't have the typical desired effect on me, nor does he have the conviction.

He's like a little child throwing a fit because his favorite toy has been taken away. I watch with a mild smile playing on my lips, which he notices after a while, falling silent.

"I'm tired of you being noisy. Can't you keep it down? Is it so hard to do? Always fidgeting, always talking, asking questions, scratching, coughing. I can't stand it! Can't you be quiet for a minute? It irritates me, you know that. I need you to stay put, to let me concentrate on making it back to Seattle," he says, and I'm stunned again.

He talks to me like I'm a teenager, as if nothing happened. We simply ended up in a lifeboat for some odd reason and now we need to make it home. The whole siren hunting thing evaporated.

"I can hum. It'll make us move faster," I say, before I can stop myself.

"Did I give you permission to talk? No." There goes the gun again in my face. "And, no, no humming. I forbid you." He clears his throat. "No humming on this lifeboat, no talking, no singing. I just told you this. Unless I ask you a question or I tell you it's okay to talk, you're not allowed to open your mouth. Nod so that I know you understand." The metallic coldness is back in his voice, he's recovered from his lapse into vulnerability and is no doubt mad at me for being the catalyst.

I nod.

Chapter 14

I won't cry, I won't cry, but I almost do.

"Good. Remember this." He shakes the gun at me and falls quiet. It's like he lost his ability to threaten me and express his anger clearly, sounding mechanical and broken. He reaches up, closes the hatch cover, and then leans forward to study the controls.

The waves drone on, licking the lifeboat. Papa pushes a few buttons and shifts a long stick that's got a round black grip on it, and a motor comes to life. He grabs on to the steering wheel with one hand, places his guns on his lap with the other, gives me a meaningful look, and tilts his head down, glancing at Hunter, who has stayed silent this whole time.

"Are you all right, son?" he says.

Considering it safe, I lean a bit more to the right and peer down to see better.

I'm sitting facing the round windows of the upper level of the boat, but Hunter reclines in the seat below in the opposite direction, so I can make out his face in the shadow. It has a dead look about it. He lifts his eyes to both of us as if to merely register where the voice is coming from, seeing nothing, glazed over and passive.

"Yeah, fine," he says.

"Good." The upper sides of Papa's cheeks pull his muscles into a grimace that's supposed to look like a smile. He's back to his nasty self, but not owning it like he usually does, forcing it. I have changed something in him, I think. Yes, I'm positive.

His attention is on Hunter right now, and on steering the boat. Its engine purrs quietly, and he shifts gears to pick up speed.

"It's unfortunate. Your failure," he tells Hunter without looking, turning the steering wheel and occasionally glancing at me. "We will have to try this again. Three times is a charm."

My heart falls. So he made him do it once before me, and is now planning to remove my voice, even after everything that's happened. It's like he possesses some kind of stubbornness that gives him reason to go on no matter what. To hold on to, so he doesn't fall apart.

I want to pinch myself. Do I really understand my father's motivations now? What will happen if I simply ask him? I'm still not sure, afraid to inflict pain on Hunter in the process. So I keep my thoughts to myself, looking out the window into the gray fog.

Despite everything, I still love you, you know, I want to tell Papa, studying the low hanging clouds and the brightening day.

My father jams the wheel in a set position and turns sideways to face me. His gray hair glistens in the growing light, his eyes sunken.

"Well, we're on our way back, which will be another hour in this thing, possibly more. I take it you're both comfortable, because we have a lot to talk about. Let's start with an explanation of your behavior, Ailen. Please. I'm listening."

This is the father I know and I automatically flare up.

"What? What behavior? You were about to kill me, and you're asking me for an explanation of *my* behavior?" I say incredulously.

His fear of me is gone, or suppressed, and the sonic gun is no longer wavering in his hand, its aim is steady. He has this pained expression on his face, then a shudder of disgust, as if digging in a pile of rotten fish with his bare hands. We're back to ground zero.

"Shhhh. Talk quietly, please, you give me a headache with your voice. Where do you get your ridiculous ideas? It was an operation to be performed for your benefit, which you, as is typical, made into a mess. We will get to that part. Now, answer my question."

I gawk, unsure of what to say, and glance at Hunter for support. He shrugs, looking at me and through me at the same time.

Chapter 14

"Come on, Ailen, it's just a question," he says. I think I hear a trace of tears in his voice and such finality that it makes me shudder. Like he's decided on something serious and doesn't give a damn anymore. It wasn't me who sucked the life out of him. It seems as if he's feeling the impossibility of getting out of this predicament, and that he's given up.

Without thinking, I turn and look Papa in the face.

"How about *you* answer my questions first? How about you explain to me *your* behavior? Your incessant need to hurt. Where, exactly, does it come from? How about you open up and admit that your mother never loved you, she hurt you, she yanked your trust right out of your little chubby hands, just like you yanked out mine, when I was little. Because you don't know any better, because everything has been taken from you by force and this is the only way you know. You don't know how to give, because nobody has ever given you anything, have they?"

His eyes widen; I press on.

"Wait, I don't need you to explain anything, I got it. You simply never grew up. You stopped maturing at that age when Grandma hurt you. You're like this little boy forever stuck in his childhood, playing with expensive toys, making rash decisions, enjoying your games, feeling entitled—like a proper asshole. No, wait, it's worse. At least assholes mess up their shit. But not you, oh no. You don't like to do the dirty work. You always hire someone else to do it for you. Am I right? So tell me, how much did it cost you, Papa? Your heart? Your soul? What will it take for you to wake up and admit your pain and stop running away from it? It's what you do. It's what you taught *me* how to do. You taught me to suppress it, and I grew up a coward, just like you, afraid to face it. So how about it? Did I get this right? Why don't *you* explain my behavior to me? I would very much like to hear your perspective." I pause to catch a breath.

As soon as I'm done talking, terror raises its ugly head in my chest. I dared to talk back to him. I watch his face, frozen.

He winces as if in pain, but he never interrupted me. He tightens the grip on his gun, but I think I detect a flash of surprise and a hint of fear.

"Are you finished?" he asks, his face ashen.

"Yeah, for the time being," I say, licking my lips, suddenly afraid I hurt him.

"Alright. Let's go through this again. Here are the rules. I talk, you listen. I ask, you answer. What part of the word *answer* do you not understand, Ailen? Take a lead from Hunter, now that's a smart boy right there."

In this moment, my father is no more than a tired, shrunken man, resigned to doing the only thing he knows how to do. Mechanically, he raises the sonic gun and points it at me.

I stare at the muzzle, wondering how many shots it takes for a siren to die, realizing that even if I can last for a while, Hunter won't last after a single blow. I steal a glance down and lower my arm, inconspicuously, I hope. Hunter shifts forward and grabs it, clasping his fingers tightly around mine. He squeezes three times, as if trying to pass a message. My mind reels, but it doesn't make any sense. Three is my favorite number, that's a start, but there's nothing else I can think of.

Papa's voice drones at the end of the tunnel.

"...again. Remember, noise is chaos. You have to organize your mind, learn to obey. Now, one more time, answer my question." He makes himself say it, stubbornly pressing on.

I drop Hunter's hand and sit straight as a rod. A stream of words pushes its way out of my mouth in a stutter, before I can arrest it or even realize what I'm saying.

"That's it! It's what you did to Mom, isn't it? She loved you, so you brainwashed her, to control her. Because you couldn't stand the idea. No, you couldn't *understand* it. Nobody has ever truly loved you before, so you didn't trust her. You thought she

Chapter 14

had some kind of a hidden agenda to make you lose your mind and then use you and dump you, right? So you decided to protect yourself, to..." I reel with words, stumbling, not knowing what to say first. It makes perfect sense.

"You..." I begin again, staring at him, shaking from sudden understanding. "You pathetic piece of shit, you thought you could—"

Bam!

I get my answer. A sonic shot fires in my belly and I'm momentarily deaf, sliding down into the reclining seat, clasping its side to prevent myself from falling. The lifeboat rocks wildly side to side and I think we will turn upside down.

Chapter 15

Salmon Bay

After what seems like an eternity, the boat rights itself, but I'm hardly aware of the world around me, swimming in agony. I made the mistake of exposing my father's pain, in front of Hunter, and I expect he'll never forgive me. But I know that I struck gold, that my hypothesis is true. I saw it in his eyes before he shot me. I saw it in his broken posture, in his trembling hand, in his slack mouth, as if his teeth have been kicked out and his lips sank in, making his cheeks hollow and his eyes dead. It's like he's sorry he's being this way yet he has no choice; it's far too ingrained in his nature to change things, and it might take years and years, decades, and only if someone out there would be willing to put up with his shit, to let him spew it out and revive his soul all the way. That would have to be me. He has no one else left.

I'm not sure I'm up for the job. I watch Papa pull back, his eyes wide with surprise, as if he's conscious for the first time of what he's doing, conscious of hurting his own daughter, of what he just did. Then the mask of this is gone and he's back to steel.

Chapter 15

"Quiet!" he yells. "I will use the gun, if I have to."

I'm numb all over. My vision is blurry, my hearing echoes, and bitter saliva fills my mouth. My right arm hangs loosely over the side of the seat and I feel Hunter grab it again and squeeze it three times. I wish I understood what he wants and curse my brain, wanting to kick myself. Tears spring from my eyes. I hate it, I hate it.

I hate it!

The slow purring of the motor reminds me that we're still floating somewhere in the Pacific Ocean.

"Let us continue. We have a lot to cover, like I said before. I would prefer that you don't interrupt me again, is that understood?" He looks at me.

I manage a nod.

"Good. I'm sure Hunter is eager to hear the details of this particular job, aren't you, son?"

"Yeah, I can't wait," Hunter says through his teeth with a quiet contempt that's barely detectable.

The thought about putting Hunter in danger cools me, and I know that my father knows it too and is using it to his advantage.

"I want you to understand that siren hunters don't make mistakes. Because if they do, they find themselves dead." This is said to Hunter. "I decided…since you two are so inseparable, I'll send you both on a job. Yes, I think it will be a good lesson for you to learn."

Hunter squeezes my hand three times again. I raise my head, nauseated and reeling.

"You what?" I say, but it's so feeble that my father doesn't hear me. He doesn't look at me; he directs his eyes to the seat beneath me.

"Hunter, you'll be in charge." Now he shifts his gaze up. "Ailen, you'll do what he tells you to do. Is that clear?"

"Wait, you—"

"Do you want another taste of this, or shall I try one on your boyfriend this time?" he asks, and whatever trace of his vulnerability was left, is gone.

Hunter squeezes my hand again, three times. What does he mean? Three is my favorite number. Okay...it takes three minutes for an average person to drown. Does he mean for us to drown together or something? No, it doesn't make any sense.

"You'll go to the siren's feeding ground, the one under the Aurora Bridge? They love fresh suicide jumpers, don't they? I want you to get rid of the sirens: Raidne, Pisinoe, Ligeia, and Teles."

What about Canosa? I want to interrupt, but catch the words just in time before they roll off my tongue.

"If, for whatever reason, they're not there, or if they manage to escape you, you'll track them down, and you'll finish them there. You will go as far as you need to go to succeed. If you manage to complete this," he looks at me, "Ailen, I'll let you keep your voice. You have my word."

He didn't mention Canosa. Canosa was the one who found us. They must have made a deal. She must have helped him catch me so that she can remain untouched. She bought herself her freedom.

A pang of pain pierces me, one that's worse than the physical pain from the blast. She betrayed me.

"You got it," Hunter says from below. I open my mouth, but he squeezes my hand again, and I close it without saying anything. All right, I'll play along.

"Ailen? Do I hear your agreement?" My father raises his eyebrows in question.

"Yeah...sure...we'll do it," I slur.

"Excellent." I detect irritation in my father's voice, the sweetest sound in the world, second to Hunter's soul.

Chapter 15

"Any questions?" he says.

"What if we fail?" Hunter asks.

"You're asking the wrong question, son. I thought I made myself clear. Siren hunters don't fail. I hope you understand that I'm giving you a second chance. Please, don't prove me wrong."

The message is clear. Do it or die.

Hunter squeezes my hand again, and I think I get it. Three minutes under water. He really does mean it. He told me how he'd die, if he had to—the whole motorcycle racing and crashing thing. I squeeze his hand back three times, to indicate I understood.

"Don't forget, siren hunters don't leave witnesses," my father throws out, while steering the lifeboat wheel and shifting gears. He continues droning on.

"Let me repeat the rules for you, one last time." His voice blends into the ocean rumble, and I let my head hang off the side of the seat to watch Hunter.

He adopts a cheerful expression and nods with enthusiasm. The gleam in his eyes is the feverish glow of someone ready to die who doesn't give a shit anymore. It makes me mad. If he doesn't care, that means he's decided to make a spectacular exit. I want to scream, to grab him and shake him and tell him that this is serious, tell him to wipe that smirk off his face, but I can't. Papa's watching. And I'm afraid to make another move, because I don't want to be rendered into a vegetable, and I don't want Hunter to get hurt any more.

Father finishes his speech with a few broad strokes of his hand and a gallant tilt of his head.

"Remember, Ailen." His eyes rest on me. "If you complete this job, your lover boy will live." He smiles, the impenetrable mask of indifference back on his face, his body tense.

I don't know if I can muster enough hate to radiate out of my eyes, afraid to utter a sound, because he points the sonic weapon at me again. Its muzzle imprints in my retinas, I stare at it so hard.

I nod and close my eyes.

Weakness takes over me and I let myself drift off into a near slumber, pulling my arm up and rolling to the other side of the seat, like into a cradle, pressing my face into the cool wall and quietly humming, seeking to reconnect with the water for strength, feeling it answer me, speeding us up little by little, so Papa won't notice, wanting to get out of this enclosure, and...

And then what? I don't know, I'll think about it when I get there. Right now I'm tired, so very tired, that for once, I don't care. I'm *tired* of caring, tired of everything.

Evening light streams through the circular windows, a dusty shade of periwinkle, getting darker by the minute. It looks like it took us the rest of the day to reach the shore. I suspect it's a good thing that we're about to arrive in Seattle under the cover of night, because I'm sure the Harbor Patrol would want to investigate what a lifeboat is doing, floating freely along city canals. We come to a halt, back at our marina, under the Aurora Bridge.

My father kills the engine and I stop humming, holding my breath.

"We made it, faster than I thought," he says.

I let my breath out. He didn't notice.

"All right, I'll be watching you two. Off you go. Use one of my rowboats, if you need to," he says into the dark, because at this point, the inside of the boat is rich with black velvet, punctured by street lights poking their way through the windows.

"W—" Hunter begins from below.

"We're done talking about this. I want you out. Now," my father says impatiently.

"Sure," Hunter mumbles. He cracks his back, and pulls himself up to my level. "Ailen? You all right?"

Chapter 15

"Yeah," I say. My tongue feels wooden, my arms and legs stiff.

"Now!" Papa yells, and that makes me move.

Hunter positions himself between our two seats, grabs the sides of the opening and worms out of the hole, his feet dangling down for a second before they're gone. He leans in and sticks his arm inside, offering his hand.

I take it, not because I need help, but because it feels good to pretend to be a real girl, so I allow him to assist me with my exit, plopping down across him over the hole in the boat's top cover, swaying to the lake's gentle waves, and studying each other in the dark.

I inhale the tumultuous city air and look around. The noise of the busy neighborhood hits me square in the chest. To my left, at eye level, people scurry across the Fremont Bridge as if they're trying to beat the crawling cars to the other side. To my right, traffic darts across the Aurora Bridge, a good 160 feet over Lake Union, the world's second most famous location for suicide jumpers.

I tilt my head up. Dusk spray-paints the air in rivulets of lilac haze, seagulls squawking their hungry calls and darting around at random. The smell of fallen leaves mixes with an impending wetness threatening to gush from the scattered clouds. The air is cold, yet not freezing, pleasantly tasting of early autumn.

I stand and glance to my right again. I jumped off this bridge two days ago, into what? Into this. Into being trapped again, worse than before, with no foreseeable end to my torture.

Hunter takes my hand, and we hop off the boat onto the wooden pier, barely visible in the descending night. We land in the middle and fall over.

"We'll be all right," Hunter whispers into my ear, pulling himself up and giving me his hand.

"Oh, yeah? What the hell was that about, the whole hand

squeezing thing?" I whisper back, now standing next to him, my face touching his. An electric current of warmth passes through me and sears me to the spot. I don't want to move, and don't want him to move, hoping to stretch the moment longer.

"Oh...that." He falls silent, and the gap between us widens.

"What, you forgot already? Well, I think I know what you meant, and I don't like it. Not one bit, do you hear me? I think..." I take a breath to tell him what I think and realize that I don't really know, it could've been just a convenient number, just a friendly way of squeezing someone's hand three times.

Hunter looks at me quizzically, waiting.

"You'll have plenty of time to talk later," my father calls from the boat, and we both turn around to listen. His head pops up from the open hatch, a sonic gun in his right hand, pointing at me.

"I forgot to mention one little detail," he continues. "About timing, just so you don't think you have a whole year ahead of you. You don't. In fact," he checks his fancy Panerai watch, "you have till the end of tomorrow. That's when I expect you to come back. Back here, understand?"

I suddenly think about how in the blue sky will he know that we actually did it?

He must be reading my mind, because he says, "In case you're wondering, my handy little radar here will indicate to me whether or not you've done the job. Amazing technology, isn't it? Now, get lost." He quickly darts his eyes to the sides; I'm sure the real gun is tucked in his pants. He points to a couple of rowboats bobbing on the water, tied to a slip post. I suppose because the sonic gun looks like a miniature loud speaker, he's not afraid to brandish it in public.

I squint into the distance. Occasional yachts break up the slow drone of the freeway, and the night darkens fast. I realize my father wouldn't dare shoot Hunter here, in the open. The

Chapter 15

water steals my mind with its welcoming lull. Nothing prevents us from swimming away, into the open ocean, into freedom. Nothing.

His head disappears into the hatch.

"Come on," Hunter says. He tugs at my hand and steps carefully along the edge of the pier, sliding into one of the rowboats and helping me hop in after him. I let him.

We plop into a familiar position, me on the front bench, Hunter on the rear one, automatically grabbing the oar handles, ready to paddle. We face each other through stretching time, for a second or maybe a whole minute, not talking, just staring, until the sky opens up into a rapid drizzle. Raindrops trace our faces, but neither of us makes an effort to wipe them off. With the last wave of his hand through the window, my father's face disappears into the darkness of the lifeboat; its engine purrs and the whole thing lurches forward. There are no goodbyes, no last minute instructions, not even yelling. We're two puppies dropped into the pond, to survive on our own.

We silently watch the boat maneuver out of the marina and into the canal, drifting at first, then picking up speed and making its way west, toward the Puget Sound.

"Strangely enough, I feel sorry for him, you know. There is not much hate in me left, mostly pity. What about you?" I say and wait for some reaction, but Hunter says nothing, pressing his lips together into a straight line.

"You have decided something and you don't want to tell me," I say.

Hunter sits motionless, obviously ignoring me. This is so unlike him that at first I stare. I want to make him talk, but then decide to let him be, for once.

"Fine, I understand, I get it," I sigh and shake my head, attempting to untangle my thoughts into some coherent stream of logic. "This just doesn't make any sense," I say quietly.

"What doesn't?" Hunter speaks up, like the previous part of the conversation didn't happen.

"Nothing does. None of this...*stuff* that's happened to me—to us—from the morning of my birthday until now. I mean, I feel lost...and confused." I glance up.

"And I'm sorry," I say, hearing the sound of the lifeboat engine trail off into the distance. "Whatever it is, this thing, it's my fault you got dragged into it. I should've never—"

"Ailen, stop it. One way or another, I would've ended up doing this. You only accelerated the pace." Hunter sighs. I feel like he wants to say something else, but he doesn't, perhaps embarrassed. Instead, he unties the ropes and pushes the rowboat out of the marina, post by post.

"What do you mean, pace? You didn't plan on becoming a siren hunter all along, did you?" I ask, breathless for a second. I sense an oncoming grip of hunger stirring my hate, fueled by Hunter's soul blaring its echo at me. My gut is doing it against my will, according to the laws of our imminent ending. One of us will kill another, as long as we stay together. We'd have to avoid each other to survive this incessant need to eradicate, to tear, to pillage and scream and stomp. My hands curl into fists involuntarily and my heart rate spikes a notch. I keep it down.

"You know what I mean, so stop asking," Hunter says. There's that teary look again that he's trying to control, and a grimace of irritation lurks somewhere beneath it, too. I wonder if he's battling some siren hunter urge to twist off my neck, but I decide this is not the right moment to breach the subject.

"You almost cut out my vocal cords," I throw back, unable to hold it down.

"I wouldn't have even come close," he says quietly.

I feel bad that I reminded him of his pain and quickly try to change the subject. "Can you at least tell me why you squeezed my hand three times? Back on the boat?" I ask, but I think I

Chapter 15

already know the answer. "And wh—"

He drops both oars and places his hand over my mouth. It burns with his warmth that's somehow on fire. The rowboat gently bobs and we drift under the blinking street lights, gliding over their reflection in the water.

"It's very simple, okay? I'll say it one time only, 'cause it's very hard for me to say it, so don't ask me to repeat it again." He licks his lips.

I nod.

He takes both of my hands in his and looks me in the eyes. "If you go, I go. I can't live without you, Ailen, would you get that into that stupid brain of yours?"

I know he's serious, yet I'm afraid to let the real meaning of his words sink in. I launch into the first thing that pops in to my mind, to fill the silence with something, some small talk. "But your mom—"

"Shhhh." He places a finger on my lips, shushing me. "She'll understand. She was in love once, too."

"So, you meant it?" *Do you seriously wanna die?* I want to add, but I don't say it aloud, still clinging to the hope that I'm wrong.

"Yeah, that's right. Only I changed my mind," he says.

I want to scream at him that this is not funny; it's not a good joke, it's mean. But it doesn't feel like it's the right thing to do. What he says feels important, serious, real.

"You changed your mind?" I manage, hoping it's a good thing. "To what?"

"Okay, so if you knew you'd die, in like, ten minutes, what would be the last thing you'd wanna do, right before your death? What?" His face is close, his eyes ablaze with sick fervor.

My heart drops. It's my turn to stare and not answer, holding myself still, wanting to leap at him, bury my nose in his scent, stretch him all around me like a blanket, curl up inside and never come out, living on his aroma of pine and the off-key melody of his ignited soul.

"Exactly. So forget about the motorcycle. Who cares about that; it's just a toy, a bunch of metal parts on wheels." He presses his hands on my face. It's already dark, but an even darker shadow from the bridge covers us completely as we pass along, slowly drifting.

"When we were in the lifeboat, it crossed my mind—no, earlier, in the lab—I'm...I don't expect you'll ever forgive me, and I'm...so very sorry I didn't fight your dad harder, I tried."

He pauses.

I briefly shake my head, indicating that it's okay, I don't mind, wanting him to continue.

"Anyway, I thought that I might not come out of this alive, and neither would you. So I thought...before it's too late, I...um..." He licks his lips again, and I can tell he's very nervous.

"I want you." He spits it out in one slur, kind of like *awantoo*. So it takes me a second to understand what he said.

My mouth slowly hangs open.

Chapter 16

Fremont Bridge

The rowboat bumps its nose into the latticework of the low wooden fence that runs along the bank underneath the Fremont Bridge. The bridge itself looms about thirty feet above us, groaning and rumbling each time a car passes overhead, tickling me with a human soul concerto. A cold breeze ruffles my hair. I barely register any of this, enthralled by the idea of what Hunter said, hearing the blood rush to his cheeks, and feeling his eyes burn me with light in the velvety darkness. My mouth is dry. First, the impossibility of his proposition renders me speechless, then it turns into a vivid image of the *possibility* of it actually happening and my eyes widen to the rapid beating of my betraying heart.

"If I could choose how to die, I'd choose to die from loving you. From...feeling your skin under my fingers. Like this." He pushes both sides of the clumsy, oversized fisherman's jacket apart, tracing the lines of my collar bones underneath; and a different type of hunger sears me from neck to knees.

"Of course you want me, I'm a siren, right?" I swallow.

"That's how it's supposed to be. It simply means that the charm is working, or the magic, of whatever you wanna call it." My voice comes out feebly.

"No. It's not like that." He takes his hands off my neck and holds my face.

"I know it's hard for you to believe, but please, for the umpteenth time, *please* believe me when I say this. I don't care what shape you're in. You're Ailen to me, always have been, always will be. *Always.* I just want to feel you, all the way, at least once, before I die. Is that so hard to believe? Don't you want the same?" His voice catches at the end, his head tilted to one side, childlike and earnest.

"Me?" I suppress the urge to dive and hide under the boat. "You really want me, *really?*" I whisper, beginning to shake like a sick person shakes from a high fever.

"Yes, *you*. Really." He looks at me with those blue eyes of his, and I lose it.

A catastrophic yearning to be held, to be loved, boils over and sweeps away my hatred, anger, anxiety, guilt, all in one smooth swipe, sending them up into the sky in an invisible stream, as if the lid held over my heart flew open. I tip forward and place my lips on his.

Slowly, like a man who's dreaming, he takes me into his arms. Then he's kissing me. Wind gusts throw raindrops under the bridge and onto my face, but I hardly feel them.

Nothing matters right now. Only this closeness.

With Hunter's help, I shed the sticky, unpleasant jacket, then the pants, and then my logic and sanity, all together. I throw them on the bottom as I try not to tear Hunter's hoodie off, wanting to feel the warmth of his energy.

"You want to do it right here, right now?" The last of my doubts escapes when we break the kiss to take a breath, Hunter wiggling out of his pants, goose bumps springing up on his skin

Chapter 16

and making him shiver.

"Yes, right here, right now," he says, and chucks his sneakers.

"Okay," I say, and then I can say no more, because we tumble in a bind between the boat's benches, our legs twisting on top of each other in an awkward dance. The front bench begins cutting into my neck under Hunter's weight, so I twist my head, breaking the kiss, muttering, "Sorry, just a second."

I turn around and punch my fist into its wooden boards, breaking them clean in the middle with a crack that echoes down from the belly of the bridge. Sitting up, I break the back bench as well, tearing at the remaining pieces with a fervor akin to one trying to break out of a coffin after being buried alive. Sodden wood creaks under my fingers.

"Whoah!" Hunter exclaims. "I like it. Do you always break stuff when—"

"Shut up!" I slap him, lightly. He grins, openly ogling me. We both grin like lunatics, naked, sitting in a boat in the middle of a lake canal, risking being discovered at any moment.

I gather the remaining wood chips and throw them overboard, clearing out as much space as I can, quickly, in the heat of rushing blood, not wanting to lose the magic of the moment, like it's happened before. I'm determined for this to go all the way.

"One more thing."

Hunter throws his arms up with a sigh. "What now?"

I pick up the fisherman's jacket from the bottom, tear off a long strip of the resin fabric with my teeth, and hum to move the boat closer to the fence. I tie the strip loosely, pass it through the ring on the very tip of the bow and around a slimy wooden post, fighting off Hunter's hands groping me from behind, yet secretly liking it. "Just let me finish!"

"I'm sorry, I can't help it," he whispers.

As soon as I'm done tying the knot, he turns me around.

Fremont Bridge

"Let's spread the jacket on the bottom so—"

"Fuck it," he says, falling over me, pinning me to the bottom of the boat. Without another word, we descend into a tangled mass of kisses, sighs, and awkward searching that quickly grows into deliberate holds.

"Dude, you're so warm," I say, when Hunter's face leaves mine, tucking into the fold between my neck and shoulder. I guess I'm unable to stifle the reflex to talk-talk-talk, anything to shoo away my clumsiness.

"I was gonna say the same thing," he says from below.

"Me? What—"

"Wrong choice of words. In the opposite way. You're so *cool* to the touch, I like it."

"You're weird," I whisper, willing the last of my resistance to go.

"So are you. Now, will you shut up already?"

He buries his face in my stomach and I let my mind go.

Waves sway the boat gently, creating a steady rhythm, letting me float in it, beat in unison, feel alive, feel *together*. This is the very thing parents hope to prevent their teenagers from doing, and I get why. Without alcohol, without weed or acid or any other kind of bravery enhancer, without it all, lovemaking itself is like a drug—it gets you so high, gets you obsessed, and you can't stop doing it. But why can't we be addicted to it? Why is it looked down upon, as something dirty, something forbidden?

It feels like love. What's so bad with being addicted to love?

I feel it fully for the first time, without being dizzy or high or drunk, and I grow divine.

If I could part into a million fingers, only to entwine with Hunter in a million possible ways, I would. If I could turn into wind, to penetrate our connectedness in every gap, to fill it with my hushed exhales, I'd do it in a heartbeat. If I could trail his kisses to draw a map of our love, I'd stare at it every day until

Chapter 16

I'd go blind. Even then, I'd still stare, tracing the paths with my fingers, immobile, dwelling on the memory of our final doom, beautiful and humid, filling every space inside my dead heart with life, with love, with music so heavenly it has no name. Only an exotic sound—outlandish in its timbre—that explodes in your ears with a splendor of pleasure beyond which immortality fades into nothing.

"I love you," Hunter whispers in my ear. "It was great. It was fucking awesome."

"I love you, too. Yeah...it was," I whisper back, barely conscious of both our bodies collapsed against each other, slick with Hunter's sweat and a sheen of salty moisture on my skin. We're panting into each other's hair, tired.

The low moon shines on us with her watchful eye through a break in the clouds, creeping to the edge of the bridge's shadow where we hide.

Fumbling, we help each other get dressed. I stick Hunter's head into his hoodie and help him wiggle in since his fingers fail to find the neck opening. He hugs himself, pulling up his knees to his chest. I secure the fisherman's pants around my waist and sling over the cold, unbending jacket before mirroring his position.

We sit across from each other, dazed.

"I can't believe we actually did it. It's like, unreal," I say, trying to separate myself from the dizziness, blinking at the reflections on the water to make sure they're there.

"No, it's something special. We just had the best joint ever, Ailen, and it's called *making love*." He pronounces it *makiiing loooove*, in his typical theatrical manner, and grins.

"Did we just have sex, like, right here, on the boat?" I say, still unable to believe it.

"Thou misses the correct expression, my dearest. It is but called *making love*. In the darkness of the night, under the bridge, to the gleeful eye of the moon itself, spying on us like a barren bitch who never saw two people shagging," he says in the low baritone of a stage performer, pointing at the moon.

"Stop it! Or I'll slap you." I scowl, but I know Hunter recognizes it as fake. In fact, I loved the whole experience but am scared to openly admit it.

"Go ahead, that'll make me horny again." I can see his grin in the darkness, wide and crooked, his teeth shining white and reflecting the faint moonlight.

"Though I admit, you felt kinda cold, you know, as compared to the other times. Must be a siren thing and all. So I get it. Man, does that make me a necrophiliac?" he says.

"What? Fuck you!" I push him in the chest.

"Gladly. Here, let me get myself worked up again, okay? Just a second." He rubs his hands for warmth, then his belly and sides, with a genuine concentration of an athlete warming up for a marathon.

"Uh-uh-uh. Almost there, thank you for your patience." He looks so comical that I laugh.

"Stop it! You're making my stomach hurt," I say, forgetting to be quiet. My voice rolls under the bridge, echoing in a series of bells, reverberating through the night around us. Hunter's burned soul melody envelops me with a familiar warmth, off-key but desirable. I stop caring about what will happen. Sitting here together, on the boat, makes me happy. I feel at home. Hunter's voice, his very presence, tunes out other noises.

I look at the moon. Its light falls on the water in a silvery film, a path with broken dancing edges. It's beautiful.

I think back to looking down at this very spot from the Aurora Bridge, aching inside, feeling the desire to end my life. Feeling overwhelmed by it, to the point of not being able to stand living another minute, wanting to go underwater and never surface. To be rid of this mind and body that I hate so much;

Chapter 16

to be rid of myself.

"Hunter?"

"Hang on, I'm not ready yet..." he starts. When he sees my face, his expression turns somber.

"What is it? What's wrong?" He takes my hand.

"Do you ever feel like you're faking it?" I say, looking at the point where the silver road of the moon's reflection ends on the horizon.

"Faking what?"

"You know, life. Like you're pretending to live just to get by. To show everyone that you can, but really you don't give a damn. Really, you don't care."

"Is that how you felt? When, you know..." He takes my other hand into his, cradling both of them, and the contrast in our body temperature makes me want to cry all over again.

"What's one reason not to die?" I say quietly. "I remember skipping stones with you into this lake as kids. I was so happy then. What happened to me, Hunter? When did I change? When I was ten, twelve, fifteen? When?"

"You mean, when you decided to turn it off, 'cause it hurt so bad it was easier to survive this way?" he asks.

A light breeze sways our boat.

"I wish I knew how it came to this. Look at me," I say and nod toward my body. "I'm a dirty plastic bag of a person who got stuck in a puddle, torn. A plastic bag without a bottom because it fell out, and without handles because they both broke. Remember that dancing plastic bag in *American Beauty*? The movie?"

"Yeah. What about it?"

"It's like that, only afterward, it's filled with too much water and stomped on in the dirt."

"That's not true." Hunter reaches for my face, but I turn away.

"Yes, it is. I couldn't hold that weight anymore, that's why. I turned empty, dry. Like an abandoned well."

I take one of my hands out of Hunter's hold and dip it into the lake, to feel it, to connect.

"I can fill you in. I just did, didn't I?" Hunter says and falls silent, perhaps realizing that this is the wrong moment to be funny.

I pretend I don't hear.

"Sorry, I'm sorry. Bad joke. Stupid." He passes a hand through his hair. "What do you want me to do? How can I help?"

"I wish we could just drop it all and swim away. Into the open ocean, you know?" I say, twirling my hand.

The boat careens left and right in the tiniest waves, soothing. Street lights flicker on and off on the surface of the lake. Stars sprinkle the sky.

"Promise me something?" Hunter says.

"What?"

He palms my face, darkness reflecting around his pupils.

"Promise me that, right after what I will tell you, after you hear what I have to say, you won't argue with me, okay?" He lets out a big exhale and waits.

"I promise," I say, holding my breath.

It takes another second for Hunter to start talking again, and he says it quietly, but firmly. "When you go, I go."

"What? So you did mean it for real. Hunter, you can't! What about your mom? Who will take care of her?" I ask.

"Please. I asked you not to argue." He makes an impatient face.

"But—" I begin.

He pulls me closer. Our noses touch—mine cold, his warm. Then our lips. Then our tongues. Moonlight splatters our faces joined in a bizarre moment of dare, a dare to those who don't believe anymore. I lose myself in it.

Chapter 16

A moment later, a fraction of a thought passes through my mind, wondering how come the moon is shining on top of us, we're supposed to be in the shadow of the bridge. It feels like déjà vu, like the kiss that we exchanged at Blake Island, before Canosa carried Hunter off to sea. I ignored it back then too. Canosa! Where is she now? A sinking feeling freezes me. The strap of orange material I tore from the fisherman's jacket must have failed, got torn, or maybe...

The boat revolves around, first slowly, then picking up speed, tracing a full circle. That nagging feeling of being watched returns full force, and I break the kiss.

"Hunter!" I grab his hand, warning him.

"Wh—" he begins and stops talking.

Three sirens circle the boat. Teles, Ligeia, and, of course, Canosa, my big sister. I nervously glance around for Raidne and Pisinoe. Canosa smiles broadly and gives me an encouraging nod. "Don't worry, they're busy. Continue. Please, continue, we didn't mean to interrupt," her voice jingles merrily. "It's rather entertaining. Wet and sloppy, but in the absence of any other variety, I'll take it. *We'll* take it."

Chapter 17

Fremont Canal

I flick my eyes to Hunter in panic, as if asking, *What do we do now? We haven't even discussed how we're going to catch them, or with what—nothing!* He winks at me, as if saying, *It's okay, I got it, just follow my lead.*

"Hey girls. Long time no see," he says, squeezing my hand three times. "A bit too cold to go skinny dipping at night in September, don't you think? I like your hair, though, as always. Your hair looks awesome."

They giggle.

"Hunter Crossby, where have you been? We missed you. Oh, we missed you so much!" Ligeia says, tilting her head to the side, causing her wet locks to roll off her bare shoulders. No doubt a practiced movement.

"Shhh! Shut up, remember what Canosa said," Teles hisses into her ear, clasping the edge of the boat.

"So? What I say is none of your business, so get off me. Get your fingers off me! You're annoying," Ligeia says. They remind me of typical high school mean girls.

Chapter 17

"What's up, Teles?" Hunter says.

"Oh, nothing, nothing in particular," she says, and lowers her head as if she's blushing.

Meanwhile, Canosa is quiet. Her stare is so demanding I can feel it on my skin. Her hair glistens in the moonlight, wet and braided with lust. I guess I expected something, anything; an acknowledgement about what she did, a nod that said she's sorry. There is none of that, only a self-indulgent gaze and egoistic demeanor. Like I owe her something, like it's my fault, like somehow I have wronged her and not the other way around.

"I'm waiting," she finally says.

I stare back. "Waiting for what?"

"For an apology," she says, like it was the most obvious thing in the world.

All caution evaporates from my mind in one instant.

"Really? An apology. You're asking for an apology? You stinking traitor."

Hunter steps on my bare foot, but it's too late. The words escape me at an alarming rate.

"All this talk about siren family, all this bullshit you've been feeding me. For what? To serve your own purposes. You turned me into a siren for your sick little game with my father. I'm no more than a pawn to you, and as soon as you're done with me, you'll dispose of me.

"Well, fuck you! You're a traitor and a liar. You made a deal with my father and sold me out. Sold both of us out. Me and Hunter. And you weren't *ever* going to show me where my mom is, were you? In fact, I'm not even sure you were here when she jumped. It was just another lie, to get me going, to make me do stuff for you, wasn't it?" Hunter stomps on my foot again.

Canosa twirls a lock of silver-white hair around her finger, an amused expression on her face.

"Answer me!" I demand.

She ignores me, using the trick my father pulls all the time. She swims around the boat to the back of it.

"Hunter Crossby, still holding on to your catch, I see." She nods in my direction. "Nice one, I must say."

Hunter faces her.

"I don't know about that. She's a slippery little thing. Kind of hard to hold on to," he says with a significant glance. I don't know if he means it as a compliment or another joke.

"Splendid, ain't she? Not bad, not bad at all. Thank you for the show, it was mesmerizing to watch. Heartbreaking, in fact. My girls here almost gagged with desire."

Ligeia and Teles nod energetically.

"I'm glad you liked it," Hunter says.

"I'm hungry." Ligeia suddenly sticks out her lower lip like an upset toddler who's about to throw a fit. "Are you?" she asks Teles, grabbing her hand and drifting to where Hunter sits.

"Canosa, can we please eat him now?" Teles says, the perfect sidekick, so gullible I want to throw up; her cute chubby face has adopted a grimace of childish pleading. "He sounds so yummy!" She looks back at Hunter with carnal lust, transforming from a cute maiden into a fierce fiend.

Canosa promptly fists Teles' forehead. "Don't you remember what I told you? To keep your mouth shut at all times?"

Teles mumbles something in response, and I see a faint smile play on Ligeia's lips. It must have been the desired effect she was looking for, moving up a rung in her boss's favor.

I shake my head. I keep getting distracted from the reality of our predicament. We have no chance of escape, no weapons to fight the sirens with. They caught us at a vulnerable moment. We were idiotic enough to forget to even ask Papa for sonic guns, I mean, how stupid is that?

I feel Canosa does not intend to let us go this time, and Papa and his guns are far out of reach. A feeling of wrongness creeps

Chapter 17

into the air, a feeling of being very close to death, close like never before, as if being watched by death itself.

"Enough idling," Canosa proclaims, and all three sirens clasp the edges of the boat, Canosa behind me and Ligeia and Teles to either side of Hunter. "Do it." There is metallic ferocity to her voice, a command.

Whatever she means by *it*, is not good. My spine turns to ice. In a split second, I weigh my options. I could scream and rouse the entire lake, but that would send Hunter into the water where the sirens would get him. I could scream very loudly without engaging the water, hoping somebody would call the cops. And then what? By the time they come, it will be too late. I could attack the sirens. Three against one? I don't stand a chance. Or, I could simply do what I've always wanted to do…let go of the fear. Let go of this miserable life, stay together with Hunter in the face of death, until the very end. The chase will never cease; I'll never have peace, no matter where I go.

Hunter's words ring clearly in my head, *If you knew you'd die, in like, ten minutes, what would be the last thing you'd wanna do, right before your death?*

I look Hunter in the eyes.

"I'd want to be together with you," I say.

He passes a shiver and says, "Me too." Looking me in the eyes, he takes both of my hands and squeezes them three times.

"See, I told you it would happen. I'm glad we had the time of our lives. This is the perfect moment, I think. Are you ready?"

The sirens begin to hum, in a barely audible baritone at first.

My heart, already down to my knees, drops further to where I can't feel it at all.

"You sure you wanna do this?" I ask.

"Yeah. The first part is done, isn't it? Like I said, perfect timing." He smiles with the finality of someone who knows death is near but refuses to give in to its terror. His hair moves in the light breeze.

The sirens' humming unnerves me, because nothing is happening.

"We don't really have a choice, do we?" I ask.

"Yes, we do. We're making it right now," he says.

"You made up your mind a while ago, didn't you?"

"You got that right, turkey." He grins, but underneath his bravado he's trembling like a leaf in the wind.

I study him, his arching eyebrows, the cocky grin that splits his face in two in the manner that I love so much, and his hair bunched up over his forehead, barely visible in the darkness. I realize I didn't know he wanted to kill himself too, all this time, but it makes sense; that's why we're such close friends. That's why he was the only one who got me, understood my playing with death, my daring, my willingness to risk life and not caring much for it.

I smile. I'm ready to die.

I expect terror, or resistance, or something, but there is nothing. I'm empty, and the decision comes easily, like relief after a long, bumpy ride. I must be at the point of complete exhaustion, from myself, my own mood swings, and my constant decision doubting—the perpetual up and down of balancing on the precipice between life and death.

I want out.

"Okay, then. Let's do it." I squeeze his hands back three times and relive the moment before I jumped, the few seconds of utter despair that pushed me over the edge; only now, we're doing it together. From the corner of my eye, I watch the sirens drifting, holding on to the boat and twirling it around slowly.

"Go ahead, girls," I say calmly. "Whatever it is you're going to do, we're ready."

For a moment, Canosa breaks her humming.

"Ailen Bright, I'm amazed. What's wrong with you, silly girl?

Chapter 17

You're giving in just like that? What a pity," she mocks, and I think perhaps she expected resistance and it was part of the plan.

"All right, let's see what you do when your boyfriend here calls for help. Ligeia, he's all yours. Teles, get her," she cackles, dropping her poison into the silence.

I notice now that we're covered by a thick bowl of fog, our rowboat sitting underneath it. That's what they were weaving with their humming, creating an invisible pocket to outside eyes.

Ligeia breaks her humming, tilts her head to the sky, and begins to sing. The air rings with her high pitch, amplified by the emptiness over the lake, reaching high, all the way to the top layer of the fog, then twists in a reverse vortex and heads directly toward the boat, dropping its force onto Hunter; his eyes hazy with her song, a thin trickle of smoke streaming from his mouth in ribbons.

Mesmerized, I focus on his eyes, arrested by the beauty of the pause before the storm, when everything's standing still, about to erupt.

"Hunter! Don't listen to her, listen to my v–" I begin. Teles' fingers wrap around my neck, cutting off my hysterical speech and my attempt to lunge at Hunter and rouse him from Ligeia's spell—my promise to die together forgotten. I want to save him; I don't want to see him perish. I gag and rain my fists on Teles' head. She doesn't flinch and only laughs. I thrash around, rocking the boat, but she squeezes tighter and I go slack.

Ligeia's song intensifies, droning in my ears. Hunter's soul-smoke strings out of him, a rainbow gone wrong and stripped of all color except a dull white. It smolders.

"How do you like it, sister? I say it's a *fair* price to pay for calling me a fat slab over the years, what do *you* say? Is my hold too weak? I can make it tighter, would you like me to?" she whispers into my ear, so unlike her previous childish self. She clamps her fingers to the point where I think my head will explode from the water held in it.

This is the true nature of a siren—this lunatic duality—toddler-like and capricious on one side, sinister and unforgiving on another. How patient they must have been, waiting to deliver their revenge on me.

You forgot something, girls. You forgot that I'm a siren, too. I'm *of your own making, and I haven't even gotten close to showing off my malevolent side. Would you like me to? I can, you know.*

I attempt to claw at Teles with my nails, lift my legs to kick her, but she digs her fingers into my gills and I cry out.

At last, I cease resisting, but unrest grows deep inside my gut, a tiny bud of fury that badly wants to bloom.

"Good job. Take it like a martyr. Now *this* is what I call fair," Teles whispers into my ear.

All I can do is stare at Hunter, unable to discern if it's his soul that's pouring out of his mouth, or the surrounding fog pouring in.

Maybe there are places for death, places that attract people to them like a magnet. Maybe this is one of them. It was my mother's place of death, and hundreds before her. This is our place of death, and we're a speck of life about to be swallowed.

Ligeia's song makes waves. The boat tilts precariously, then flops back upright and tips to the other side. Hunter's face drains color rapidly as more of the thick, coiling substance oozes from between his lips, lilac and bloodless.

My body goes numb. I feel the last of my resistance leave me. Even my attempts at breathing stop, my diaphragm relaxes. Perhaps responding to this, something passes between us all, me, Hunter, and the sirens—a question so dark that it has only one answer.

Down, down, down.

Mom, if you hear me, if you're over there somewhere, I'm coming, I say inside my head, before Teles cuts so deeply into my

Chapter 17

neck that I feel like my head will break off and fall off my shoulders. My hands feel cold and clammy, so do my feet, so does my heart. I'm giving in to this willingly.

Drowning in the bathtub water wasn't enough. I want to drown in the dead waters of the Styx, the river that Greeks believed connected Earth and Underworld, the great marsh of human misery on the way to extinction. I want to be dragged into the labyrinth of muddy streams, accompanied by the ever-present Siren of Canosa, carrying a zither, her right arm over her head in a moaning sign, her left on my shoulder, guiding me on my afterlife journey.

The boat tilts further and begins sliding down a whirlpool like a coin circling down a spiral wishing well. Blue is my favorite color. The water is not even blue; it's black, the color of burnt weed, a bad trip from a drug that's worse than teenage love. A trip with only one possible destination: death.

It doesn't come to claim me, however.

A car honks somewhere above in the fog.

Someone gasps on the shore, a human soul.

Teles lets go of me.

Mad splashing trails around the boat, and then Ligeia's song abruptly dies, ending on a high-pitched cry.

Canosa yells, "Teles, no! Stop it! Get back to her! I said, *stop it! Now!*"

The whirlpool stops. The boat spins one more time from inertia and eases out. The fog breaks up into dirty rags, letting in the night, until it gets completely blown away by a light breeze. The velvet darkness of the sky consumes us.

The air pierces with girl-fight calls.

"You stupid cow!" Ligeia whines. "I almost had him. Look what you did! You're such an idiot; I would've left you half! Get off me, Canosa told you, did you hear her? Get off me!"

I tense, a bud of fury poking at my ribs, gingerly, eager to get out. Canosa is yelling and fighting with both sirens. Teles hisses at her, and then lashes into a long string of swear words. Light penetrates the darkness and I see Hunter's soul slam back into him from Ligeia's lips as Teles puts her in a headlock and pulls her underwater. Hunter slides to the bottom of the boat, eyes closed, clothes sodden, and clinging to his exhausted frame with his legs bent and twisted at an unnatural angle.

A strong feeling paralyzes me. Shame floods me with a staggering force. Shame for thinking only about myself. Shame for being so selfish, for pulling Hunter into this and agreeing to double suicide, without asking him for a valid reason, without trying to convince him otherwise, simply going along with it.

Is this what you call love? I mock myself, wanting to slap myself in the face.

But it's not too late. No, I can fix it. I will pull him out of this, alive.

He's still unconscious, still in the same unnaturally twisted position, but alive. I can hear his soul. It's beating faintly beneath the white noise of the sirens' cacophony. His impossibly delicious sweetness of homey noises and endless comfort; the fragrance of summer wrapped around the beautiful scores of Vivaldi violins. My heart rate speeds up to incredible highs, pounding in my ears and calling my hunger upward.

Horrified, I lick my lips, shaking off the desire to fall on him and suck his essence out, to make it mine. Time slows down; so does my heart. The world around me acquires a liquid viscosity that I can grab at will. I inhale and hum, moving the rowboat silently to the shore, away from the sirens who now resemble a bunch of snarling sharks in a feeding frenzy.

I hum some more.

The water swells and falls in a series of heavy breaths, lassoing around the boat, pushing it to the shore. The waves crest, frosting with foam, and rise higher, until we're bobbing on top

Chapter 17

of the gigantic surf that's bubbling in tune with my inner boiling rhythm.

At once, it recedes and we're thrown onto the bank, the boat's hull hitting the grass with a dull thud, its wooden planks groaning under impact. I collapse on the floor of the boat, banging into Hunter's knees.

Hunter moans, opens his eyes and stares at me, looking as if he's seeing me for the first time in his life. I'm terrified about what will happen next, staring back at him, sensing the boat slowly sliding underneath me and back into the lake.

Our first encounter on the boat, almost in the same place where we are now, flashes through my mind. My turning into a siren, jumping out of the water on my first hunt, trying to sing out the first soul I detected, only to open my eyes and realize it was Hunter, Hunter all along. Grinning his crooked smile with that familiar dimple in his right cheek, his hair bunched up, raindrops on his eyelashes, his eyes blue. And me, gaping at him, thunderstruck by the magnificent melody of his soul. Now, like then, I lunge at him out of fear.

"Say something! I need to know you're okay. Say something, please!" Tears spring up in the corners of my eyes.

He swallows, his pupils growing large, to the size of two black pools, glistening in the night.

"Ailen?" he croaks. "Is that you? What the hell happened?" His chest heaves as he glances about.

I listen with all of my being. And there it is, the faint crush of a delicate summer flower broken off its stem, and a faint whiff of smoke emanating from between his lips with every breath. It will never stop.

"Do you love me?" I dare to ask.

"Of course, I do, why are you asking? Where the *fuck* are we?"

Moonlight paints the night with her white glow, fading,

yielding to early dawn. The boat drifts a few yards and I hum to guide it back to the shore. In the distance, the sirens' hysterical battle chorus—their boom of otherworldly rage—ceases, giving way to one frustrated cry, perhaps at the realization that we're both gone.

"Let's get the heck out of here," I say, and before I can add the fact that his house is only ten minutes away, he gives me this piercing look.

"Isn't that what we planned all along?" His eyes reach deep inside of me, his face full of sadness; I sense a hidden idea behind his words. "He'll never leave us alone, your dad, you know that, right?"

"Yeah, I know."

We leave the rest unspoken, perhaps afraid to say it and realizing the futility of escaping. I choke on my helplessness. We don't have a chance to choose our parents; we are given them the way they are, whether we can bear them or not.

I can't take a single breath, can't close my mouth. My eyes fill with tears, heart pounding. I gag, wanting to take in some air, but I can't. I try to rip myself open, to let this feeling out. I want to turn back the time, to reverse everything that's been done.

"Come on, Ailen. Let's do it, before somebody else helps us. I'd rather die on my own terms," Hunter says with a terrible finality.

He takes my hands into his. "Double suicide."

Chapter 18

Mount Rainier

Memories refuse to appear. There is nothing there. It's like I've been gutted of my past and there is only now. Only Hunter's eyes, blue and scary in their determination. And my own fear; fear of letting him go, fear of not succeeding at killing myself, of being left alone, to suffer for who knows how long.

"Why?" I ask. Now that we're away from danger, or at least there is an illusion of being away from danger, suddenly I don't want him to die, maybe don't even want to die myself.

His voice is tired. "What changed? You promised me. If you go, I go. Unless we decide *how* we do it, somebody will decide for us. Like those siren girlfriends of yours. You see what I mean?" he says.

"You're right," I admit.

"When you jumped off the bridge—I hope you take this the right way—I was jealous. Jealous of your...how do I call it? Well, it was a brave thing to do, it took serious guts."

"Suicide is not about bravery." I glare.

"Hang on, just let me finish. What I'm saying is, it gave me the boost I needed. A kick in the ass, in a way. I've thought about...taking my life for a couple of years now—when my mom got cancer, and again when Dad left. Anyway, I came close, but chickened out at the last minute." He falls silent.

"You never told me," I say, shocked.

"Of course I didn't. I didn't want to freak you out."

"What exactly did you do?" I ask.

"I stole a bike and rode it really fast." He grins.

"Jesus. You did? For real?"

"Yeah. It was awesome, at first. Then I was turning and I lost control. Out of the blue, the stupid back tire decided to lock up," he waves his arms showing me how far he was leaning and how fast the tires were spinning, "and I skidded for a few feet and rode into a ditch. Thank God it was simply dirt and not rocks or something. I left the bike and hiked home. It took me three hours, lots of time to think about lots of things. After that, I was too afraid to try it again." He plays with my fingers, pressing them like piano keys.

"And you were never found out? Whose bike was it?" I ask.

"I dunno. Just some bike off the street. I hot-wired it."

"Figures. So you lied to me. When I asked you if you ever thought about killing yourself."

"Well, I just, ah...evaded the question. Sorry." He hangs his head for a while, and then looks back up. "Does this mean you're up for it, then?"

"I jumped, didn't I?" I motion with my head toward the lake. "That was suicide attempt number two for me. No, wait—three. Four? I don't even know what number it was, to be honest. I lost count. I guess I'm game. What else can we do? If you go, I go." I shrug my shoulders.

"Awesome," Hunter says and kisses me, as if I just agreed to go on an amusement park ride with him and not on a ride to

Chapter 18

extinction.

A wild surge of feelings spins my head and I have no room for a single breath, gulping his warm presence like a starving, caged animal that was thrown a bone for the first time in days. The echo of Hunter's burning soul envelops me, melts me.

We part, panting, electrified.

Hunter's face is contorted in a menacing rage. He quickly forces it down and smiles. I mirror him back.

There will be no happy times, after all. There is no way for us to be together. There is no other way out. So be it.

This dare to death itself fills me with a strange excitement. It's something I finally have control over. I hope I can shriek so loudly that my voice will pass the speed of sound and I'll simply explode. Wouldn't that be something?

Hunter grins the smile of a boy who doesn't care if his newest mischief will cost him his life, because it's too exciting not to try. To exit this world as spectacularly as we can, to be seen and heard and talked about for a long time after we're gone. *Now* they will notice. *Now* they will cry. *Now* they will regret. *Now* they will hurt. But we won't care—it won't be our hurt anymore, it will be theirs to live with. We will be free of it by then, free and happy.

The air around us fills with purpose and a feeling of relief. The decision has been made and suffering leaves our conversation. We're back to planning it, like it's a vacation.

"So, how exactly do you propose we do it?" I ask.

"Are you thinking what I'm thinking? Because I think we got ourselves a new toy." Hunter pulls me by the hand.

"What toy?"

"Right there. See?" He points at the parking lot in front of a two-story office building, the parking lot where some of the unfortunate suicide jumpers land.

By now the morning is in full swing and I can hear the souls of commuters. Thankfully, it's still early and there are hardly any people here. At the far end of it, next to a pile of rags left over by the homeless, a bike leans casually on its stand. It's hardly noticeable, blending into the shadows, an unusual silver-gray color with bright white letters on the side of its fairing.

Hunter stops abruptly and drops my hand. "Holy shit, Ailen. It's a Ducati 748! They must have done a custom job, look at the silver. Gorgeous. Stock only comes in yellow, red, or black."

Hunter breaks into a trot and squats next to the bike. I follow.

"No, it's not a custom job. This looks like original factory coloring. Man, I think I know what it is. There were only one hundred of these babies produced, Neiman Marcus limited edition. It's a 748L! Look at the metallic shading, carbon fiber fender, Christ…" He continues mumbling under his breath, stroking the bike, admiring it.

"Um, is that supposed to be cool?" I ask, not impressed.

"Are you fucking kidding me? This is what we need." He passes his fingers through his hair and wipes the palms of his hands on his jeans, standing up.

"No, you're not thinking that," I say, and tug on his sleeve.

"Oh, yes, I am. Got my tool on me, too."

"You're out of your mind."

"So what? We're talking life or death here, no?" He pats the bike's leather seat.

I bite my lip, trying to suppress my rising excitement. I know it's wrong—very, very wrong—and yet I can't help but wonder how it would feel to ride this beast behind Hunter, hugging him, pressing my face into his back; how we would look on this silver drop of speed glistening with that wet, after-the-rain shine.

A glance at the pile.

"Oh my God!" I shriek, unable to believe my eyes.

Chapter 18

"What is it?"

"My hoodie!" I pull it out and unfurl the clammy roll of cotton, instantly recognizing the large white letter S in the multitude of blue folds. "It's the one I lost when I jumped! It must have floated to the shore." Beside myself with joy, I unzip the fisherman's jacket, toss it to the ground, and pull my beloved hoodie over my head, feeling its dampness next to my skin.

"That's cool," Hunter says absentmindedly. He rummages inside his jeans pocket, kneels next to the bike, hugs the front of the fairing with his left arm and sticks his right into the bike's guts. A quiet click later, he is up on his feet again, mounting the bike, pushing the start button. The engine roars to life. My world explodes with brilliant noise. I cover both ears.

"This is how I wanted to go, remember?" Hunter shouts. He beams at me, but there is no laughter in his eyes. Just an empty calm. I'm drawn into his darkness, wishing for vacuum. I want him to suck me in, keep me blind, and never let me go.

"Care for a ride?" His hand doesn't shake. Long slender fingers. An upturned palm. And this look.

"Yes," I say and give him mine. I lift one leg and slide on the back seat, feeling the heat from the exhaust penetrate my clothes and scorch the bare skin on my feet. I manage to find passenger pegs and unfold them by grabbing them with my toes and pushing them down.

"Hey!" A man in a black all-leather suit is running toward us, a silver helmet swinging in his left hand, bike keys dangling from his right. His closely cropped scalp sports graying hair and the sinister features of a weathered rider.

I feel ashamed at the excitement of stealing something that belongs to him. At the same time, the sinister side of me, the siren, grins greedily. *Tough shit, mister, bad timing!*

"What the hell are you two doing? Get off my bike! Get off, get off!" The heels of his riding boots click on the asphalt.

"Hold on!" Hunter holds in the clutch and waddles, rolling the bike backward, out of the parking lot, so that he can turn into the road. The man closes in on us; another ten seconds or so and he'll grab the back of my hoodie. Just then, Hunter stops, shifts into first gear, and gives the gas. The bike roars. I wrap my arms around his waist even tighter, clasp my fingers together, and turn my head.

"Back off!" I shout, with evil glee.

My call cascades across the parking lot in a powerful acoustic wave that bounces off the bridge's underbelly. The man freezes in place, his mouth open, the tips of his gloved fingers a few inches away from the bike's exhaust.

I flip him the finger.

And we fly.

The ride is choppy, each speed change a jolt. Hunter is out of practice, but he quickly adjusts and, gradually, the movement becomes smooth. Heart-quickening. We're a silver drop of speed, first on empty neighborhood streets, then against slow-moving highway traffic, a sea of gray prone to commuting boredom. If there is a way to go in style, it's by cutting into this fabric of mundane and ripping it apart. Those who follow the rules stay inside preconceived road lanes. We cut on top of them, oblivious to honking, mean stares, and flared-up indignation.

Live every minute as if it were your last. Experience a million lives in a moment against half a life in a hundred tedious years. This is my one minute of fantasy that's better than nothing.

We dart along Highway 99, across the Aurora Bridge and into downtown Seattle that busts with life while the rest of the town is still just waking. The city is swarmed with souls, carrying their bodies into cars, sipping their first cups of coffee, and puffing the air with delight after each gulp.

I hug Hunter tighter and press my cheek against his back, expecting to crash any second. Together. Because he weaves in

Chapter 18

and out of gaps between cars like a madman, begging for it to happen.

A cop car is leisurely patrolling early commuters. We whiz by it. I hear the cop spill his coffee, curse in surprise, and flip on the lights. Red and blue flashes in my peripheral vision. Hunter's body trembles with what must be adrenaline. He shifts into fifth gear. The bike jerks and lurches forward.

The police siren goes off from behind us.

Bweep! Bweep! Bweep!

"We've got to lose him!" I yell over the wind howl.

A few seconds later my left knee nearly scrapes the ground as we veer onto the dark swallow of the off-ramp and come off Highway 99 right by Seattle's two stadiums.

Hunter speeds up to fifty miles per hour, sixty, eighty. He runs the red light, turns left onto the road that leads to another onramp, rides up the hill, swerves along the loop, and gets on to a relatively empty Interstate 5 to the surprised looks from north-crawling traffic and honking from the cars heading south. Another cop comes ablaze from behind us. Great.

Hunter shivers violently. My hair ripples in the stink of traffic exhaust. I lean forward and yell, "What's wrong?"

"I'm freezing!" he shouts back against the tide of air. "I can't feel my fingers!"

"Shit," I say into his back.

I feel Hunter's temperature drop as we fly in between road lanes, oblivious to the angry shouts and beeping and the blaring sirens behind us.

I breathe into Hunter's sweatshirt, inhaling the lightly moist scent that reminds me of wet laundry. Its fabric balloons and ripples in the wind. Suddenly I know. Humidity. Water vapor in the air. Perhaps I can move little droplets of water faster and make the air warmer by speeding them up?

It's worth a try.

"Don't freak out! I'm about to scream! I want to try something!" I shout. There's no indication that he heard me.

I tilt my head at the sky and open into a guttural animal wail, a wild a cappella. It starts out soft and then gradually grows in volume. I hike it up a pitch, higher, *higher*, overpowering the cacophony of traffic punctured by the blaring police sirens behind us.

Hunter's body goes tense; I rub my hands up and down his stomach to tell him it's okay, to hopefully relax him.

My yowl explodes into a solo opening for a reckless opera, its staccato rhythm designed to match the rhythm of water atoms—three of them, one oxygen and two hydrogen—their lot connected by a chemical embrace.

Listen to me, I command it. *I want you to dance for me, okay? I want you to move faster, move as fast as you can and create hot steam.*

They hear. The atoms. A great many of them in about a twenty-foot diameter around me. They shift and scat and jitter in tune to my yelling.

At first, I create a tunnel of dry air that parts the rain into pouring, rattling sheets. But I can do better. I can produce a bubble of warmth. I can bind tiny basic units of water to my voice.

The air in my lungs is running out and I badly need another breath but am afraid to break the flow. I continue bellowing, losing myself in the sound.

I feel Hunter's core warm up, stop trembling, and relax. At the same time, the gush of wind against my face rises in temperature. My fingertips tingle with the buzzing heat.

"Whatever it is you're doing, it's awesome! Keep doing it!" he shouts at me.

I take another deep breath, and launch into more wailing, turning the little sphere of climate around us almost tropical.

Chapter 18

The traffic thins out. We keep riding fast with the cops still on our tail, but now I think I also detect a distant whoop-whoop of a helicopter.

Time stretches, or maybe it shrinks, I can't tell. City buildings give way to low-strung malls and houses skittered along the highway.

Two patrol cars catch up with us, flanking our stolen motorcycle. I can see an officer gesticulating, ordering us to slow down and pull over.

"Eat this!" Hunter shouts and guns the bike. He whizzes ahead and skids across two lanes to the right, veering onto the closest exit, a cloud of smoke dissipating behind us. The engine emits some coughing noises, stretched to its limits. The off-ramp slope is so steep that the front wheel of the bike lifts off the ground for a second and then we thump down as Hunter brakes and nearly lays the bike down in the turn.

"Woo-hoo! We popped a wheelie!" he yells in delirious excitement. We speed across the little bridge over the highway. Both cops whiz by underneath, too late to react, but sure to turn around at the first opportunity. We make it to a suburban road, crest it, and suddenly there is Mount Rainier.

It's a beautiful sight and it takes my breath away. Over the jagged line of uniform rooftops, a valley of trees, and a strip of houses miles away, a magnificent expanse of sky towers its heavy brow. The morning sun breaks through the clouds and, in that pocket of pink, an enormous mountain glistens with snow, pristinely white in its splendor. Multiple ridges give it a rough yet peaceful appearance, its sheer vastness making me feel small and unimportant.

"Mount Rainier?" I say into his ear, standing up on the pegs.

"Yep. Ought to go out in style, right? Ever flew off a stratovolcano?" He falls into his comical speak, shouting over the racket of the motor.

"Ladies and gentlemen, welcome to our performance, the one and only show. Against a backdrop of glacial ice, with Rainier Valley for the stage! Today! Don't miss it! There will be no reruns! We will make sure to donate all proceeds to future suicide victims, of which, let me assure you, there will be many!"

"That's not funny!" I interrupt him.

"Says who?"

I pinch him lightly.

The topic dies and we continue speeding along mostly empty streets. A minute or two later I pick up the distant wail of the police siren again.

"Cops!" I yell. "A few miles behind!"

"Can you shroud us in fog or something?" Hunter yells back, gunning the bike and running a red light to the honk of a lonely car at the intersection.

"Ahead of you, punk, already planned!" I lie. Well, just a little bit, to appear superior, because I still feel wounded by his stupid joke.

A blue shimmer of atmosphere rushes past us as rolling blankets of fog creep up the sides of the road. Hunter turns and we fly onto a narrow back road hidden in the woods, full of twists and turns to enjoy one last time.

Yellowing trees frame our flight with their canopies of burnt foliage on top of tufts of green as if their gigantic, hairy heads have been dipped in fire. The damp smell of fallen leaves mixes with the crispness of fall, fresh and chilly. An obnoxious mechanical blaring is on our tail, together with helicopter blades whooping above us. Another minute and they'll see us.

I tilt my head up and open into a song, the one I sang to Hunter, one of my Siren Suicides favorites.

"There you are,
Without me you cry.

Chapter 18

*I surround you,
Love me or I die."*

Thick mist rolls off my skin and licks us under a cotton-candy blanket of fog. Its edges touch the ground on all sides except in front, leaving a wide enough gap between the sky and the road for Hunter to see where we're going.

*"I adore you,
See me or I fly."*

All other noises hush. I listen for the police. Their annoying ululating has diminished. Hunter gives me a thumbs up with his left hand before gripping the clutch handle again.

*"Can you hold my heart?
Can you hold my soul?
I can't be apart."*

The words ring so true that I'm ready for our fall, watching this spectacular ride through a cloud of my own creation, singing until my throat turns hoarse and I can't sing anymore. I close my mouth and press my cheek against Hunter's back, letting myself get lost in the scenery. Slowly, the fog recedes to greenery on our left and a huge flat lake on our right. The road comes up to the base of the mountain after which it disappears around the bend into nothing. The mountain itself is not visible behind the thick layer of forest.

I concentrate on listening into the distance behind us. Apart from a few souls and a few passing cars, there is nothing. At the same time, Hunter slows down and stops on the side of the road.

In front of us towers a wooden park entrance, a twenty-foot-high structure of two cut-off tree trunks on each side and six more on top of them forming a roof. The actual gate is fastened to each front pole and is currently open. Two metal chains hug the middle top beam and hold up a wooden board that reads, MT. RAINIER NATIONAL PARK. Up ahead are wooden cabins with windows and a flag in the middle of the road. In fact, the road parts in two around the entrance station where you're supposed to stop and buy a park pass.

"We've lost them. The cops," I say, as I get off the bike and stretch out my legs.

"*You* lost them. Thank you." He turns and takes my face into his hands, the bike idling softly.

"Ah, it's nothing. How are we going to get past that?" I point ahead. "I have no cash on me. Do you?"

"No cash needed, baby. We will gun it, as always."

"Right," I say, avoiding his intense gaze. Beyond the entrance station, the base of the mountain is covered in dense vegetation, the road zigzagging up and out of sight, vertical rock on its right side, a void on its left.

"I've never been here before," I say. "What's it called? I mean, what part of Mount Rainier are we going up?"

"Paradise," Hunter says.

"Seriously? It's called *Paradise*?"

"Absolutely and irresistibly correct. Paradise Ridge. I've been here before, err...contemplating. There is this nice drop-off about—" He shifts closer to me. "What's wrong?"

I sigh. "Nothing."

Hunter gives me a quick peck on the nose. "I don't believe you. Talk to me."

I try to make out the mountain's peak in the clouds, golden in the sun. "Do you really want to know?"

"I do. I really do," Hunter says. "I think I know. This is my bridge, in a way, and to you it must feel like—"

"No. No, that's not what I mean."

Chapter 18

"What do you mean then?"

"You never told me why you want to kill yourself. I told you, but you never told me. And I...I want to know." I fall quiet, biting my lower lip.

Hunter looks away. He appears to study a nearby bush sprinkled with bursts of yellow salmonberries.

"The week when my father left, I thought I could fix it." His eyes brim with tears and he flaps his hand at them, pressing his lips together so that the next words come out suppressed as if they were never meant to be heard by anyone.

"I was stupid and arrogant, thought I could fix anything, but then I couldn't. There is no magic glue for family, you know, no magic pill for cancer. I felt so useless, just wanted to lie down and die..."

"And you decided you couldn't hold the weight anymore? It was too painful to bear," I quietly chime in.

"Yeah. You're stealing my words." He stretches his lips into a hint of a smile.

I simply hold his hand.

"Then I got angry. I picked myself up and decided to fight no matter what. We had no money for medical insurance, so I went out and got a job, a real paying job." There are tears in his voice.

"It was fake though, a false hope. It only pushed back what I knew would happen all along. She doesn't even recognize me anymore, has to ask my name every day. So what's the point? What is the fucking point?"

He grabs my shoulders and shakes me. I let him.

"At least you have a mom," I whisper.

He falls silent, as if I slapped him on the face.

"At least you have a dad."

Touché.

"Yeah. I have a dad. A control freak, a sicko woman-hating

asshole creep." I stop to catch my breath, tears spilling down my cheeks in two angry lines.

He cradles my face.

"I'm sorry, I didn't mean to upset you. How can I make you feel better? What can I do?" His eyes widen and all I see is the sky reflected in the two blue pools of his irises, pulsing with care. It fills me with a brilliant pain that's borderline pleasure and hunger, rearing its ugly head to hear Hunter's burning soul—an off-key shuffling of slippers on the floor, clanking dishes as the dinner table is set, and birds chirping, all against the background of Vivaldi's "Summer" season.

It takes an enormous amount of will power not to lunge and tear him apart. My chest lights on fire and threatens to burn me alive from the inside.

"Let's just do it," I whisper through tight lips, hoping against all hope that, by the sheer force of my yelling, I will explode and finally stop existing; images of Hunter smashing on the rocks into a million pieces pollutes my head.

I take a deep breath and exhale the pain, numb. "Have you ever given someone a ride of a lifetime?"

We exchange a smile.

"What's a ride of a lifetime?" he asks innocently.

"You know, the killer kind," I say, mirroring his tone.

"Oh, how curious. Nope, I never have."

"Well, can I be the first? Pretty please?" I play coy.

"You? Of course. Always. And forever."

I lean in and he's kissing me. Desperate to feel all of it, I press hard. Lips, tongue, my whole face. We gobble each other up. There is no room for breath, no room for thought, only this.

His hands grip my hair. I ball up the collar of his clammy shirt into fists, watching clouds drift by, revealing blue sky. Blue is my favorite color. Three is my favorite number. It takes only one minute to fall down ten thousand feet. I close my eyes,

Chapter 18

trying to imagine what our bodies will sound like, flying down the mountainside, crashing through pines and onto the rocks. I decide that I will see Hunter through his fall, to make sure he dies peacefully, and then I will wail over his dead body and burst into nothing.

Pulling against desire, as if against a strong magnetic force, we break apart.

"It's time," Hunter says.

"How long to the top?"

"Well, it's not exactly *the top*. It's a drop-off from one of the ridges. One of the observation points. Twenty minutes at the most."

"Oh, right," I say and mutter, "I love you. To death."

"I love you more." He grins and gives me another peck on the lips. "You're so beautiful, you know that?"

And I don't know how to parry that, dropping my eyes. A surge of excitement runs through me, pins and needles. My hands shake.

Hunter turns and revs up the bike.

"Shit, we're almost out of fuel. Get on!"

"I'm on!" I shout, clutching him from behind. We whiz up the path and past the entrance, ignoring the shouts of the ranger who sticks his head out the window, surprised.

Up we go, high, higher, taking tight turns at incredible speed, waiting for that perfect drop-off to come.

How ironic is it to experience the last twenty minutes of your life as the most vibrant and happy? The sky's aglow with September morning, and I gobble it up with my eyes. I suck the cool wind, full of autumn smells, through my nose. The thick brush is dotted with the distant tinkle of deer souls. Above all, Hunter's burning soul, although smoldering, is still the sweet penultimate note to finish it all off.

I begin to count the minutes. Seven pass by, thirteen left until we reach our spot.

Each turn makes my heart stop. We ride higher still, twisting together with the road.

"Right there!" Hunter yells and points across the valley. I dare to glance to my right, and then down—and I wish I didn't. We're riding on the top edge of a narrow valley with a river at its very bottom. He points to a cliff across the valley. So our drop won't be a spectacular 14,000 feet high like I thought; more like 500 feet. Still, it's breath-catching. A layer of fog palms the tree tops ever so gently, torn into patches of needlework by the sun.

Six minutes left.

We take a sharp right turn together with the road. Douglas firs, red cedars, and hemlocks recede, giving way to occasional pine clumps against open clearings tickled with berries and dew. I hug Hunter tighter. He covers my hands with his left palm, hot and sweaty despite the rapidly dropping temperature.

I press my knees into his thighs and squeeze hard. I feel his stomach muscles roll under my arms. I imprint my face in his back wanting to melt into him and become a permanent impression—one solid being instead of two.

Four minutes left.

Pieces of crumbled rock fly from under the bike's wheels and skitter down into obscurity. I turn my head back a little to see the mountain. The sky has cleared of clouds. The sun shines down the valley, rendering it gray, covering it with a layer of milky thick mist, just like I've seen on postcards.

One minute.

I nuzzle my face all over Hunter's back, trying to absorb as much of him as I can; reveling in the shape of his ribs that curve out from a delicate spine to the smooth sides of his torso, tense with apprehension. As if in answer, Hunter guns the throttle.

Chapter 18

The bike sputters and coughs up a phlegm of purple exhaust.

"We're out of fucking fuel!" he yells. "Right on time!"

"I love you!" I yell back, wondering if these would be the last words I tell him, rubbing my hands all over him in a mad urgent caress, feeling his face, touching his lips, sliding my fingers down his neck, panic rolling over me and pulling me under.

"I love you more!" he shouts with delirious glee. His voice is sharp with shrillness. We are near. I can see the drop-off ahead of us.

Thirty seconds.

This is our final stretch. I clench my arms around his waist, not worried anymore if I cut off his breath or not. Hunter grunts and grabs my hands briefly, crushing my fingers.

Ten seconds.

We go in a straight line, right into the sun, into the split that divides the horizon, light blue and dark blue. Blue is my favorite color.

Three. Two. One.

Chapter 19

Paradise

"YEAH!" Hunter's voice echoes into space as he takes his hands off the bike handles and intertwines his fingers with mine. At the same time, I reach out to him. Joined, we spread our arms like wings before the wind tears off our madness feathers. The bike roars, sputters, and falls out from under us, crashing over treetops along the steep incline. On inertia, we arch away from the slope and propel down into the rocky valley. Wind flaps our shirts and Hunter is falling face first, I hover over him. One second passes, and then another. I'm hit with a full-blown panic attack. What the hell are we doing? The air is thin and freezes my guts. The wind, rumbling loudly, tears at me with its fingers and the rush deafens me.

My mind reels with big red pulsing letters forming one word: WRONG!

As if to tell me—wrong way, wrong decision, wrong direction. But it's too late to turn back. Too late for anything at this point. Another five seconds or so and we'll be mush at best, slime at worst, to be scraped off the rocks as our final act of to-

Chapter 19

getherness.

This is a hundred times worse than jumping off the Aurora Bridge. This is so scary that I think my heart will stop beating and I'll slide into a coma before we hit.

Hunter's fingers clench mine with the force of a corpse in its final death grip, bone-crunching and icy. We tear through the milky fog. A clump of pines is lined up as spikes, ready to puncture our fall. I briefly think about creating a pocket of air to cushion our landing, when the direction of the wind shifts. We hit a dense air mass at the wrong angle and spiral out of control. My thoughts ruthlessly tossed aside, my body takes over and my siren survival instinct kicks in.

I scream.

Desperation passes through my vocal cords and exits as a battle cry, a death growl, a rebel yell, all combined into one. We're two seconds from hitting the ground when the mist shifts. Droplets appear out of thin air and multiply at an alarming rate. Water condenses around us and wafts down in a river of rain. I forget my promise to Hunter. All I want right now is to save him. I don't want him to die. I clench my arms into a tight hold, curl my knees and lift my legs up, twisting in the air, surrounding Hunter with my body like a blanket, my back to the ground, acting as a protective shield.

Crack!

We crash through pines at the very bottom of the incline. Branches snap across my back, their furious hands slapping my face and covering me in a shower of needles. I lose all sense of direction, closing my eyes and keeping only one goal in mind. *Protect Hunter. At any cost, protect Hunter.*

Thud!

My back lands on the wet ground, softened by all the water. It's like I managed to create a floating sphere of liquid and landed in the middle of it, bursting it apart. A shockwave travels through my spine; its force seems to break every one of my bones, stretching every muscle to its snapping point. Still, I don't release my arms, pressing them tighter. It doesn't matter what happens, I won't let Hunter go.

I can't quite pick up the echo of his burning soul, or his breathing, or the beating of his heart.

Nature itself seems to be unperturbed by our fall, hurrying on its way. A cold whiff of rapidly moving mountain river fills my nostrils. Despite my pain, I smile and take a deep inhale, noting the aroma of moss, passing fish, and evergreen trees.

A huge Douglas fir towers over us in a protective gesture. It's solitary, standing all alone, a long way from the cluster of firs yards away on either side. A silver line of river glistens about twenty yards behind it.

Guilt crushes me. I'm alive. Before I descend into the dark tunnel of self-loathing, I hear something through the diminishing ringing in my ears. There it is again. A flood of elation pulls into instant happiness unlike anything I've felt before.

I can hear the echo of Hunter's soul! He convulses and coughs up blood. Warm liquid trickles down my fingers.

"Oh my God! Hunter! You're alive, you're alive!" And I laugh, though it comes out in hysterical bursts.

"We're alive, Hunter. Did you hear me? We're alive."

He breathes in short wheezing gasps and doesn't answer me.

"Are you all right?" I ask again.

Silence is my answer.

I can't move my arms or wiggle my fingers. Nothing works. I can't pinpoint the exact moment when my body stopped melting from an internal fire of pain and succumbed to the freezing numbness. I try to wiggle my toes or move my legs. I don't feel them at all.

Are my bones broken? It feels like they are—all of them. How exactly can I help Hunter if I can't move? I realize I didn't

Chapter 19

think about this scenario.

A loud thunder cracks in the near distance, sounding like an explosion.

"There goes the bike," I say.

Silence. Hunter doesn't react.

"Hunter? Can you hear me? I can hear you breathing. Can you say something, anything, please? Or just nod to let me know that you heard me?" My voice catches. His hair tickles my nose. More blood seeps from Hunter and onto my left sleeve. He shakes in a violent fit and is still.

I give up trying to make him talk. "Hey, it's okay. We're alive, and that's all that matters. It was an idiotic thing to do. I'm here, I'm with you. It'll be okay," I whisper.

No response, only shallow wheezing. Hunter takes a deep breath and produces a barely audible, "Fuck."

"Oh, God. Oh, God, you can talk. You're alive. We didn't die. That was the stupidest thing we've ever done, you hear me? It was fucking retarded. I don't care what you say, but I'm not going to do this, not ever again. It's not our turn to die, okay? Fuck this, fuck suicide. Do you hear me?"

Rapid breathing.

"As long as you don't die on me, you don't have to answer. Just keep breathing, okay? Keep breathing and keep living," I whisper.

A tickling sensation runs through my torso down to my legs. My muscles begin knitting together of their own accord. I feel them mend, limbs tingling. My skin is itchy as if a million red ants bit me all over. *Stand aside, creeps, I'll be reborn here any second,* pops into my head. It sounds like something Hunter would say.

I rest, happy to feel his warmth in my embrace, and feel my eyelids slowly droop and close completely from weakness.

How much time goes by, I don't know. The only thing I

know is that I'm still broken but repairing myself fast. I dare to flex my fingers. They work, but my hands still can't move. I notice that Hunter's breathing slows down.

No. No-no-no. Don't panic. It's okay, it'll be okay. All I can do is breathe into his hair and wait, listening to the faint violin moans of his burning soul, knowing that as long as I can hear it, he's living.

I can now move my arms. Carefully, afraid to hurt Hunter, and in what seems to take an eternity—inch by inch—I pull my left arm from under him, letting him lie on the rocks. After that's done, I prop myself up on my elbow and promptly collapse back onto the ground, hitting my head on stone.

I hear souls and snap my eyes open. A hundred feet away, a couple of deer step out from behind the trees. They flick their ears, approaching cautiously, sniffing at the air and keeping their distance. Their slender legs click against the stones. Their souls sound like rustling leaves and animal trilling. I clear my throat, thinking whether or not I can lure one in to feast on it. It would do me good. I suppose I could sustain myself on animals alone, come to think of it. Why not? It would take more of them, in terms of quantity, to match one human soul. As if reading my thoughts, they sprint and are gone.

The sun is as bright as it was during our fall, and appears to be in the same position. I'm guessing it's around three in the afternoon. I wonder if the ranger decided to pursue us or didn't bother. Did anyone see us sail off the cliff? Has anyone heard the bike explode?

I try lifting myself again. My arm shakes like crazy. Beads of cold perspiration break out on my forehead and my gills puff up, inflated. Reaching the river to get moisture into my system dominates my every wish. I lick my lips and pause for a few seconds to make sure the dizziness goes away. Slowly, I prop myself up on all shaky fours and gently roll Hunter onto his back, holding

Chapter 19

his head and laying it down carefully.

I don't want to see what I see.

His face is mush, scraped and bruised and swollen, one bloody mess caked into a mask of pain. His eyes are two slits that are glued shut. His hair appears to have become an old wig from a prop shop that needs to be thrown away; it's matted and greasy and dirty. His clothes are a shredded heap of cotton from another life, the color of mud.

His legs are bent; his feet are still in socks, but his sneakers are gone. His right arm is limp and his left sticks out at an awkward angle. I touch his cheek.

It feels like his scream will never end.

"Fuck that hurts don't touch me talking hurts! Oww..." he wails, gradually falling into quiet moaning, occasionally coughing.

"I'm sorry I'm sorry I'm sorry," I mutter, cursing myself for my own stupidity.

Hunter sobs. Tears trace two clear lines on the sides of his filthy face. For a moment, he opens his eyes wide. His bright blue irises are the only two things of clean color, as lovely as the sky. He closes them, whimpering. I decide if I look at his face any longer, I will start sobbing, so I get busy. I squat, ball up the bottom of his sweatshirt, and rip it open in one yank.

"Your ribs look like they're intact, so that's a good thing." I gently hover my hand over his shoulders and stomach, afraid to touch him, eyeing his bright red bruises on either side of his chest. There are no cuts, and I sigh in relief.

"Looks like your arm might be broken. Can you move it?"

I dare to touch it and Hunter wails, then coughs up more blood and stops moving. I hear his smoldering soul dance in his ribcage like a moth at the light, wanting to flee, thrashing, breaking its delicate wings. It cries out to me, begs for mercy.

Terror envelops me.

"No-no-no-no-no. Don't you die on me now!"

I pry open his eyelids. His mouth falls open and the first tendrils of mist curl out. Mist and smoke. His soul! There is no time to think. My tears transform into a soft, velvety humming. It drips into a song, creating a stream of calming water, drop by drop, puddle by puddle.

"Look up,
The sky is gray.
Can you see me?
Tell me."

I take his cold hands into mine, lowering my face over his so that our lips almost touch. I sing and I sing and I sing, pouring out my wish to take his pain away. His soul skirts around me and up into the sky, ready to flee his body.

"No!"

His bloodied face turns old, his eyelids falling into their sockets, buried in wrinkles, hollow.

"NO!" I yell at him. *"No no no no no!"*

I try again.

"Speak to my love,
It won't survive."

My song doesn't seem to be working as it usually does. It comes out ugly, torn and disjointed. But I don't care. I don't want him to die, not now, not after all of this. What else is there to do except to try to bring him back? He's not fully gone yet. I hear his faint breathing, a slow beating of his heart like a flickering light. Now it's on, now it's off. I choke on tears and sing more.

Chapter 19

"Did you love me?
Tell me, did you love me."

I call to the mountain, to the river, to the trees and grass. It seems like they sway in sorrow together with me, it seems the ground itself is wailing.

"Memories
Have left me now.
I want to know."

My voice rises and it soon turns into a shriek that bounces off the ravine cliffs, for all to hear. Something shifts in the air from far away, moves in closer with lightning speed, as if all it was waiting for was my location.

Canosa. She's not alone. And she's on her way to find me.

Chapter 20

Nisqually River

My wail dies, kicked out of me by Canosa's impending presence. For a few moments I'm disoriented, not fully understanding where I am and how I got here, held fast in the flow of the melody that I managed to produce with my pain. I blink, tearing myself out of my choral daze.

Hunter.

He's injured. He died, didn't he? An otherworldly melody, piercing in its beauty, touches my every nerve and sends me into bliss. I have revived him, after all. His soul is back to its splendor of homey sounds, the comfort of shuffling slippers on a parquet floor, the banging of pots in the kitchen, a late summer wind filled with bird whistles, and laughter. Hearty laughter. And no burning. I want to give in to it, to bask in it as if it were the sun, and soak up its warmth. But I can't, not after what just happened.

Involuntarily, I let out a cry of dismay.

"Can we do without screaming, please?" Hunter croaks, as if he was awake for a while. "I thought paradise was supposed to

Chapter 20

be a quiet place, a place without headaches. Man, I'm thirsty."

My thoughts about Canosa vanish in an instant.

"You didn't die." I kneel over him, a surge of happiness making me tremble.

"Thanks for letting me know. I was just wondering about that." His lips part into a grimace of pain across his bloody face. The dusk of the pre-evening sky matches the lavender blue of his eyes.

I gasp, at once exhilarated and miserable, because all of this is so absurd, so unreal, and then I remember.

"Hunter. I need to tell you something important. I'm sorry that I don't have a properly prepared speech for this. I didn't think we'd live. But if I don't say it now, I won't have the courage to try to say it again." I pause.

He closes his eyes and groans. I can't tell if he's listening or not, but now that I started, I'm unable to stop.

"I'm leaving. And...I don't want you to love me anymore," I say quietly.

He props himself up on his right elbow and winces, but doesn't cry out. "What? Sorry, I missed it. What did you say?"

I raise my eyes at him, unable to repeat the "I'm leaving" part, and burst into, "Are you hurt? How are you feeling?"

Everything inside me trembles.

He just looks at me blankly.

"Did you seriously just ask me how I'm feeling?" He's shaking. "How would you feel if you were me? Huh?" He shakes his head. "All right, I'll tell you. I'm feeling fine, thank you very much, considering I just fell more than five hundred fucking feet off this cliff, almost smashed to pieces, and am probably crippled now. Thanks to my siren girlfriend who decided to save me. Did I ask you to? Nope. So then, why in the fuck are *you* the one crying? I'm the one who has every right to come apart." He's glaring at me, his bloodied face angry with fire.

I wipe my face. "Sorry."

He's on a roll, rattling off insult after insult. I'm taking in his resentment, abashed at its ferocity. I remember reading in some magazine that when you prevent someone from committing suicide, instead of thanking you, they shower you with indignation. Because in that scary moment—when they've had it, when they finally hoped to find relief from their pain by parting with life—you interrupted, and they are overwhelmed with tremendous devastation. Most internalize this new pain and never show it. But a few are capable of throwing it in your face. Hunter is certainly the latter type. Here he was, hoping to end his torture once and for all, and here I am, having broken my promise to help him.

"One minute I'm flying through the air, and the next, I wake up on the bottom of the world, broken but alive. I'm supposed to be dead, all right. I'm supposed to—cut it out!" He makes an angry face, complete with snarling and bared teeth.

I recoil. On one level, I'm glad he's distressed. One can't fall in love while in the state of shock and confusion like he is right now. This will make my job easier.

"We can't stay here," I say as calmly as I can. "Canosa heard me singing. She and the others are coming. We have maybe a few minutes, at best, before they get here. I'll need to carry you. May I?" As I say it, I wonder if I'll be able to lift him in my state, let alone carry him.

In an attempt to prop himself up on both elbows, Hunter shifts his weight to the left and collapses on the ground. He opens his mouth into an agonizing cry. "I think my arm is broken. Fuck!"

"I thought so. I'm sorry. I'm..." I reach out to him again, but he yells with such intensity that I fall back on my butt.

"I said, don't fucking touch me!" Tears spring up in his eyes; he swats at them with his right hand, grinding his teeth.

Chapter 20

I blurt it out. "Why are you so mad at me?"

"Because you let me live! Isn't it obvious? I thought we agreed to die together. Then why in the hell did you stop me? Because you were too chicken to let me go?" He scowls in pain.

"I...I only wanted to...Hunter! I couldn't *not* protect you. I'm sorry I failed you. I really am." I'm trying not to cry.

He's suddenly somber.

"Hey." He reaches out with his right hand, and I take it. "Hey, I don't know what came over me. I'm sorry, baby. I'm the one who should be sorry. Will you forgive me?" He suddenly comes apart and screws up his face.

"It's just that..." He looks up at me, lost.

After a pause, he says, "Ailen? Tell me it's not true. Tell me we're having a bad trip. Tell me we took some strong medicine-grade shit. For fuck's sake, did we *really* just fall down that cliff?" He motions with his head. "This is not happening. It can't be happening. Wait, did you say something about leaving?"

My ears adjust to a sudden change. I put a finger across my lips. Hunter falls silent, his eyes widening.

It's quiet. In fact, it's too quiet, and the feeling of being watched creeps into my senses again.

"I don't like this silence," I whisper.

Hunter nods. I scoot next to him, studying the valley and the road above us, listening to the forest life, to the faint gurgle of the river. I detect the distant motor of a car. A couple of cars. A mouse here, a bird there, and deer. Three of them, grazing on the grass a couple hundred feet away. Their souls rustle softly in the wind, pine needles crunching under their hooves.

Pine needles fall.

Pine needles fall on my head. I brush them out of my hair, and then look up and meet two eyes. The two eyes of Canosa, who descends head first down gigantic Douglas fir boughs, using them as ladder steps, hissing. Her siren sisters are behind her, their long hair hanging down in hunks, making them look like inverted blooming cattails. My only thought is: How did they make it here without a sound, how did I fail to detect them?

There is a stillness in the air, and I know that as soon as I make a move, even attempt to breathe, it will erupt.

Canosa glows with an ageless hunger. Perhaps a thousand souls have sunk into her, perhaps a hundred thousand. That white mane over her eerie face, and those large green eyes. Their chill makes me shrink. It's impossible for me to get any colder, yet I do. I crust all over with a layer of frost and terror. I know she's fed up with me and came here to kill.

"How the hell did you get here so fast?" I manage.

"Ailen Bright, silly girl. Nice to see you in one piece," she says. That's her opening point. I get it.

Without breaking our gaze, from the corners of my eyes I see droplets of water caught between fir needles. Ligeia's and Teles' hungry faces peer from above, glistening with anticipation. They both have changed, as if they grew up—that's the best way I can describe them. Cold, distant, bent on feeding their lust, savoring the idea of swallowing Hunter's soul.

Raidne and Pisinoe appear behind us. I'm one injured weakling against a pack of nacreous girls on the prowl.

"Girls, you got your reward. Have fun," Canosa says.

And I'm born. A note rises to my throat, forcing my lips open.

I scream a war cry. It's so loud that the trees seem to sway in response, the mountain itself pulses to my rhythm, and the ground shifts under my feet. I scream an animal scream, a wild call to protect my territory. It means, *Back off, or I'll claw at your eyes, I'll rip out your heart, I'll feast on your flesh, I'll grind your bones into a thousand pieces and spit you out to rot.*

Hunter squints and covers his ear with his uninjured hand. I'd rather have him deaf than dead.

Chapter 20

The sirens answer me with a guttural wail.

It booms through the expanse of the gorge and echoes off the vertical walls of rock, whining and howling and moaning. They're hungry, but they're waiting for their alpha to make her first move.

She does.

Canosa lets go of her grip on the fir's thickest bough about ten feet from the ground and propels herself forward with inhuman speed, landing on my back. She attempts to stuff my gills full of fir needles. I anticipated the trick so I crane my neck as far back as it will go, raising my shoulders at the same time. Fir needles fall under my sweatshirt, sticky with sap.

Canosa tosses me to the ground. I reach back and grab handfuls of her hair. We roll away from Hunter. Dirt stuffs my eyes, tiny pebbles flying into my mouth. Bitter, crunchy. Canosa tightens her grip on me. She's strong, but I'm faster, even though I'm not fully healed yet. I twist in her grip and nail her in the face with the back of my head. She lets go with a cry.

"How is that for a greeting?" I say and begin crawling back toward the tree, to Hunter.

Canosa stares me down, no doubt calculating her next move.

This is a girl fight unlike you've ever seen. The immature bickering is gone. This is real. This here is an alpha siren, animalistic and primitive to the very marrow of her bones. Her nostrils flare and her eyes search me, lips tight. She pulls herself back up, no shred of clothing on her petite yet womanly body except thick strands of hair so long it touches her feet.

She glances up. A signal. Ligeia and Teles let go of the tree with a cry, propel over my head a good fifteen feet, and squat down next to her. Raidne and Pisinoe snarl at me, waiting. I know they're just along for the ride. They don't care if I die or not, only Canosa hungers for my death, or, perhaps, she's not done playing with me yet. But I am. I don't want to be part of this anymore. After this morning, I've finally had enough of dying.

"Bravo," I say, sitting up, feeling for Hunter's hand and squeezing it once. Then, quickly, two times more. He squeezes it back three times.

"In simple speak—which I'm sure you require—congratulations," I continue. "This will give you bragging rights. How many sirens did you bring with you to take me down? Will that be really enough against *one* injured newborn? I mean, after all, I'm what—barely a week old? If I were you, I wouldn't take any chances. Oh, look at me; I'm such a terrible, horrible monster." I growl theatrically, to see how much I can annoy her.

Canosa stiffens.

"You forgot how to talk? I see. All right, I'll talk for both of us. I understand your plan now. This is what it was all about. To torture me as much as possible, to see pain on my face, which resembles my father's face to some extent, right? Oh, and my mother's as well—so, two birds killed with one stone. I get it. Then you waited for me to fall off the cliff and break all my bones to become an easy target. Sorry it took me so long. Truly. I apologize for the inconvenience." I let go of Hunter's hand and stand, attempting to perform a curtsey, failing horribly and nearly falling off my quivering legs.

"Hush! Ungrateful girl," Canosa says with a flick of her hair. I would imagine she's missing a mirror to check how magnificent she looks. "Have you lost the rest of your manners? The world does not revolve around you or your pitiful desires. Why would I expect any more from a motherless child?"

That stings. I cringe, willing myself not to react.

"I came here to thank you," she continues. "Thank you for a job well done. Now, if you could please step aside and let us finish it, I would be delighted." She points toward Hunter and assumes the stance of a boxer, legs spread far apart for balance,

Chapter 20

arms bent close to her sides, hands in fists.

"If you came to thank me, why did you have to bring your sorry sidekicks with you? Because they had nothing else to do? Or to stand by in case something terribly awful should happen? Are you afraid of me? Ailen Bright! The little girl who turned out to be so dangerous, so frightening! And she's not alone! She's with her terribly dangerous friend, only injured from a fall off the cliff over there, no big deal." I motion at Hunter who throws me a terrified look, asking with his eyes, *What the hell are you doing?*

"Oh my God! Everyone! Run and hide," I finish.

They fire a chorus of hisses at me.

"Nice speech. Hold it, girls," Canosa pushes Raidne and Pisinoe back, having started forward. They shout their displeasure to her, visibly annoyed.

Hunter manages to sit up. His uninjured hand pokes around for a rock the right size, to fit into his palm. I hear his laborious breathing without looking, backing away from Canosa and toward him, spreading my arms in a protective gesture.

Ligeia purses her lips and wipes the dirt off her face, sneers, showing rows of jagged teeth that I hadn't noticed before. "You little thief. You stole my catch. Again. And I wanted to call you my sister."

"We'll split him in half this time, okay, *sister*? You promised," Teles says, her voice melodic yet harsh. Her hair, curly and thin, barely covers her voluptuous body.

"Oh, so you act on command only? Canosa is your boss, right? The big sis. Lovely arrangement," I murmur with distaste.

"Quiet. Back off, both of you," Canosa interjects.

My mind races. What should I do next, how can I overpower five strong sirens while my bones are still hardening, my muscles still knitting together, my skin still closing, and Hunter so badly injured and weak?

"Nice outfits. I still prefer you with your hair up, though. Like, totally naked," Hunter suddenly says. We exchange a look. He nods, assuring me to trust him. "I hear there is going to be a girl fight, just for me? Why, thank you, ladies. This should be spectacular."

"More like a party in honor of our jump," I chime in. "I think we broke the world-record, surviving a fall over five hundred feet. Drinks should be served momentarily. Care to join?"

"Nah, I don't know. I'm not dressed for the occasion." He motions at his torn sweatshirt.

"Hunter Crossby," Canosa says, acknowledging his existence for the first time. "The unfortunate siren hunter who happened to forget his weapon. Pity. But it's very nice to see you again. *Alive.* How's the mom?" Canosa asks.

I sense Hunter tense all over, emanating hatred, and then it's gone, washed over with self-control.

"Fine, thanks. How's yours? I forget the name. Let's see... Terpsichore? No. Melpomene. Nope, not that. Sterope? Chthon? There were four, right? Nice names, too. Listen, I always wanted to ask you how this works. Did they all fuck the same guy?"

I break into a wide smile. I know that what Hunter said is mean and primitive, but I can't help it.

A fizz of anger erupts from Canosa's lips. "Make him shut up. I can't stand this insolent nonsense." She flicks her hand and assumes the stance of a nonchalant observer.

Ligeia and Teles shriek in approval and advance on me.

I widen my stance, feeling pressed into the corner of a gigantic basin framed by mountains, their ridges its rims, their vegetation its dingy, slippery coating. The only thing that's missing to complete the picture is water. Canosa watches the scene with her lips stretched into a smile, her body stiff with anticipation.

My heart sinks. This is not a girl fight, this is slaughter. Per-

Chapter 20

haps she'll leave me alive, just to play some more. Perhaps she'll kill Hunter in front of my eyes, just to see what I'll do, how I'll react. She's bound to win.

Ligeia descends on Hunter, pins him down, laughing. In my mind, she's a squirming maggot that wants to eat his soul, to tear him apart and suck on his guts, devouring him whole—bones and sinew and hair. He cries in pain and then falls silent. She must have propped open his eyes. The first tendrils of fog reach my peripheral vision, and the air temperature drops ten degrees.

Ligeia begins to sing.

"You said we'll split him in half this time! Don't you dare eat him whole!" Teles shouts. I lurch forward and saddle her, pinning her wrists to the ground.

"I was just wondering," I say. "Would you like some gravel for dinner instead?"

She begins screaming.

Chapter 21

Douglas Fir

I have obstacles in my path to saving Hunter's life, and they need to be eliminated. Teles happens to be the unfortunate first. Somehow, the fact that my entire life I have called her a sister and adored her chubby marble cheeks doesn't matter anymore. I scoop handfuls of crushed rock and stuff them into her mouth and gills, pushing hard with my thumbs to make it go deep. She writhes in agony like a leech on hot sand.

Mist dims the valley, hiding the Douglas fir and rolling over us before it reaches the river like a giant bleached tongue. At any second, I expect Canosa to jump out of the haze at me and tear me apart, but she's disappeared. There is no time to wonder where she went or why. I have minutes left before Hunter's soul takes a hike in Ligeia's chest.

I lower my face directly over Teles' and shout into her open mouth, making her body shimmer as if aglow. My ringing holler rises an octave higher, stretching the range of my limits, approaching the upper register of the highest female voice possible, a painfully shrill soprano. If a sonic gun can cause a lethal vibra-

Chapter 21

tion, so can my voice. Can't it? It all comes down to air waves reaching a speed faster than the speed of sound, to produce a sonic boom, much like a mini-explosion.

I force my pitch higher, louder, until it begins trilling like a piercing whistle, becoming diaphanous, almost translucent in the musical sense of the word. If I measure its speed in numbers, it would have to reach beyond 751 miles per hour to break the sound barrier. My every fiber palpitates in tune and I lose myself in this shimmering sensation, reaching a crescendo. At last, my air goes out, and my scream abruptly stops.

An invisible force throws me on the rocks. I hit my head hard on a boulder. In front of my eyes, the inflated body of Teles pulsates for a split second like a gigantic balloon filled with too much water and then it simply bursts into a million droplets. I get drenched. Water drips off my hair and runs down my cheeks, a poor imitation of tears, because I have none. For a moment, I see the indentation of her shape in the fog, a faint outline burned into my retina. I blink and it's gone.

"I blew her up," I whisper, unable to believe it, letting the knowledge sink in. I relive the episode while looking at my upturned palms. I'm afraid to lick my lips; somehow, that seems as if I'd be licking off a piece of Teles. A shudder of disgust overwhelms me. I wipe my face with my sleeve until it's almost dry. It hits me that I really did it—I willed myself to do it. Delirious, I open into a victorious cry, pitching my voice to an impossible height.

"I DID IT!"

I wait for the usual horror of guilt to cover me with its wings and to painfully peck at my equilibrium, but it doesn't. I'm in my element, and I feel divine. I roll onto all fours, ignoring the jagged rock edges cutting into my palms and knees. I lift my head and focus on my next target, like a predator sizing up the distance to its prey. Knowing that victory is on my side.

Douglas Fir

The best part of believing in yourself is having others see it. I'm superior to Ligeia right now. I know it, and I know that she knows it. Her every pore speaks to me clearly, her stunted body tells me a million words of submission. She heard me, and she saw Teles explode. In fact, she's doused in her remains, silver drops falling off her chin and onto Hunter. Their shapes appear in two gray clumps amidst the receding fog. Ligeia stops singing. She hovers above him as if in a dream gone wrong, her face distorted with hatred and anguish at the same time. Her hands fly up to cover her ears.

"I'm sorry, Ligeia, but that won't help you," I say, lunging for her. I cover the fifteen feet between us in one powerful leap, astounded that my body is functioning like new, expecting it to falter at any second due to the exertion from my sonic cry.

I spearhead into her chest and throw her off Hunter, clasping her shoulders and beating my head repeatedly into her ribcage. We land on the rocks, her limp body in my hold and me pressing my knees into her hollow stomach. She coughs up Hunter's soul. Curlicue after curlicue, it makes its way to its rightful owner. He gulps it up, convulsing.

Satisfied, I scream into Ligeia's open mouth. She doesn't resist, knowing her fate. I drive my voice into a familiar crescendo. The nightmare repeats and she pops. I'm thrown off her by the force of the explosion, shivering from exhaustion. Yet, in a way, it fuels me, driving me to keep going. My actions and responses become automatic as if, instead of slaying another siren, I merely squashed an annoying bug and am on an extermination spree.

Raidne and Pisinoe have gone into hiding. I can almost taste their fear. I discover Raidne behind a tree. As I sing her to oblivion, she doesn't even resist. It's as if she'd been waiting for or wanting an end all along. I'm briefly touched by our similarities, but I have to focus. I hear shuffling further in the pines. I follow the sounds and find Pisinoe approaching a doe. She stretches her

Chapter 21

arm out and the deer doesn't move. She pets its neck. "I petted it, so it's my pet," she whispers. "My first pet. I finally have a pet." She turns to me. Her eyes are soft and misty. It's senseless, I know, but I can't stop now.

I kill her.

One more, Ailen, one more. Canosa, wherever you are, your squalid presence is my next target for elimination.

The fog has become so thick it starts to feel like light rain, although it makes no difference. I wipe my brow as best as I can and search for Hunter. A mere hop away, his body is curled up in sediment mud, his hands over his ears and his eyes squinted shut. I take a hasty step.

"Spectacular. Who would've thought you possess such talent," Canosa warbles softly, striving to instigate my usual self-doubt.

I refuse to waver. Nothing has the desired effect—not her white mane nor her devilish sneer. None of those things changes the fact that, for once, I'm not afraid. And we both feel it.

"I'm glad you approve," I say, eyeing her uncertain movement. She carefully skips from stone to stone, balancing casually on a boulder about seven feet away.

"Come on, Ailen Bright. I thought you could do better than that. Look at me, I'm still standing." Her face glows subtly in the mist.

I'm suddenly unsure of the outcome, thinking that there is a chance that I might lose to her. She seems eager to confirm.

In the flight of a bird, her hair acts as the white, feathery wings of an albatross; she sails over me in an incredibly beautiful jump and lands next to Hunter, rolling him onto his back and smacking her foot into his chest. He groans. His breath rises in a mushroom cloud of steam and into the cold air before she chokes him into silence.

I arrest the urge to lurch at her and, instead, take a breath.

My throat is ablaze from so much screaming. Tired of the pretense, I decide to be simple and ask the question that's been bothering me from the start.

"What do you want?" My voice catches at the end.

Canosa senses my uncertainty and giggles like a little girl.

"*You*, silly girl. I want *you*. Haven't you figured it out with that smart brain of yours? You disappoint me." She purses her lips. "Well, *now* you know. I'm very pleased. There are only two of us left, thanks to you. Isn't it splendid? You made my job easier and, for that, I'm eternally grateful. Come." She stretches out her hand.

I freeze, my eyes on Hunter.

"Oh, leave this mortal to his suffering." She presses her foot harder on his chest. He only moans, his eyes still closed. "He's boring. The whole world is ours for the taking, Ailen Bright, you and me alone. Let's go fry some big fish, together. Sound like fun?"

"Wait, what?" I'm taken aback. "You wanted to dispose of your sisters all along?" The idea is so incredulous that, for a second, I lower my guard and start to think that maybe this is her intention, to shift my focus and make me vulnerable so that she can attack me. I begin to hyperventilate, frantically digging for the source of my calm, willing it to come back.

"Well, no, it wasn't like that. I wasn't sure of you, at first. When you were born, all I wanted to do was to, um, get rid of you, to hurt your father. But you've proven to grow up into something else, forever stubborn, not giving in to his persistent violence. Nerves of steel. I liked watching your spirit resist from the confines of my bronze self, forever hugging the faucet, waiting for the perfect moment."

"And what perfect moment was that?" I ask.

"You have decided to take your life. You have matured from a young helpless girl to a strong willful woman who chose death

Chapter 21

over pain and fear—you were ready to be turned into a fully-fledged, ferocious siren."

"I don't understand—"

"Listen," Canosa hisses. "This is how it works. You sing to one too young, she simply dies. You sing to one too old, she withers on the spot, becomes a walking corpse, a ghost of her previous vitality. Ever seen those women, dry like fallen leaves, bitter, odious, distorted shadows of themselves? Those are the ones who didn't *quite* turn out. Pity. I made a lot of those mistakes when I was younger. Way too many." She pauses dramatically, pointing her finger at me. "And then I found you." She smiles and it looks like she means it. Her face alights with pride.

"Your soul grew ripe that night, ripe and juicy." She licks her lips. "You turned the whole bathroom into a smoky hell. I thought I would cough and blow my cover! I knew it was time. Time to reap you. Oh, the sweet sound of your soul—your dreams, the flutter of you leafing through book pages, the tinkling of your favorite music. I admit, you were the tastiest girl I ever turned."

I recoil. "Who gave you the right? It was not up to you to decide. I didn't ask you," I say, trembling all over.

"Oh, but you did, the girl who doesn't remember. You asked for my help. I merely obliged. Your mother truly missed the opportunity to polish your behavior, to teach you when it's appropriate to say hi and goodbye, please and thank you. Shame-shame-shame. How very disappointing." She falls silent and studies me, shaking her head slightly in disapproval.

I grunt something unintelligible, awash with blinding fury.

"Is that a *yes* I hear?" Canosa asks, and it blows the lid on my tumultuous pot. Terror surges through me first, and then confusion, anger, dismay, childish helplessness, and, finally, elation. I have power and I know it.

Above all, I have my voice.

I can sing.

"You haven't heard anything yet," I say quietly.

Her eyebrows fly up in surprise, a hint of fear flashing across her features. It's obviously not the answer she expected.

Time stops. My body shakes violently, ready to explode. I put my feet together and stand tall, strung into a line about to leap skyward. I sing my way through the drizzle, searching for the frequency of the rhythm, for the very tempo that causes Canosa's particles to move, her little water cells that make up her essence. It's different from screaming into the mouths of Teles and Ligeia, where I could sense their vibrations and mimic them. We're separated by about seven feet, and I have to match her pulse to lead her to an exploding crescendo. I want to unravel her, octave by octave, note by note, until she is no more. With each musical stroll into this lethal madness, I grow bolder, wilder, until my confidence is back and I'm on a roll.

Canosa takes a gulp of wet air to sing back at me, bidding to duel. She doesn't realize that she's made a big mistake. Her singing gives me her pitch, the key to her melody, straight to the core of her tempo. Her siren DNA.

I'm like a homeless runaway dipped in rain and mud and madness.

My earth-shattering cry continues to grow in volume and ferocity. It proceeds to uproot young trees from the ground. Another beat, and it lifts Canosa off of her feet and throws her into the air. Her limbs flit and twist. Another octave higher and the leaden sky itself is out of place, a foreboding glaucous mass, quivering to my command. I'm the conductor. I unify all moisture around me, set its tempo, and tell it when to beat and how fast.

First, raindrops tap on my temple. Then, all at once, a rush of rain slaps me in the face as if someone overturned a bucket of water on my head.

Chapter 21

A deafening tearing noise erupts, mixed with a creaky groan. The gigantic Douglas fir, in the shadow of which we ended our fall, leans dangerously and then falls a few feet in front of me with a detonating crash, showering me with needles and twigs. I stop.

Canosa is gone, swept away by my voice. Or dare I hope she exploded? Wouldn't I have heard it?

Beneath the heavy rain, silence is absolute. I'm afraid of it; it's somehow wrong. I have created a wasteland in roughly a mile radius. There is nothing around me except dirt.

"Hunter?"

Chapter 22

Mud Lake

A feeble violin moans in the gloomy yonder and falls silent. I spring up and dash in its direction, my feet slipping in mud puddles, my breath ripping my chest. As quickly as it surfaced, the sound disappears. I stop to listen. There it is again, coming from the pile of rocks and dirt a good fifty feet from the fallen fir tree. I stumble, fall, pick myself up, and sprint to the source of the melody.

I stop in front of a hillock and start digging like mad, fingers and nails, one frantic little mole. I throw stones off the pile in all directions, muttering gibberish, hoping against all hope that I'm right. Stones give way to gravel, gravel gives way to dirt. When the dirt shifts, a hand emerges and grabs on to me for dear life.

"Hunter!" I shriek.

I clear his face from the debris. He coughs and opens his eyes, bright blue in contrast to all this dirt. He gulps for air, licking his lips.

"Water," he mouths, without an actual sound.

"Just a second!" I say and dash to the river. Up close it turns

Chapter 22

out to be no more than a brook about thirty feet across. It gurgles its merry stream and I dip into it, wade deeper, and exhale in relief as I dunk my head and drink the melted glacier water. Savoring its sweetness, I inhale it through my cracked gills and wash my face, the icy water chilling me properly. I stumble out, sliding on mossy pebbles with the precious liquid caught in my palms. Carrying it carefully over to Hunter, I trickle drop by drop between his cracked lips.

"More," he croaks, so quietly that I barely hear it.

I repeat my journey, elated, feeling as if I'm flying, ready to make the trip to the stream and back a million times.

"You're alive," I say on repeat, digging the rest of his frame out until he's free of dirt, lightly pressing him against my chest.

"You're alive, you're alive, you're *alive*. I'm so sorry I hurt you, I really am. I lost control, I sort of forgot about everything else. I needed to get rid of the sirens. Ligeia was sucking out your soul and..." I notice his incredulous look. "Are you badly hurt? Will you ever forgive me? Can I—"

"I can't hear you," Hunter utters in a long slur, obviously disoriented. It sounds more like *acanthearya*.

I fist the end of my wet sweatshirt sleeve and wipe his lips clean. "I said, I'm sorry. I said—"

He grabs me with his left hand, bewildered.

"What? What is it? What's wrong?" I ask, alarmed.

"I can't hear you. I can't hear myself talking. I can't hear nothing." His voice is quiet and garbled, words hardly separated from each other, sounding like one long string.

Paralysis pins me to the ground. I feared this might happen.

"You can't hear me?" I repeat like a parrot. "How about now?" I yell into his ear, denying what he told me, not wanting to acknowledge what it means. He doesn't cringe at my voice, which confirms that I must have damaged his eardrums. But wouldn't he be in terrible pain right now if I did? He doesn't look like he is.

"Come on, let me carry you, let's figure out a way to get out of here. We'll go to your house and you'll take a bath and a nap and feel better and see your mom and…" I chatter nonsense in hopes of making him feel better, but mostly I hope to make myself feel better. I scoop him by the shoulders and struggle to sit him up. I slip in the mud and fall on my knees. He grabs my arm and insistently pulls me closer to him.

"Stop…I'm deaf…STOP!"

Strength drains from me. The feeling of dread returns, brought on by the horrible mistake I made. I can't reverse it no matter what I do.

I break into hysteria.

"What do you mean, stop? What do you mean, you can't hear me? Listen to me! I killed them, I killed them all. The sirens, they're gone! Well, I'm not so sure about Canosa, but…but even if she made it, I don't think she'll bother us anymore. She won't dare. You should've seen her fly, it was epic. We didn't die, you hear me? We can live, we can run away, we can…" I grope for the next thing we can do, thinking that in some perverted sense it's great that he's deaf, because maybe, just *maybe*, it will prevent him from reacting to my siren voice and we actually will have a chance of creating a future together.

Hunter shakes his head no. It makes me angry.

I shout obscenities at him, wave my arms for added effect, but all I see in response is pain flitting across his face, and I know I went a little too far.

"You can't be deaf!" I yell at the end of my tirade, and break down crying. Hunter reaches out to my cheek, smearing tears off my face. I grasp his hand and kiss his grimy fingers, one by one.

"I'm sorry. Sorry. I didn't mean it like that…it's just…I was…I'm overwhelmed with all of this shit, okay? It's getting under my skin and it's a little too much. I want to forget about

Chapter 22

everything that happened and run away, hide some place quiet, you know. Together..." I trail off, not sure what else to say, ignoring the futility of it, which Hunter confirms.

"I...can't...hear...you." He spells out each word carefully, moving his lips in an exaggerated fashion, and gradually the meaning sinks in.

"You can't hear me?" I repeat idiotically.

He reads my lips and nods, wiping hair off his forehead and leaving a dirty streak. He props himself up on his healthy arm, and I help him sit up. We stare at each other, into each other.

"Did I blow your eardrums? I did, didn't I," I say quietly. I cover my mouth with one hand, horrified, holding his hand in the other.

The moment is ripe to feel tears rolling down my cheeks instead of raindrops, but they won't come. My tear ducts are as dry as bone. The sky cries for me, rain dripping down my face and soaking my tattered sweatshirt.

"Oh, God. What did I do. What did I do."

Hunter slides his hand out of my grip and taps me on the shoulder. Then, stumbling over each word and stopping to make sure I understand him, he begins to talk, slowly.

"Ailen. I didn't ask you to save me. The deal was to die together. But you're a stubborn turkey, eh? You always do things *your* way. Well, it's *my* life and it's up to *me* what I do with it. I decided to call it quits a long time ago. I planned for it, carefully, in case you didn't know. Now I'm alive and deaf. Crippled. You know how weird it feels talking and not hearing yourself? It's not just weird, it's scary. I don't want to carry this pain around for the rest of my life. If you can call it life," he sighs, visibly exhausted by his effort.

I open my mouth.

He shakes his head. "We were supposed to exit life, *spectacularly*, once and for all. I thought falling down over five hundred feet would do it. I shouldn't have dragged you with me. I should've done it alone."

He holds back tears.

"Shoulda-woulda-coulda. Hindsight is twenty-twenty. You know who I am right now?" he asks, the tone of his voice bordering on annoyance.

I shake my head, scared to look up.

"A disabled teenager with a single parent who's dying of cancer. Hunter Crossby, nice to meet you." He shifts from talking to nearly yelling, which sounds even scarier because he fails to pronounce the words clearly and they sound like a broken string of vowels and consonants.

"A siren hunter who can't hear. What a joke. I don't know what else to do. This is all I know. It's what your father taught me to do. To hell with sonic guns, why bother? You exploded them with your voice, just like that. What's the need for me after this? Nice job, Ailen. Go brag to your papa." He yanks his hand out of my grip.

He never ever used to call my father "papa." Not once.

His face is livid with anger, and he glares me down.

"Remember how I asked you if you ever wanted to kill yourself?" I say. "Well, have you ever felt like death is not enough, like the mere fact of your existence poisons everything around you, ruins everyone you touch? It's like in that legend about King Midas. He asked Dionysus, the Greek god of grape harvest, to grant him a special wish. To turn anything he touched into gold. You know what happened to him? He died of hunger. Know why? Because the food he touched turned to gold. Even his daughter turned to gold when he wanted to hug her. I'm like that Midas guy, except everything I touch turns to dust." I suppress the oncoming tears.

Hunter looks at me, but from the expression on his face, I can see that he didn't hear a word I just said.

Chapter 22

Rain splatters over the fallen tree trunk. The brook warbles and rolls and gurgles. The air turns dark and impatient.

Hunter starts to shiver. I keep forgetting that it's me who feels good under the rain, not him.

I hear his soul, grasp at its tune as if I'm drowning. Yet, somehow, it doesn't sound like home to me anymore, doesn't sound like anything at all. It's just a melody empty of meaning.

Hunter opens and closes his mouth like a fish out of water, but no words come out. He averts his eyes and looks into the darkening distance, not seeming to see anything at all.

"It hurts, you know, not being able to hear you," he finally says in a small voice, as if his whole body shrunk. "I love listening to your voice. Loved it." He's in pain, I can feel it, and I squat next to him, to comfort him. He shrugs away and I freeze, my arm raised. I slowly lower it and hug myself, tight.

"I want to die. Can you please leave me alone? Leave me."

I can't believe what I'm hearing. I want to reach out to him, to stroke his hair, to kiss his face, to hold him. My arms stay firmly crossed over each other.

"Your father told me, you know." He slurs his words, but the undertone of bitterness is unmistakable. "Sirens poison our very spirit. They do it sweetly, quietly, with a hundred percent rate of success."

He turns his head to look at me. "Why can't I simply quit you? Why? Can you please get out of my life, *please*? Can you simply leave me alone? It's all I'm asking." I sense an urge to hurt me in his eyes, a childish wish to strike out just because. Just because it will make him feel better. So I take this virtual blow and nod. I wanted to prevent him from falling in love with me again after all, didn't I? I succeeded. It's time to let him go, but I can't move.

"Fine. If you won't go, I will," Hunter says.

He turns his back on me, pulls up his legs, and awkwardly

pushes himself up, using his only healthy arm, moaning in pain and slipping in dirt. I stretch out my arms to help, but then drop them, knowing he won't accept it. He stumbles forward a good ten feet before looking back. I never saw his eyes that cold.

"I don't ever want to see you again, you hear me?" His voice catches at the end. "Never." And then, after a pause, "I can't even tell if you heard me or not." He turns away and stumbles forward.

"Mission accomplished," I whisper. I want to beg him not to leave, I want to scream and yell and thrash, but my muscles atrophy. One phrase echoes against the walls of my empty core: *He left me, he left me.* I need to accept it. But I can't help myself and lose it completely.

I wail. I pour my grief into an odious animalistic howl that has no words, only pain. Its voluble garble disperses across the valley in loud echoes, and I howl harder. I lose myself in my anguish, screaming freely, at the top of my lungs. What I fail to take into account is the effect my voice has on the elements, water in particular. By the time I figure out what's happening, it can't be reversed.

Called on by my incessant misery, liquid seeps out of the ground and pools into puddles; puddles overflow, forming rills that quickly join with the flowing river about thirty feet away. It spills over its rims and rises a foot, swallows the banks, rapidly covering dirt with mangy streams. I abruptly stop, watching with horror as the surrounding mud turns into a pond filled with broken tree limbs and tawny fluid.

There is a sucking sound from the ground itself, as if it's a gigantic sponge that some ancient, monstrous hand squeezed. At once, water surrounds me, rising rapidly from my knees to my waist to my shoulders. The rumble is overpowering.

"Hunter!" I yell, thrashing about in the muddy liquid of my own creation.

Chapter 22

Hunter is about ten yards away, clutching the Douglas fir trunk, bobbing in this watery madness. He struggles to pull himself over with one arm, to saddle on top of it.

I want to help him but his request to get out of his life holds me back. Now is the perfect time to let go and die for real. Now there is truly nothing else left to live for. Nothing at all.

This knowledge makes me calm and I know what to do.

Water comes out from all surfaces at once, covering my shoulders, gurgling, filling up the basin between the mountain ridges, turning the valley into a gigantic bathtub filled with liquid mud, with my pain, with Hunter's pain, with my father's pain, with my mother's pain. Even with Canosa's pain and the pain of the sirens. It soaks it all up, the brown mess of life that stinks, that's hard to face, that we shove into the backs of our minds hoping it will vanish.

Hunter shouts something at me, pointing into the distance and then back at me. I can't hear him.

Clouds give way to a clear lavender sky. Mount Rainier looms its white splendor over everything. I watch as rapid fluid darts down its slope at maybe fifty miles per hour. A loud rumble fills the air, announcing melted snow mixed with soil and other forest debris. It sounds almost like a musical mudflow, with me directing its performance. Except, at this point, I'm not doing anything anymore; I shifted something and set it in motion with my wailing, the glorious vocalist of erosion.

I watch the catastrophe unfold with insane glee, my feet barely touching the ground underneath the murk. The noise of the rushing water is deafening, but it appears that the worst of it is over. It's gradually quieting down.

Something bumps into me and kicks me out of my delusion. It's a tree trunk. Uprooted firs fight for space, their branches overlapping each other. Several yards away, dunking in and out of the water, Hunter clutches a floating Douglas for dear life.

He frantically motions at me. I can't make up my mind if it's safe to swim to him and help, when a distinct rhythmical plopping enters my range of hearing.

An elongated object bobs on the surface about a mile away. It's hollow. I concentrate on it, trying to discern the exact shape by the sound and why it attracted me in the first place.

Then I know why. It's a boat. A rowboat. It slips across the surface of the liquid mud. It's empty. I can't discern a human soul within it. Perfect. The least I can do is guide it here and let it be Hunter's ride, if he decides he still wants to live. It's better than having him hang off a tree trunk.

I hum, creating an undercurrent, thinking that once Hunter spots the boat and makes his way into it, which I'm sure he will, I can secretly hum him back to civilization and maybe he'll change his mind about dying.

The boat appears in the distance, no more than a dark dot gliding through evening mist.

"It's for you, Hunter, just so you know that I love you," I whisper.

Hunter doesn't even look at me. I don't blame him. There is nothing to look at; I'm a cold, undead girl submerged to her neck in thick brown soup.

You're a monster, remember that. Won't you ever forget your place?

The boat is now about fifty feet away, and Hunter notices it too. It looks empty, two oars trailing on each side, their handles sticking out of the rusty oarlocks, screeching. Its hull was once painted bright blue; now it's faded into an unidentifiable shade of ultramarine. It bobs on the waves, its weight disproportionate with the shape and size of its wooden body, submerged too deeply in the thick gumbo of dirt that I conjured.

I open my eyes to see what's wrong and float very still.

The boat is ten feet away from me, and about ten feet away

Chapter 22

from Hunter, dead in the middle between us. What I took for silence is not silence at all. I hear it now. Quiet, but there. The familiar flap of butterfly wings, the broken flute, and a crackling, smoldering fire. My father sits up in the boat, his face pale yet smug and satisfied.

Chapter 23

Cascade Range

This is my nightmare.

"You never cease to surprise me with your...methods, Ailen. Nonetheless, excellent job. Four sirens gone, and Canosa damaged. I'm pleased with you, very pleased indeed."

Somehow I'm still floating, taking in every detail of our encounter in a series of snapshots. My father's open forehead, his gray hair carefully combed back. His stern eyes peeling me apart. His ever-present classy boating outfit, complete with a fancy maroon waterproof jacket and brand-new khaki pants. I sense a whiff of his signature cologne and want to gag.

"Out of all boats, I had to pick the one with you in it," I whisper, every word slow to emerge.

"Kids," he actually addresses both of us, "sorry to have left you hanging. I certainly didn't think it would take you this far from the Aurora Bridge to do the job. But a job is a job, right? You did it. I will hold to my word. You both will live. Ain't that good news, Ailen? Where is that smile, show your Papa, please?"

Chapter 23

He looks at me with a new expression on his face, one I don't recognize. Half awe, half fascination, and perhaps a hint of jealousy mixed with fear. All under his mask of fake parental love. Forget gagging, I want to outright vomit.

He leans out of the boat and I have the sudden urge to pull him underwater and keep him there until he is no more.

"Will you accept my apology for abandoning you two?" my father says. My jaw drops. He has never apologized to me in my entire life. Never. Not once.

He stretches out his right hand, his gray hair moving in the evening breeze and his lips forming a perfect smile.

When I fail to give him my hand in return, he pats me on the head lightly with a contained grimace of disgust. My father always hated wet things, especially wet, dirty things. Promptly, he unzips both of his jacket pockets and takes out two resin gloves, the thick orange kind that fishermen use for fetching their catch out of the water. They squeak as he pulls them on.

"Looks like your boyfriend is injured?" he says to me.

"Hey, son, you all right?" This is directed at Hunter.

Hunter merely nods.

"If you don't want to talk, that's fine with me. We'll have all the time in the world to talk later." My father is obviously in a very good mood and I exhale in relief.

Hunter seems indifferent, staring blankly.

"Well?" My father raises his eyebrows.

He apologized to me. He praised me for a job well done. He *heard* me and spoke to me like to a normal human being. It took for me to die to get this. It's what I wanted my entire life.

I follow the boat and help my father prop Hunter up and over the side of it.

"Did you forget how to talk? Or did she stun you with her theatrics?" my father asks Hunter.

"Hello," Hunter mutters and falls silent, slumping into a

wet, shivering pile on the front bench, giving me a look full of accusation.

"I don't blame you. I'd be speechless, too. Look at this. She flooded an entire valley! My God." My father's cheery mood fueled by the aftermath of the destruction makes him blind to what's going on.

"Ailen? You coming?" My father stretches out his gloved hand, speaking in a jovial tone as if we're departing for a summer picnic.

Did I finally earn his approval? Is it possible that he feels remorse, or guilt, or dare I imagine, *love* for me?

I fasten my eyes onto his blank gaze. His pupils widen, two dark pools into the unknown. They don't frighten me like they used to. Although the lilac of the dusk solidifies by the minute, I see his eyes clearly for what they really are—merely two orbs full of protein liquid. I could reach out and pop them with my fingers, or I could scream and make them boil. Either way, the source of my nightmares—those two terrible spheres of menace—are gone, replaced by a pair of vulnerable globules, old and tired, sunken from years of internal conflict. My father's whole demeanor is that of a disappointed old man who's trying to make ends meet, doing the only thing he knows how to do well: hate women. What sorry existence it must be, how much pain must he carry around and suppress on a daily basis.

I choose to believe the unbelievable.

"Sure," I say.

I steady the boat from bobbing and propel myself up and out of the filthy soup in one leap, landing softly between him and Hunter onto the boat's floor. My feet splatter mud in all directions and I watch with horror how the beautiful maroon fabric of my father's jacket turns brown in several spots.

I feel him burning a hole in my head with his stare and I dare to lift my eyes, expecting a blow. It doesn't happen, and I

Chapter 23

sigh in relief, noticing wonder in his eyes. Wonder and uncertainty.

"Don't worry, sweetie, it's just a jacket." This is new as well, and I stare, struggling to comprehend the change.

He gives me another pat on the shoulder and smiles. "Let's go home." He picks up the oars and plunges them into the dark water.

"It will take us forever," I manage.

"But you can hum us faster, can't you? We don't have to go far. I left my car by the campground, over there." He motions west. "It's high on the ridge, so it evaded your…what shall we call it…forceful flooding."

"Sure, I'll do it," I nod, overtaken by his attention. An alarm rings a thousand bells inside my mind, but my heart covers it with a blanket of hope, hushing it.

It's my trap and my curse, this elusive happiness. I'm buried alive by my desire. Despite it, I clutch to the silky rope of the promise of his love, elusive as it is.

I've got nothing left to lose at this point, do I? Then why not risk it? Why not throw myself into mad belief?

So I hum and hum, passing hours as we make our way to a campground that resembles a ghostly peninsula in the night, completely devoid of campers and sitting smack in the middle of the mudslide, swollen with tree trunks, silt, and even snowmelt.

"That took, what, less than an hour? You could make good money doing this, Ailen, did it ever cross your mind?" my father exclaims. I nod. No other remarks are exchanged for the rest of the journey.

Time loses significance and staggers along in a series of boring practical moves, like getting out of the boat, pulling it ashore, slushing through wet grass to the dark parking lot. My über-organized father, nonplussed, turns on his super bright flashlight. I help Hunter limp along, eager to enter the comfortable confines of Papa's Maserati. Surprised that we're not asked to clean up, we both file into the back of the car and sink into the enveloping leather. I realize I forgot what it's like to ride in a car, to bask in its quiet whirring. I take Hunter's hand, and he lets me. I squeeze it and wait. He doesn't squeeze back at first, then he does, and I feel a tired smile spread over my face.

How we make it out to the highway is less about driving along a road and more about wading through a dark tunnel toward some unattainable light at the end—light and life and normalcy.

My journey home is paved with anguish. Three days ago I was in a different place. Three hours is how long it takes for me to return to its precise location. Three minutes to surface out of sealed-off wonder, taking in my house through the tinted car windows like a ghost from the past. Instantly I can't breathe, sensing that I'll die right here, in this place where I grew up, where I was born.

We arrive in the dead of the night.

My father parks the car by our garage door, kills the purr of the engine, and throws me a large black fleece blanket to cover myself up. Apparently, he's worried that my glowing skin will freak the neighbors out.

I open the door, throw the blanket over my head, shuffle around the car, and help Hunter out, ignoring my father's hushed urgency to be fast and quiet and discreet lest we be discovered by neighbors who—thank you very much—are still under the impression that I died from my suicidal jump off the Aurora Bridge. I would imagine I gave Mrs. Elliott and her elderly friends enough juicy details to speculate on my passing and how it must have felt.

I make my legs move, dragging them up the steps to my house that, with its lights turned off, resembles a huge casket. *No more running for you, Ailen Bright. Where would you even go?*

Chapter 23

Hunter breathes rapidly in front of me, taking each step with great care, moving slowly and moaning; his damp hoodie brushes my face as I nearly stumble into it. Having endured Hunter's soul melody during the three-hour ride, I don't know how to find the strength to suppress my growing hunger. It's overpowering.

We emerge on the porch and wait for Father to quietly fumble for keys. Hunter leans on the railing, his head turned away from me. Afraid to bother him, I leave him be, clutching the edges of the blanket tighter around my head, creating a hood.

Velvety black at this hour, with only two street lights dotting the night on either side, lies our street. Wet from recent rain, puddles glisten with the reflected light. Expensive cars are parked along its right curb, while recycling and compost cans have been rolled out neatly in between.

You hypocrites. You like to flash your perfect façades to everyone, but you don't dare talk about your familial secrets. You hide inside your beautiful houses, pretending like you have your shit together, when, in fact, you don't. I spit with vigor, thinking about my father and his nightly violence toward my mother, covered up in the morning with the proper social stance of a respected businessman with a wife who's gone a little cuckoo. But whose doesn't? That was always his counterpoint. *Women were made to haul water,* his words echo in my mind as I stare at our manicured lawn, so disgustingly pristine in the moonlight.

"Welcome home," my father says, slowly opening the door into darkness with a barely audible squeak. Hunter steps in, and I follow, Father shutting the door behind us.

Hunter immediately staggers into the living room and plops down on the couch, hands over his ears, all without having uttered a single word, silent for more than three hours now. I throw a worried look to see if Father is alarmed by this in any way.

"I'm afraid we won't be able to turn on any lights at this

moment, I hope you don't mind. Go on, take a seat." Father motions me to the same couch, and then proceeds to carefully remove his dirty boating shoes. After he sheds his rain jacket, he flattens the collar of his shirt and smoothes his hair.

I carelessly drop the blanket onto the floor and, without wiping my bare feet on the rug, I walk over to sit next to Hunter, feeling like I'll never get out of this house again.

I recognize the outlines of the familiar furniture in the gloom of the living room. To my left stands our dinner table of cherry wood, a thick oval top balanced on a single spindle leg, four chairs tucked under it. The lucid tulip shades of our chandelier hang over it. Swarovski crystal, twinkling like drops of water suspended in the air.

I remember climbing on top of the table and pushing the chandelier to swing, watching the shadows dance on the walls and pretending I was underwater. Papa hit me hard for that, and without warning. I flew several feet and split my chin on our polished parquet floor. There was a lot of blood, but I didn't utter a sound. I flinch at the memory, remembering clearly how Mother was bringing out the casserole and a set of candlesticks, ignoring the scene out of fear and averting her eyes as if nothing happened. I can almost smell the bubbling hot cheese and the burnt matches after she lit the candles. I was five.

I blink and look to my right, to the big window unobscured by blinds, because Father likes his light. In the blackness outside I see the street lights on the Aurora Bridge, 3,000 feet of its steel stretched from my house to Hunter's, where his mom is probably thinking him dead at the moment, if she is thinking anything at all in her state.

I turn my head and notice Hunter's gaze in the same direction. He quickly lowers his eyes. I wonder what is going through his head, but I don't dare ask. Not that he'll hear me anyway. I suppress the urge to grab his hand and press it to my chest. I

Chapter 23

shift a little to the right, just so I'm farther away from his maddeningly sweet melody.

"A perfect blend of art and science, wouldn't you say?" Father interrupts my willful stupor. He lifts a glass sphere from the coffee table and turns it this way and that, squinting at the water against the moonlight that filters through the glass, causing fish to scatter in all directions; they bump into the sphere's walls, into each other, locked in their glass casket until they die.

"Yeah..." I trail off, looking at it with a new understanding.

"Hey," I say, unable to bring myself to call him Papa and yet not feeling comfortable at this particular moment to say "Father" either. "Hunter needs to see a doctor, like, soon. His arm might be broken, and I think I..." I want to say, I made him deaf, but arrest it mid-sentence, biting my tongue. "I think I shook him up pretty badly. We fell off a cliff about five hundred feet, so—"

"Don't you find it fascinating?" my father continues. His usual treatment is back, so I close off and ignore him, incredulous at his ability to shut out the most horrific facts, yet understanding it fully. This is how he must have survived his own horror—whatever it was—by making horrible things sound normal. You fell off a cliff over five hundred feet tall? No big deal.

"It's not very polite to ignore me, Ailen, you know that. Don't you have anything to say?" He places the fishbowl back on the table, comes up to me, squats, and lifts my chin toward the window. I freeze at his touch—warm, yet not comforting. He peers into my face, as if it's my turn to be his orb. *I'm not transparent, Papa, I'm empty. I have no soul. There's no use looking.*

"You really need to take Hunter to the ER," I repeat, feeling the urge to kill rising in my chest in large, vehement waves.

"I'm sure he can speak up for himself, can't he?" my father says inquisitively.

"Sorry," I say, not knowing for what. It's a habit.

"No need to apologize. You're my star, after everything

you've accomplished. Albeit, a bit messy. But I understand. We all love a little fame, don't we?" He pats me on the shoulder.

"Hunter needs to see a doctor, now," I press on. "He's in pain." I turn my head and see him slumped in the corner of the couch, soundly sleeping; by some unknown miracle, I don't fall on top of him right there and then. Watching him sleep is like watching a delicious homemade pie steam its sugary aroma, fresh out of the oven, placed directly under your nose after you've had nothing to eat for a whole week.

"I see." Father is back on his feet and then sits across from me on the other couch, a low glass coffee table separating us, the glass aquarium balancing dully in the middle like an enormous transparent egg.

"You're that fond of him, are you?"

I swallow rapidly but don't answer.

"He seems okay for now, don't you think? Sleep will do him good. Meanwhile, I want to show you something. I want you to pay close attention, please." He sticks his thumb and forefinger into his shirt pocket, takes out a small object, and places it on his upturned palm. It glistens in the hazy moonlight.

A pearl.

While I look at it, he pulls out a sonic gun from under his feet and places it on the table top with a cautious smile. I recoil. I thought he trusted me, but he's still afraid, after all.

"Let me explain something to you, perhaps it will help us understand each other better. Do you know what this is?"

Do you take me for an idiot, I want to say, but the gun makes me answer his question literally. "A pearl?"

"Not just any pearl. It's a natural pearl. Do you know the difference between a cultured and a natural pearl?" The way he says it make me feel dumb. The way I'll explain it, he won't hear. So I give him an excuse to shine.

"No, I don't," I say.

Chapter 23

"Of course you don't. Most pearls in stores are cultured, grown on pearl farms. It's a fascinating process, really. They take a tiny mother-of-pearl bead, or a piece of sand, and implant it into a mollusk—the host." He pauses, waiting for a reaction.

I nod, unsure where he's going.

"This one," he puts it on his palm, "was made by nature. It's perfectly round, which is extremely rare. Look."

He lifts it against the faint light diffusing through the window and pinches it between his manicured fingers. "Very pretty. The closer it is to an ideal spherical shape, the more expensive. Until the last century, they've been valued above all other gems. Know why?"

I shake my head, playing along.

"Not for their beauty. For their rarity."

He gives me a long look. I shift uncomfortably. Something sinister wakes in his eyes; I can't place it. He leans over the table, his other hand on the gun.

"Tell me how natural pearls are made."

I stare.

"Do we need to talk about pearls right now? Hunter's—"

"By a *parasite*," he interrupts me.

A film of greedy fever rolls over his face like parchment. I have a sensation that I'm looking at a marionette controlled by an evil puppeteer, struggling to remember the last time he gave me an in-depth lecture like this one and coming up blank.

"The parasite enters a mollusk's body so that it can't be expelled. The mollusk fights back by producing calcium carbonate and protein, to cover it up, layer upon layer, until it's completely enclosed. Dead. It becomes a cyst, a cancerous growth. That's what a natural pearl is, Ailen."

He closes his lips on my name with an audible smack, then shifts back into the groaning couch cushions, apparently satisfied with my reaction.

Cascade Range

My mouth goes dry.
I get it.

Chapter 24

Brights' House

A lonely car honks once behind the window. A few late-night commuter souls clink into a tired escapade from a party, trailing home. Hunter's soul smolders in a faint but delicious concerto next to me. Darkness presses on the house, smelling of gasoline and nightly perspiration. My tongue tastes bitter.

A parasite, I repeat in my mind over and over. He means me. Enclosed in a beautiful shell. His most precious pearl. A work of art and science combined. Extracted from a broken mollusk discarded after delivery. I shrink into the soft leather. Revolting disappointment overwhelms me. A sudden temptation takes over, and I throw my next words at my father like I don't care.

"You forgot something," I say levelly.

He raises his eyebrows and taps his fingers on the sonic gun in a steady rhythm, lifting his feet on tiptoe so that his silk socks press lightly into the freshly vacuumed carpet.

"Please, enlighten me," he says.

"You forgot to check if the parasite is still alive." I savor the pause.

"Oh. Not for long, actually. Turns out, I have grown rather fond of the parasite I happened to produce." He stretches his lips, but his eyes don't smile.

"We'll be staging your funeral tomorrow morning. To quiet the city folk and stop the rumors, let people know we found your body and just weren't ready to disclose the news. You know, the works. To give you a proper goodbye."

"What?" I almost choke. "Why?"

I just sit there, reaching out and grasping for the meaning of this news but finding nothing to hold on to.

"Where would you like to go?"

"What?" I force myself back. "I'm sorry, I got distracted. What did you say?"

"I said, after it's over, where would you like to settle? You didn't hear anything at all, did you?" He shakes his head. "How typical."

I gape. "Sorry. The whole parasite thing, and then the funeral thing...why do we need to do it? I don't understand."

"I'm doing this for you, Ailen. *We* need to do this for you." He studies me, making a clear emphasis on the word *we*.

"*We* need to do this? For *me*?" I repeat.

"Yes, for *you*." He clears his throat. "I made a mistake, as a father, and I apologize. I failed to...to see you as my daughter, above all, siren or not. I want to make this right again. I want us to feel like a family and put an end to this incessant conflict."

I simply stare, dumbfounded. Something smells fishy.

"Once you're *buried*, we'll be able to leave Seattle and start a new life, you and me. I will close my business and open up a new one in another city. What do you say? Sound good? Is there a particular place you'd like to go?" he asks again.

His knuckles grow white, his skin stretched over the hand holding the gun, yet his face lights up. There was only one other

Chapter 24

time when he was glowing like this, and it was when we returned from my mother's funeral. Another fake funeral, because there was no body to bury and her casket was empty. He excused his happiness on account of not having to look for her body anymore. He said the funeral brought him much needed closure. Back then, of course, I had no real idea of what is so clear to me now: it was him who pushed her to jump off the bridge.

"You're serious? You mean this? For real?" As I say this, my traitor heart bursts aflutter. Hopeful, childish, full of naïve excitement. His crimes forgotten. His violent behavior evaporating from my memory like it never existed.

"Of course I mean it! How is that for a birthday present? I didn't forget, see?"

I study him, wanting to make sure there is not a hint of deception in his eyes, not a twitch in his facial muscles. I'm scared, terrified to believe. It's too good to be true, too easy, too all of a sudden. I swallow back tears.

"Can this be true?" I croak.

"Can't an old man change at the sunset of his life? Come on, Ailen, give me some credit. Look at me." He places the gun down on the coffee table and raises both arms in surrender. "I admit, I'm a little afraid of you. You turned out to be a fierce little thing. But I'm proud of you. I'm very, *very* proud of you."

I want to hug him, but I can't make myself move. I've never hugged my father, or been hugged by him in return.

"I don't care where. Anywhere. You pick," I say and mean it.

"All right. I have an idea. How about Italy? On the outskirts of Rome, away from heavy population, say, in some small village, so that every weekend we can take a trip to the—"

"—Baths of Caracalla, to listen to the opera," I finish automatically, fetching this knowledge from the depths of my memory.

"Precisely. That's exactly what I meant. How did you know?"

He looks at me quizzically.

"I just do. I'm your daughter, after all..." I trail off, blinking tears down my cheeks, mortified that he'll see me crying.

"Interesting. Perhaps it confirms that we're truly related." He grins.

I gasp. "What do you mean by that? Are you implying Mom cheated on you? How can you even fathom such a thing? She would never...she loved you." My voice catches.

His face wrinkles in pain. "Let's drop the subject of your mother. We have other, rather exciting things to discuss. About the funeral—"

I can't stop. "Did you really think that M—"

"Silence!" His scream is so sudden and abrupt that my teeth click as I close my mouth. This feels comfortable in a twisted way. My father is back to normal, and thankfully, I know how to deal with him amidst his angry fits.

I feign rapt attention.

"You will pretend to be a corpse, for lack of a better word. I'm sure you can manage—your skin is perfectly white with characteristic blue undertones. Would you be able to lay still for several hours?" he asks.

"Sure," I manage, afraid I lost his love before I even had a chance to bask in it.

"Excellent. Hunter will stay with you while you get ready. I thought you'd like that."

I steal a glance at Hunter's face; it's bloodied yet peaceful with his eyes closed; his hair bunches up over his fist and his chest slowly rises and falls with each breath. *I need to stay away from him.*

"And where will you be?" I ask.

"Funeral business, of course. I have to leave in a few minutes to pick up the casket," his eyes drop to his Panerai watch, "see to the funeral parlor, prepare the boat—"

Chapter 24

"The boat?" I ask.

"Ailen. How else do you think you'll be able to extract yourself from the casket—by digging yourself out of the grave in the middle of the night? I certainly don't think it's a good idea. We will be giving you a burial at sea."

I blink. "Wow. Why?"

"Because it's the only way you can safely break out of the casket. You'll tear off the lid, swim to Ocean Shores and we will meet there, okay?"

"Ocean Shores? Is it that small town on the coast where you and Mom went one summer? Why Ocean Shores?" I have so many questions that my words are momentarily paralyzed, bunched up in my throat in a mass of screaming.

Father walks over to Hunter and shakes him awake, prodding his arm with his delicate fingers, announcing, "Your arm isn't broken, it's sprained. You'll live. Now, listen to me. Your job is to see to it that Ailen preps for her funeral. She needs to take a shower and put on a clean change of clothes. I don't care what, as long as it looks decent. Can you do this for me?"

Hunter's eyes open wide in a struggle to understand. "Wha..." He winces.

I can't tell if it's because he's realizing once again that he's deaf, or because something hurts, or if he was able to make out the word *funeral* from my father's lips.

"Let me repeat." Father launches into a detailed explanation of the type of casket he picked out and why it would be easy for me to open, the time people will come to pick me up, how long the ceremony will take, and where we will go afterward. But I only half listen. My other half imagines things that I didn't dare to imagine before, like life with my father. In another city. Starting new, from scratch.

Suddenly, I realize that *funeral* is a very lovely word. It means a happy ending. I think that a funeral is my new favorite thing.

It's where families get reunited, to witness the passage of a loved one to the other side. Like birth, only the other way around.

Hunter nods, perhaps afraid to speak up, stealing quick glances at me.

Father is done with his tirade.

"You got everything, son? Can I count on you?" he asks.

"Yes." Hunter nods.

"If he forgets, I'll remind him," I say, to get Father to leave the house faster, eager to get ready and move away from Hunter so I can have a little break.

"Your job is not to remind him, but to get ready. Do you understand?" he asks.

"Yes," I answer.

"Good." My father excuses himself and disappears upstairs to change, then comes down donned in one of his finest Italian wool suits, black, with a black tie contrasting against his crisp white shirt. It takes him less than ten minutes to transform from a recreational fisherman to a gallant businessman. During this time, I dare not move closer to Hunter, dare not talk to him, remaining in the same position I was.

In the foyer, Father adjusts his cufflinks and slides into his black shiny leather Italian shoes to complement the look, addressing me without raising his eyes.

"It's close to five a.m. now. Be ready by six, please. I should be back by then with the casket." He sticks his arms into the sleeves of a trench coat, picks up his umbrella, and then jingles the keys before dropping them into his pocket. A chatter of heels against the parquet floor, a click of the door latch, and he's gone.

I remain seated for a beat or two, the rectangle of the door fried into my retinas, when Hunter nudges my sleeve.

I jump up and wheel around.

"I'll be right back!" I say and raise my index finger to indicate both my fast return and my desire to go upstairs. Then,

Chapter 24

before he has a chance to say anything or hold me back, I sprint up the stairs, open the door to the bathroom and close it with a loud bang.

Somewhere in the back of my mind, I register that this door is brand new and smells freshly painted. Out of habit, and without thinking, I lock it, slide down to the floor, and break down into sobs. Secretly I wish Hunter would dash after me, knock on the door, beg me to let him in. But he doesn't. I know why. He's giving me space, allowing me to fume. I bang on the floor with my fists, driving the pain out of me, into the open, turning it into words, spelling it out aloud and not caring if the neighbors hear me. I simply have to purge my system of this sonorous misery.

"Hunter, I'm sorry. I want to be with you, but I can't. I love you, but I can't. I want to die, and I can't. I want to bring my mother back. I can't. I want to kill Canosa so she'd," I bang both fists on the floor, "stop," I hit again, "fucking," and hit once more, "threatening you. I can't. Can't seem to be able to do it. I don't want to be a siren anymore. I want to be normal, I want to turn time around. I want to go back to how it was before my birthday. But I can't! I can't! I can't!"

I hit the floor until my knuckles bleed the clear liquid that is my blood. I spring up and direct the rest of my fury at myself in a kind of a delirious glee, tearing at my hair, slapping my own face. There is one thing I *can* do, I realize, and it's reunite with my father.

I yank at my Siren Suicides hoodie. It's clammy and sticks to my skin and won't peel off, so I rip it and throw its dirty rags around me. I strip out of the hateful orange fisherman's capris, tearing them to shreds in the process. There is nothing else to destroy, so I turn my attention to our antique, carved-marble bathtub, the ridiculous Bright family relic. I almost laugh when I see the sirens are gone. Of course! I consider lifting it and smashing it to pieces. Curiously, it looks naked to me, boring and bland without its sirens and their mouths open in a lethal song, their arms spread like wings. The faucet bends its bronze neck, vulnerable, lonely and frail without the Siren of Canosa holding it in her delicate hands. To wash off my frustrations, I want to soak in a bath so badly that I decide to hack it into a pile of rocks afterward.

I vigorously twist the cold-water handle and nearly break it off. A frothy stream gushes from the spout. I watch it bubble, inhaling the echo of chlorine like a welcome friend. I plug in the chained resin stopper and delight in the twirling fluid. It rapidly fills the tub, making me think for a second that it's my birthday again. Instead of drowning, I'll simply take a bath and get out, before it all goes to hell.

I step over the rim and descend into cold water, rushing into submersion. I tilt my head to the ceiling and slide all the way in, letting my face sink, breathing through my gills.

This is bliss. Nothing bad happened, no time has passed. It's September 7, around 7:00 a.m., and today, I'm sixteen years old. I'm simply getting ready for my big day, to celebrate, to be all nice smelling and adorable and pampered.

The ceiling doesn't share my sentiment, however. It frowns through circular waves on the surface of the water. There are no bubbles that escape my mouth, no disturbance in my chest of any kind, no pain in my lungs. I don't need to push myself down with both arms to stop from floating up. In fact, I can make my body sink or float at will, without moving a single muscle, simply by thinking about it. No, not even thinking, it's instinctual now. I tentatively reach up and touch my gills, tracing their ragged edges, torn a few days ago but now smooth and healed into two coarse openings. Jets of fluid siphon in and out of them, matching my breath.

The doorknob turns once to the right. I hear a distinct click

Chapter 24

amplified by several feet of water and sit up, my heart pounding.

I watch the knob. It turns three times to the right.

Click-click-click.

"Hunter?" I call, forgetting that he won't hear me now, but knowing that if it was him, he'd knock first and not barge in like a Neanderthal.

"Papa?" This is my next guess.

There is no answer, but a single tentative knock on the door. I hug my knees, realizing with horror that I forgot to grab a change of clothes from my room and have nothing to throw on.

"Hang on, I'm naked! Getting out." I swiftly jump out of the tub, and, dripping water all over, grab the nearest towel, rolling myself in it and tucking in one end at the top, ensuring it's secure. It occurs to me that, indeed, it is Hunter—who else would it be? The soft concerto of his soul seeps through the crack under the door, how did I not hear it before?

"Hunter, is that you?" I repeat, not caring that it's useless. The melody of his name alone makes my heart sing.

"Ailen?" he says, as if he heard me. But it comes out muffled, strained, slurry. "Hey, uh...I got clean jeans for you." Pause. "And a T-shirt." Another pause, followed by his heavy breathing. "I can't hear what you're saying, so, can I just come in? I'll drop them on the floor and be out in a flash. I won't look, I promise. Remember your favorite number? It'll take me three seconds—" The last lines he delivers fast, in a rush, and then promptly falls quiet as if cut off. I think I hear a choking cough.

"Favorite number?" I say, thinking, *three*. Why did he ask me that? I frown, turn the lock lever into the open position, and grab the door handle. My wet palm slides against its polished bronze. Brand new and stuck, it doesn't give. I wipe my hands on the towel.

"Hang on. I can't open the darn thing," I mumble, turning it harder, afraid to break it. It won't budge, stuck.

"What the..." I curse under my breath.

A melody penetrates me. Strong vibrations come from behind the door. I try to rotate the handle again. It's no use. The song comes through the walls, like a chorus of some ancient opera. At once, Hunter mentioning three makes sense. Him squeezing my hand three times. Three minutes is how long it takes for an average person to drown. For both of us, three is like a code for death.

"Canosa!" I shriek, and hear her mad cackle. Her rotten stink poisons the air, bursting through every gap and enveloping me in its ruin. It burns my nostrils, laughing at my naïveté.

I rip the handle off and drop it on the floor. Raising my right leg, I kick the door with great force—one, two, three times. The hinges take pockets of plaster out of the wall and the newly painted wooden slab finally collapses with a groan, rousing a puff of dust.

My heart sinks.

Chapter 25

Marble Bathtub

Time has a peculiar way of turning on its head. I'm transported back to the very first time I met Canosa, on the edge of the lake. The cherry expanse of the door rolls out between us in a six-foot-long welcoming carpet. She stands at its opposite end, the way she stood back then, except she's not a gorgeous femme fatale anymore. Her face and body are distorted, her features lopsided. Half of her tissues appear dead. Her mouth is open in a grimace. Her hair is reduced to a sorry matted mess and pushed to one side; on her other side, she holds Hunter in a neck bind. The only thing that hasn't changed is her penetrating gaze, her big green eyes oozing some prehistoric, primeval hatred.

"You bronze bitch. Let him go!" I roar.

"Make another move and he's dead," she hisses.

I lower my leg, having almost taken a step.

She tilts up her head and laughs, her slick, moist breasts jiggling unpleasantly. My guts spasm in revulsion.

"Oh, I've been dying to see this pain on your pretty face.

Marvelous," she exhales. "Now, kiss your boyfriend goodbye, Ailen Bright." She tightens the headlock. Hunter claws at her fingers, choking.

There is no time to think. It's not your typical staring-and-sizing-each-other-up deal. Forget it. This is a battle for life or death, and I dive into it with zeal.

To say that I leap at her is to rob your imagination. I crash at her in a combination of an acoustic and a physical wave, ear-splitting in my shrill, all-consuming in my wake, oscillating and howling. I spearhead into her slimy stomach and we tumble down the stairs in a tangle of limbs, rolling all the way into the hall and stopping only inches from the front door. The racket we produce must have roused the entire neighborhood.

I grab at everything I can, digging my fingernails into her flesh, biting her with my teeth, even reaching up with my feet in an attempt to kick her. Hunter is half-sandwiched between us, thrashing. He can't yell, his air is cut off by Canosa's arm. I can't see his face, only the back of his head.

We cartwheel around the floor, ripping coats off the hooks from the open wardrobe, spilling about shoes, and knocking down the umbrella tree stand with a clang. Canosa's hair mashes into my mouth, her limbs bulge with veins. Her mouth opens almost to an audible cracking of her skull, and then her teeth sink into my arms, my stomach, my face.

I'm about to be eaten alive. I don't care. There is only one goal on my mind. *Free Hunter.* If I can't overpower her with my strength, I can try to overpower her with my voice. I inhale, but before I can burst into a song, my throat splits open. Using her nails, she rips out a chunk of flesh from my neck, tearing at both gills. I gurgle water, as pain blinds me.

"You disgraceful, ignorant girl! I'm sick of you!" Her voice booms around me and through me. "I will show you how to fight me. I will show you what happens when you dare to fight

Chapter 25

the Siren of Canosa!"

Canosa pulls herself up with a grunt and leans against the front door, Hunter firmly in her headlock. His eyes are closed; he's not moaning or struggling anymore. It appears he has passed out.

I want to scream at Canosa to leave him alone. I try to stand up, but my feet slide on the slick floor. My leg muscles are torn by her nails; the clear liquid of my dead blood pools between wooden planks of the parquet. I stare at my naked, mutilated body, watching skin and muscles begin knitting together with a quiet hush, itching like crazy.

Canosa props my head on one of my shoes. "So you can see better, silly girl," she whispers.

See what? I want to ask, but don't need to.

The next minute will be forever etched into my miserable memory. All I can do is watch and listen, because my body refuses to move; I can't even hum.

Canosa sits opposite me, by the front door. She pulls on Hunter's limp body, putting his head into her lap.

I can't look away, feeling the life drain from me with every one of her movements. I know there is nothing I can do. I know this is the end.

She stares into his eyes and ignites his soul. She promptly launches into a Greek song that sounds like gibberish to me. She leans over his face, holding her hair up to make sure I see everything. She grimaces in a deadly yawn and sucks out his very essence, his beautiful concerto, wisp by wisp, breath by breath, until there is nothing left. Then she smacks her lips, throws me a victorious stare, and breaks into a mad laughter that sends shivers up and down my spine, shaking every wall in the house. Just like that—without a warning, without so much as a glorious battle—Hunter is gone.

Hunter, Hunter, Hunter.

Seconds melt into hours. At first slowly, and then all at once, the weight of devastation rips a hole in my chest and devours me whole. My eyes roll back and I'm about to black out.

I feel Canosa grab me under my armpits and drag me upstairs. My feet slam against the steps, one by one. I don't care. I have no strength to stop her, no strength to look around. No will to do anything anymore. She unceremoniously drops me into the empty bathtub. I slam my head on the marble and my eyes fly open. I don't even utter a cry of pain, because I don't register it anymore. It happens to some other girl, some other body, in some long-distant other world that is of no concern to me.

"There you are. I have relieved you of your pain. Aren't you going to thank me? Look at me." She painfully digs her fingers into my chin. "Don't you turn your head away. Look at me! I've been thinking about you, ever since you blew me out of the water in that mountain valley. Have you been thinking about me, Ailen Bright? Tell me."

She hops into the tub and pins my arms under my body and crawls on top of my chest. I can't look away, drawn into her green eyes, drinking from them some sort of coldness that binds me first, then spreads through my agony, soothing it.

"You *have* been thinking about me, haven't you?"

Hunter. You killed Hunter.

"Ailen Bright. You thought you could kill me. You silly, *silly* girl." She leans closer, her hair parting in two milky curtains. "Well, let me tell you something, the girl who thinks she's so smart. It takes more than a song. You're not the first, you know. Many have tried before you."

I don't move. *I love you, Hunter. I didn't get a chance to tell you this a million times more.*

"I'll let you in on a little secret," she continues quietly. "A secret only for you and me, what do you say? You can't kill me. Nobody can," Canosa whispers.

Chapter 25

The air around us agrees with ominous silence.

"You're just dead meat that can sing, nothing more."

I croak involuntarily, because the wound she inflicted is healing quickly. She promptly reaches out and slashes my neck with her nails again. Cold slime oozes on both sides of my neck, dripping into the bathtub.

"It's who you wanted to be, Ailen Bright. This is what you are: a piece of dead meat that can sing."

I shake my head *no*.

"Go on, then. Pretend to live. Pretend we never met. How about it? How would you like to play this kind of a game?"

Hunter.

"You're not just silly, you're rude. Didn't your mother teach you proper manners? Answer me. I want to hear you say it one more time." She waits a beat and slaps me on the face, hard.

I keep staring, barely feeling anything.

My mother was never there to teach me anything, flashes through my mid. *Because of you.* I watch this thought pass, like it's a gust of wind and nothing more. *Hunter.* I want to chant his name.

"This mess you're in? You're the one who made it. You took it into your own little hands. Well, you're not alone. Thousands before you asked for me, called me, and I came." Her nostrils flare, the stink of rotten lilies emanating from her in waves.

I wrinkle my nose at the smell.

"You're a spoiled little brat, that's what you are. You think only about yourself. You disgust me." She stands.

Relieved of her weight, I try to prop myself up and slide back into a heap of jittering muscles.

"You can't balance on this edge between living and dying forever, you're smart enough to know this. Not after you've crossed to the other side once, not after you've tasted the bliss of death. It's only a matter of time before you try again," she says, in a voice of authority not to be questioned. She stands above me, her skin glowing softly in the hazy darkness of the pre-dawn that seeps through the bathroom window.

"Soon, we'll meet again, like old friends. Like sisters." She beams. "Until then, stay out of my way. It's my final warning. You let me do my business, I let you do yours. And don't worry about burying your boyfriend's body. I'll take care of that for you. I'll feed him to the fish, just like I fed your mother." She squats and stretches out her hand to me.

I understand that she said something about my mother's body, but I can't seem to grasp the meaning of it. Annoyed, she grabs my hand and clutches it with such force that I hear my bones crack.

Then she begins to sing.

I find myself entwined in the ribbon of her voice. It binds me, lifts me up, and whisks me away, to where there is no pain, no memories, no happiness, just nothing.

I let go and fall.

I fall into the vortex of her eyes, into her pupils, deeper into darkness, into what appears to be a mass of dead souls, a colorless chaos of shadowy figures composed of fog. I fall inside, becoming part of this mass. It breathes as one gigantic body, all-consuming, rhythmic. I can't breathe. I'm surrounded with a liquid that has no oxygen—it presses on me and sweeps me off my feet.

A current of this liquid propels me on toward the bottom of this crazy nightmare, ten feet, twenty, a few hundred, until my chest is ready to explode. Here the fluid turns syrupy, sticky, and absolutely black.

Is this the River Styx? Is she showing me my final journey into the afterlife?

At the far end of this blackness appears a face. Canosa's? It stands out against the darkness like an ultimate black dot, all

Chapter 25

consuming, beyond emotion, plain in its vastness. A black hole. An absolute end. I don't see its eyes, but it's looking at me, staring me up and down, and then it frowns as if I interrupted it and will be punished severely for it.

"Get out of my sight," the face booms. "You're early."

Horror raises every single hair on my body, freezes me into a piece of ice dangerously minuscule against this enormous overpowering being. I know who it is.

It's Death.

Death itself just told me to leave. I do the only thing there is to do. *Get the fuck out.* I turn and kick off, wading through thick, velvety liquid, a swamp of grief and loss. This is where everything ends, but I haven't crossed the final line. Not yet.

The syrup spits me out and I take one frantic breath. I'm in a black lake filled with black water, floating under the black sky. The water writhes with bodies, brushing against my legs like long lily stems, clammy and soft. I shriek and swim, not feeling anything except red pulsing panic. I bump into a shore, but it's not a shore, it's the rim of the tub. I'm in a tub full of water and I'm climbing out, heavy, as if I weigh a hundred tons and can't lift my own body. The dank smell of abandonment packs its mold around me.

I wiggle my fingers and move my legs, my arms. Everything seems to work. My throat feels as if it's healed itself.

A muted stillness clings in shards to my face, the floor slick under my palms and knees as I drop down and lay on the cool tiles, head turning to the side to breathe. I glance at the broken door. Yes, Canosa was here, and yes, Hunter is gone. She took him. She took him for good. For some reason she didn't kill me, she let me live. Why?

And I know.

Emptiness shrouds me in a heavy blanket.

I pull my knees up, hug myself and whimper, rocking. Back

and forth. Back and forth. As if movement will soothe my pain. As if I fit in this dark and lonely place—my misery. I push past a coldness so deep it touches my frozen bones. I want to warm up, to hear Hunter's soul. But it's gone. Gone. Gone.

This is worse than death.

"Hunter," I moan, testing my voice. It works. "Hunter. Hunter. Hunter." I keep repeating his name, as if it will bring him back.

I try to imagine the sound of his soul, to bring back that feeling of home—the clatter of food cooked on the stove, the clanking of dishes, the shuffling of feet in slippers on a wooden floor, laughter, the anticipation of a meal, birds chirping behind an open window, the buzzing of insects basking in rays of the morning sun. Vivaldi's "*Summer*," its violins.

I don't remember how it sounds.

I tighten my grip and keep rocking. Time as I know it has lost its essence. I try to soothe myself to some semblance of sleep. But sirens don't sleep, so I brood in my self-induced slumber.

"I want to die," I say. "Please, I want to die."

I rock some more. Morning light turns from a lilac to the soft gray that's typical of a Seattle dawn.

"Mom," I say. "I wish you were here. I wish you could hold me. I wish you could take me to wherever it is you are. I want to be together. Please, I want to die."

In front of the house, loose gravel crunches under the wheels of my father's car. My heart jumps, aflutter.

"Papa," I say. "Papa!"

My Papa is all I have left. Immediately, I'm afraid he'll be mad when he sees the destruction I've caused to the house and will change his mind. My head pounds with horror.

Keys jingle and the front door slams. Footsteps.

"What is this mess...Ailen!"

I hastily push myself up, take a few steps on shaky legs, rip

Chapter 25

another towel from the hook and cover myself with unbending fingers. The skin on my cuts has closed, and my muscles have knit back together, but they still seem weak. A weird sense of déjà vu makes me dizzy, like it's the morning of my birthday, all over again.

"I know you're here, sweetie. Answer me." Curses, followed by steps on the stairs. I want to disappear.

"I hope you're ready. We're leaving in fifteen minutes."

More steps.

I clutch the doorframe to prevent myself from falling. My father slowly emerges from the shadow, first his head topped with his shiny, styled gray hair, then his black suit, then his fine Italian shoes. I dare not look him in the eyes. Both shoes stop abruptly in front of the broken door, their shiny noses glistening with contempt.

"I thought I'd find you here. What the hell happened?"

With a concentrated grunt, he lifts the door and props it up against the wall, clapping his hands to get rid of the dust.

"Will you look at this..." I hear anger in his voice.

He reaches with his hand past my shoulder, turns on the light and steps into the bathroom, whistling his dismay. The leather soles of his shoes squeak on the wet tiles. Light hits me in the face. Its electric intensity colors my hands in a bluish tint. Blue is my favorite color.

My father gapes; his mouth is open and his eyes are mad, his finger pointing.

"Look what you did."

All I can do is stare.

"You know how much it costs to replace a door?"

"I didn't mean to, I swear," I say. "Well, I mean, I did do it, yes. Because Canosa was strangling Hunter. She—"

He interrupts me.

"Look at you. I spend all night preparing, organizing, arranging for caterers, scheduling flower delivery and whatnot, and picking out a casket. I haven't slept all night. I'm supposed to pick you up clean, dressed, and ready. Your funeral starts in a couple hours. I rush back, and what do I find? The house is a mess and you look like *shit!*" His finger pokes me in the chest, above the towel, and I wince at his warm touch.

He sniffs the air. "Do you smell it? What's that smell?"

I don't answer, confused.

"Answer me. Your father is asking you a question. What does that smell like?"

"What's what smell like?" I manage.

"I thought you more intelligent than this, Ailen. Think."

"Sorry, I don't know what you mean..." I say, afraid to lose the last pillar of my family, the only one who's left.

"You. I'm talking about you." Another jab, yet an exhale in relief. "You smell like the death of me. Do you know how much a funeral costs? Do you know how much it will run me to make it happen? To abandon my business here? To move to Italy with you? It will cost me a small fortune."

I shake, filled with terror. He lifts my face, takes a breath. I widen my eyes, expecting a blow, disbelieving what I'm hearing.

"Come on, don't be scared. Did I scare you? I didn't mean to," he says with almost tenderness.

Was Hunter the price for me to get you back, Papa? Was that it?

"Let's just get through this together. Tomorrow we'll start a new life. We'll sun every day, you'll have a new school and meet new friends...hmm? How about it?" His eyes narrow and I search them, wanting it to be true.

"She killed him," I say, swallowing tears.

"Who? What?" He feigns interest.

"Canosa. She killed Hunter," I say.

He frowns without surprise. "That is unfortunate. I'm very sorry. But I can assure you that she won't bother us anymore."

Chapter 25

"So you made a deal with her? Is this what you did? You paid her with Hunter?" I fall silent, processing the information I managed to spit out without realizing it was there all along, at the tip of my tongue.

"Look, sweetie, what's done is done. There's no use mulling over it. We need to get moving."

I gasp. "You seriously did it? How could you...how can you talk about it so mundanely, like it's buying groceries or something. He was my best friend. I...I loved him." As I say this, I feel the full impact of this loss and I grope for the tub behind me, slowly sliding to the floor, dropping my head into my hands.

I want to die, I want to die, I want to die.

"You're a siren. A siren can't have human friends," he says from above. There is finality in my father's voice.

I glance up. His lips press into a thin line as if saying, *There will be no arguing about this.* Broken, devastated, and desperate, I'm so afraid to lose my dream of having his attention that I decide not to press the subject. It's easier to push the pain down and forget, as if my happiness with Hunter never existed.

"And you're okay with me being, you know, a *siren*?" I wish I didn't ask this, wanting badly for the floor to part and swallow me before I hear his answer.

"Of course I am. I'm your father, remember?"

I blink. There, three feet above me, hangs his face, smiling, illuminated with the bluish electric light, resplendent with a fresh haircut and shave, yet gray and sunken from a sleepless night. Suddenly, he looks like a pitiful old man, and I want to comfort him; my grudges, my hate, my resolve to torture him, all blotted out by this new desire. This overwhelming yearning for being together, as a family.

"We'll talk about this later. Right now I need you to get cleaned up and ready, all right? Can you do it fast? Five minutes?"

Marble Bathtub

I nod.

"That's my girl." He smiles. "Now, here is what I'll have you do."

He talks and talks. He talks fast. He explains it all. The reception. The guests. The venue. The boat. The burial at sea. The speech. The passing of the casket. The plunge into the ocean. The goodbyes. All I hear is white noise. All I see are his eyes directed at me for a full five minutes. I have Papa for five minutes, all to myself. It's a miracle paid for by an enormous pain and it's worth it. If only he'd give me a hug. *One step at a time,* Ailen, *one step at a time.*

"...you'll break out, swim to Ocean Shores, and wait for me by the lighthouse. Don't worry, there is only one. It's easy to find and it'll be empty at that hour. I'll meet you there after dark. Okay?" It's the first time we touch when I don't flinch away.

"Hunter is gone. Hunter is gone, Papa. I don't know if I can stand the pain," I whisper, unable to stop my words from escaping.

"I know. But you have me now, don't you?" He smiles and I don't know if he jokes or if he truly cares; if I should be scared or elated.

"About the funeral..." I grope for words. "I thought they only scattered ashes at sea? You're not planning on burning me, are you?"

"Of course not!" he retorts. "How could you even think such a thing!"

"Okay. One more thing. Our extended family, they will be there, yes?" Fear gnaws its silky torture in my chest. "What if they notice something? I'm scared."

"You'll be fine. Pretend it's a performance, a school play. Your role is to play dead. You can do it, I have faith in you." A pat on the back. "Let's get going."

He pulls me to my feet; I lean on him, laying my cheek

Chapter 25

against the brushed wool of his black suit. I inhale his signature cologne.

Close. Close enough to a hug. This will do.

Epilogue

The body of the yacht tilts ten degrees, twenty, thirty. Waves boil, swallowing it foot by foot. There is no crew to man the pumps—not like it will help any. It's too late now.

I want to ignore this like a bad dream, as if it's not really happening. I want to pinch myself and wake up, as simple as that. It's gone too far. It's not fair. I just got my father back. He can't simply die in the middle of the ocean because I'm too weak to carry him to the shore. It would be the ultimate punishment, to watch him sink into unforgiving waves while I breathe water through my gills, floating, unable to help him.

We almost make it to the end of the deck, where it meets the cockpit. The floor tilts another ten degrees and the nose of the boat rises up a few feet at once. The fog thickens and evening dims the light. It will be dark soon.

"Hold on!" Papa shouts and lets go of my hand. "Life preserver. Right there. I just need to get far enough—"

I'm a siren, remember? I want to say, but I can't. Papa got his

Epilogue

wish, my vocal cords are too damaged to speak. Suddenly I wonder if I'm damaged enough to not be able to swim.

I clutch the metal bars in fear and listen to his laborious breathing, to the squeaking of his shoes on the wet deck. He flings his leg over the rail and reaches out to the bright orange circle affixed with ropes to its outer edge. There is a crack and the gushing of the water intensifies. With a powerful sway, the yacht dips back and starts dragging the rest of its steel body underwater. Papa slides down, hitting my chest with his back.

Too weak to hold him, I let go and we both dip overboard. He curses and thrashes vigorously to stay afloat. I bob up and down next to him, soaking in the moisture, my panic receding. I can swim, I'm all right. I will be all right. But what about Papa? I can't see him and can't hear his soul.

Everywhere I look, bubbling fountains erupt with a fizz. Wood creaks, metal parts clink and jingle. Together, it sounds like the felling of a tree—slow, deliberate, and imminent. Debris spills from the deck, towels, cushions, several plastic containers. They dance on top of the foam and then sail off into the mist.

Papa, where are you?

The yacht is not very large but it produces plenty of racket. With a final burp, it disappears into the whirlpool it created. It takes a few seconds for the ocean to swallow the last of its fifty feet of length, ten tons of its weight, its teak paneling, custom upholstered seating, and diesel engine. I dive after it.

Life preserver. I need to get you a life preserver.

In the darkness, guided by my instincts alone, I manage to squirm fast enough after it to hook my arm into the gap and yank the orange ring off the ropes. For a moment, the current drags me down, but the life preserver's buoyancy helps me break out and surface. I spit out salty water and look around, feeling strength desert me after this short adventure.

Papa resurfaces fifty feet away. He calls out my name feebly,

Epilogue

waving his arm. I barely see him in the darkening murk amidst all this fog. I sigh in relief, holding on to the orange ring and kicking with both legs, moving at a pathetically slow speed. It takes me a few minutes, but at last I reach him. He grabs on to the opposite side. His hands are white, bloodless. The platinum of his Panerai watch glistens on his wrist.

"I thought I lost you." His lips quiver from the cold. I keep forgetting that whatever water temperature feels comfortable to me must feel like freezing to him. He's hyperventilating.

His perfect hair is now a layer of wet gray hair glued to his scalp. His black shirt and jacket are soaked, smelling of wet wool. The look on his face frightens me. I sense that he intends to leave me, like everyone else has. First Mom, then Hunter, and now him.

Our faces are three feet apart. The brilliant circle of the flaming life preserver bobs between us, its four white perpendicular stripes mimicking the cardinal directions of a compass rose. Papa is between West and South, and I'm between North and East. We're on two opposite ends of the world.

I'm sorry. Sorry I screwed up.

"Are you feeling...all right?" It's difficult for him to ask me. I see a hint of physical strain on his face, a rare effort to be nice.

I nod, suppressing a horrible thought. *I'm all right, except I have no voice now, so I can't sing. That means I won't be able to feed. I'll probably wither from my growing weakness.*

Papa leans forward and reaches out with one hand. I cower, pressing my head into my shoulders on instinct. But he only brushes wet hair off my face, carefully picking at individual strands and peeling them off my forehead one by one, until it's clean to his satisfaction. Then he pats the top of my head, smoothing it until it's perfectly slick, maybe for his comfort rather than mine, a mechanical task that passes for a loving gesture. His movements are awkward and forced. I'm grateful,

Epilogue

nonetheless. This is as good as it gets.

I raise my hand and point to my throat. I hope he understands what I want to say.

"Yes, I know," he says, looking not at me but kind of through me.

"Look." He rubs his eyes, clearly unable to say something important. Or so I hope. I want to stop the clock right then and freeze time, because I think I know what it is.

"I regret it has to end like this." Then, after a pause, "Thank you for the song, by the way. It was surprisingly beautiful. Almost as good as opera." Dreamy, looking beyond me, he cracks a smile, his second genuine smile in one day. I don't know if it's addressed to me or to the memory of a particularly amazing opera performance he heard. I don't care. The fact remains.

He heard me. He heard my song!

I try to forget that we are stranded in the middle of the ocean, holding on to a life preserver. I want to be here and allow myself to feel this overwhelming thirst for closeness, and the pain that inevitably comes with it.

He studies me. "Yes, yes, I was wrong. Is that what you wanted to hear?" He shakes from the cold and looks away again.

I dare not breathe, perplexed. What did I do wrong to irritate him? I shake my head in an energetic *no.*

The fog thickens into an atmospheric milk, growing indigo by the minute. He looks aside, somewhere in the distance, past my head.

"I failed you as a father." He says it to the ocean, not to me, his head turned slightly away.

No! I yell without sound, opening my mouth, shaking my head. *No-no-no! Not at all!* After initial hesitation, I reach out to him and grab his hand. It's as cold as mine. He lets me hold it.

"Life is tough, Ailen. I wanted to get you ready for it. I was tough on you, maybe too tough. That was my mistake." He

Epilogue

steals a quick glance at me, almost embarrassed.

I squeeze his hand.

"What? What else do you want to know?" he erupts. I shrink.

"Yes, I was young and arrogant when I met Canosa." His eyes wander. "I was rowing one night, and there she was. Standing in the lake, surrounded by water lilies, singing. I thought she was mad. Who in their right mind would do such a thing? So I paddled closer." He presses his lips together. "She stole my soul. I've detested sirens ever since. You could say that she turned me into a perfect siren hunter." He steals another glance at me.

"It was different with your mother. Your mother stole my heart. I loved her so much I hated her." He sniffs and sneezes, shaking all over. "I failed to save her. She was a slippery thing, your mom. She twisted right out of my arms. She was scared of me. That look on her face, it haunts me every day, Ailen, every day."

He suddenly breaks down, convulsing in silent sobs, turning his head away from me.

"You remind me of her so much. Sometimes I can't bear looking at you." His usual polished politeness falls off, and I see him the way I never saw him. Vulnerable.

"I hope you can forgive me," he whispers to the sky.

My heart beats fast; I want to say, *What do you mean, you hope? No, you will hold on to me and I'll carry you to the shore. You can float next to me until then. Can't you?*

He stops shaking. His eyes sink deeply into his hollow face.

"It's no use, Ailen." His words are long and slurry. "You know I will freeze to death soon. Hypothermia is already setting in. Any chance of a ship picking us up in the next few minutes is next to nil. Why prolong the inevitable?"

He lets go of the life preserver.

"Have a good life." These are his last words, and he sinks.

Epilogue

The burial at sea is now complete.

I yell inside my head. I hear my voice ring as if a ribbon of thought passes through the water, through space, through the entire world. My scream uncoils and I feel every syllable tinkle. I let go of the life preserver and dive after him.

The water is murky and it's hard for me to see. I gulp it in, siphoning in oxygen. It tastes like tears, salty. I see Papa's face, his white hands. The rest is dark, clothed in black wool and melting with the dimness of the ocean. He lets out a stream of bubbles. It reaches me from below like a shimmering bridge between life and death.

I open my mouth and throw out random calls, one after another, without any coherent structure. *Hold on! Don't go! I'm coming! Don't breathe! Give me your hand!* They sink into nothing. I'm mute.

I will carry you out!

A sudden realization fills me to the brim of my emotional capacity. It pushes so hard, I want to burst.

Papa, it wasn't you, it was me. I made a mistake. You're right. I need to stop this suicidal nonsense. I don't want to die anymore. I want to live!

I say it in my head, again and again.

I WANT TO LIVE! I WANT TO LIVE! I WANT TO LIVE!

I want to laugh. I want to run around, to be silly, to dance under the rain. I want to break into song and explode into a myriad of bells. I want to feel alive!

A surge of strength comes out of nowhere and throws me into action. I kick until I finally reach Papa. I grab one of his hands. I barely see his face and I can't tell if his eyes are open or closed. Water gurgles around me. I grab on to his hand with both of mine, and slowly, step by step, move my hands up his arm, until I reach his shoulder. I clasp him under his armpits.

His soul is barely an echo of a badly out of tune flute. It

Epilogue

flickers now and then, and he's heavy, very heavy.

Papa! I shout into his face.

He opens his eyes and smiles. It's a toothy, happy smile, and it lets out a big air bubble. His last. He gulps water and convulses in my arms, then his soul is gone. It just fizzes out like a feeble candle.

I kick and thrash, yanking on his arms to swim up, but he only grows heavier and keeps pulling me down. My strength drains rapidly. My fingers begin sliding across his jacket. I grip him harder, but he slides out. I know that every attempt to recover him is futile. My muscles pass a tremor and slowly my fingers begin to uncurl. I watch with horror as his body slips out of my grip and plunges deeper. I try to grab ahold of him again and kick, but my legs hardly listen. Oblivious to my mute pleading, the ocean sucks him into the freezing liquid depths. I can't hum to the water anymore, to create a stream and push his body out. Stubbornly, I follow until I don't see him anymore.

He's gone.

And I'm still here.

Papa, I'm sorry I wasn't strong enough to save you. I'll try to have a good life, like you wanted me to. I don't want to die anymore. I want to live. I will live.

I twirl in the water, overtaken by grief, trying to find something to hold on to. Facts. Facts will carry me out. One thing at a time. First, I need to orient myself. I'm in the ocean. I need to swim up and find the life preserver, and then I'll think about what to do next. Which way is up?

I realize I lost all sense of direction in this complete darkness. I rely on my ears and my eyes. Above me is endless quiet; below me must be the air, the droning noise of the rolling waves. I turn around and follow the sound, painstakingly moving my arms and legs. The water gets slightly warmer as dim light begins to seep in. It's probably nighttime by now, and the fog must have receded to let in the moonlight; at this depth, it looks like a stream of silver fluid. It blinds me with its sudden intensity, so brilliant and smooth. I think that if I reach out to it, I'll touch it, like something solid.

It's so dazzling that I close my eyes, sluggishly wading through the brine until I reach the surface and burst into air. I try to open my eyes, but the light is so bright that my eyes water, making everything blurry. Is it morning? Was I underwater all night? The relief of being on the surface is so overwhelming that, at first, I can't even breathe. My chest sort of collapsed in on itself. I flap my arms around, wanting to find something to hold on to, to prevent myself from slipping into darkness. I let my eyes adjust to the light before opening them.

Seems like luck is on my side. Groping around, I find the smooth surface of the life preserver and curl my fingers around it, relieved. My anxiety recedes, my diaphragm relaxes, and I draw in a sharp breath, again and again and again, short for air.

"Papa, I decided I want to live," I say, coughing out water, shaking all over and hyperventilating. I'm so happy I want to cry.

"I'm alive. I can talk. I can talk?" I say, incredulous.

I open my eyes. Slowly, it all comes into focus.

I'm in the bathroom, our bathroom, the only room in our house that locks. There is the ceiling that I know so well, the monogrammed towels hanging on the hooks by the door. What I thought was a life preserver is actually the edge of the tub, Papa's beloved antique carved-marble tub, the ridiculous Bright family relic.

I frantically bend down to look.

"Oh God, oh God," I mumble under my breath.

There they are—four marble sirens. I slide from corner to corner, to make sure none are missing. They look so little, only two feet tall. Here is Pisinoe, the youngest, who always wanted a pet. Teles, slightly chubby. Raidne, with her long and curly hair.

Epilogue

And Ligeia, the shrill one, with perfect breasts. I hang out of the tub, face to face with the last creature, looking at her upside down. Blood rushes to my head and I reel with dizziness. I start coughing uncontrollably, wheezing, feeling my throat burn.

Ligeia winks her marble eye at me.

I must be really stoned, I think, blinking. She's back to cold stone. I look at her hands. They are right underneath the tub's rim, turned up in worship to the Siren of Canosa.

I sit up so fast my head collides with the miniature statue wrapping the faucet. I let out a cry of pain and twist around, gazing at her intently.

She's exactly as I remember her, a bronze faucet figurine, barely a foot tall. Her left hand holds the faucet, her right arm raised over her head in a gesture of mourning. Her hair wraps around her body in tapered, sophisticated lines. I reach out and touch her. She's solid bronze.

"You're just a statue," I say, chortling out one hysterical laugh, and coughing again. Nausea spins my vision.

I make myself look at the clock on the wall.

It's three minutes past seven. Seven in the morning?

I study my palms, warm and pink, with real blood running through them. I look at my soaked hoodie, with white letters spelling Siren Suicides across it, and my favorite jeans.

"Hunter, what the fuck did you give me?"

I lean over the edge of the tub again. A stub of a joint lies on the tiled floor, somehow defiant, as if it knows something I don't, flipping me the finger.

"Ailen? Last warning. Open the door or I'm kicking it down! One..." Papa's voice comes through the door.

"Papa!" I shriek. My heart pounds in my ears and I begin spinning as if down a whirlpool. I grab the edges of the tub to steady myself. "Hang on, I'm getting out!"

"Why didn't you answer before? I've been knocking for the

Epilogue

last three minutes. Out, now!"

"Sorry! Dressing!" I shout, full of glee.

He's alive! That means, that means...

I crawl out of the tub, water cascading down me. I strip with unbending fingers, pulling hard at the sticky jeans as they cling to my skin. My hands shake and it takes forever.

"I can breathe. I'm alive. I'm okay. It was just a bad trip," I mumble under my breath,to assert myself. Another rush of dizziness sweeps over me and I lean on the wall, coughing again.

"Two...don't make me get to three, Ailen," Papa's voice rings through the gap.

"Almost done!" I grab the nearest towel, blot my face and my shoulders, and wrap it around myself. Then I grab my wet clothes and shove them behind the toilet, hoping he won't see. My eyes fall on the joint and I bend to pick it up and throw it out the window, then I stop myself. I stand tall and walk up to the bathroom mirror on the wall.

A startled face looks back at me, wet hair sticking out to all sides in a crazy halo, deep purple circles under my eyes and my skin devoid of any color, looking deathly pale. But my eyes shine.

"Ailen Bright," I say. "What do you know, you're alive after all."

I turn around, walk over, and unlock the door.

"Papa!" I'm so happy to see him, standing on the other side of the door, meticulously dressed in his fine silk pajamas, deep maroon with barely visible rosy stripes, his hair smooth as if he didn't just climb out of bed minutes ago, a dab of cologne still wafting off of him in the delicate scent. I love it all and take it all in, wanting to rush over and gather him in a hug.

He opens his mouth and launches into a string of swear words and accusations and warnings that *One day, you just wait, one day, you will turn out just like your mother.* I ignore all of it

Epilogue

like white noise.

"Papa," I say. "I'm so happy to see you." My voice catches.

He doesn't hear me. I nearly forgot his typical conversational pattern. He yells back, waving his arms, froth forming at the corners of his mouth. His eyes bulge out of their sockets, his hands flying dangerously close to my face. Instantly, I know what will come next, and I decide that I've had it.

I take a step toward him, grab him by the shoulders, and shake him roughly.

"Listen to me!" I shout in his face. "Did you hear what I just said?"

Utter shock makes him freeze with his mouth open, his pupils wide.

I talk into the next few seconds of silence, letting my arms fall back to my sides. "Papa, I love you. But you've got to stop screaming at me all the time, okay? It's my birthday today, have you forgotten? I'm sixteen, I'm a big girl. I'll be fine. I'll turn out just fine, don't worry."

"What...what did you say?" He doesn't grasp it, his face ashen. His fingers spread, as if willing to grab something and strangle it, yet not sure what it should be, perhaps for the first time in his life.

I look into his face.

"I'm sixteen, Papa, I'll be fine. I'm okay, really. No need to freak out and control me all the time. I'm my own person, and you've got to stop this. Today. Now."

"Oh," he says, and takes a step back, away from me, bewildered. Then he takes a step forward again.

"How dare you talk back to me like this." He begins his usual tirade. "You little—" He raises his right arm to hit me.

I'm ready for it, and I intercept it midair, grabbing it with both my hands, arresting the blow before it happens. We perform somewhat of a dance, a movement that brushes my hip and

Epilogue

dissolves. I let go of his arm.

"Papa, if you hit me one more time, I will hit you back, I promise you that. I don't want to do it. So, please, don't hit me ever again." I look him in the eyes.

He falls silent, locking his gaze with mine, and I hold it. I don't avert my eyes, I don't hide. I have no fear. He senses it and glances at his feet briefly before raising his eyes back again, amidst awkward silence.

"I won't let you do to me what you did to Mom, okay? But I want you to know that, no matter what happened in the past, I still love you."

He grunts and looks to the side, as if we have a third invisible person who is part of the conversation. "See? I knew it. Same genes. It's a pathology." He looks back at me. "You're just like your mother. Crazy! It's what I was afraid of. All th—"

"No!" I interrupt him sharply. "I'm not crazy, and don't you *ever* call Mom crazy, you hear me?"

He shrinks right before my eyes, and I realize that he's scared, scared of this absence of fear I'm displaying, unsure what to do with it.

"I'm not interested in spending my morning listening—"

"Shut up!" I yell, my hands curled into fists.

For a brief moment I see a little boy standing in front of me, terrified, unable to move or breathe. Then he's back to his usual self, except shaken and pale. He's shocked into silence.

"You *will* listen to me, because I'm your daughter and I have something important to say."

"Can we talk about this important stuff later? I have to use the bathroom, or I'll be late," he nearly whimpers, and I pause, astounded.

"Bullshit! No you won't. It's fucking early and you know that." This is the first time I openly swear at him, as if a lid flies off my suppressed feelings, giving me freedom to talk, letting me

Epilogue

say what I meant to say for years.

"I have a question for you, actually. Do you know what women were made for?"

His face floats somewhere between shock and anger. His eyes bulge, veins pushing against the skin of his neck. He opens and closes his mouth like a beached fish.

"Answer the question," I say.

"Don't you talk to me like this, young lady." He's shaking. "I'm your father, and you do as I say." But I see the glint fade in his eyes.

"Women were made to love and to be loved, Papa," I say.

"Where did you get that idea?" he asks.

There is a knock on the front door. My heart expands at once into all corners of every room, making the whole house pulse. I beam, knowing who it is.

"Here." I tap my head. "Here is where I got this idea." I take a step, unable to restrain myself, then turn around, remembering one more thing.

"Oh, and...uh, I smoked a joint. It was good weed, you know. I think you should start doing it, Papa, it might do you good." I tap him on the shoulder and, before he has time to react, flee down the stairs, jumping them three at a time, skidding to a stop at the front door. I fumble with the stupid, woman-faced handle for a few seconds, my shaking hands refusing to function properly.

At last, I throw it open.

"Hunter!"

There he stands, looking at me. Droplets zigzag off his rain jacket, bright blue, my favorite color. His hands are in its pockets. It takes all my willpower to not launch at him and squeeze him really hard. I'm afraid to freak him out, so I hyperventilate instead.

"Hey. Happy birthday, brat." He grins, wipes his wet nose

Epilogue

with one hand with a loud sniffle, pulls out his other hand from his pocket, and hands me a crumpled envelope made of blue recycled paper.

I take it with shaky hands.

"Oh, thank you, thank you! Oh..." I don't know what else to say, bursting with glee. I want to jump up and down, feeling my heels lift off the floor.

"Um...can I come in?"

"Oh! Sure!" I say, and step aside, blushing under his stares at my chest, right where the towel started sliding off. I yank it up, tuck the end back in, and scowl at him.

"Hunter."

"Sorry, sorry." He raises his hands in defense.

I shut the door and hold the envelope in front of me. "What is it?"

"Open it." He lowers his hood, dog-shakes his head, and looks up behind me. "Morning, Mr. Bright. How are you doing? I wanted to be the first to wish Ailen a happy birthday. I hope that's okay?"

I turn my head. Papa stands at the top of the stairs, gravely looking down. Then he turns without a word and slams the bathroom door shut behind him.

"What's wrong with him?" Hunter asks quietly.

"I'll explain later," I say, and begin jumping up and down like a little girl, pressing the towel to my chest with one hand, holding the envelope in the other. Hunter follows me with his eyes, mimicking my movement with his head, nodding up and down.

"Jesus, girl. I make you that happy, really? Come on, open the present already." He leans on the doorframe, studying me in his lazy manner, squinting his eyes.

I grin from ear to ear, short of breath, feeling glee spread through my limbs and unable to stop. I rip the envelope open,

Epilogue

look inside. "Two tickets to Siren Suicides tonight!" I take them out and stare at them.

"What's wrong? You don't like it?"

I look up. "I saw a dream, Hunter. Well, not a dream...okay, I'll explain. I had a *bad* trip. I have to tell you all about it. That shit you gave me, it was fucking strong!"

"Shhhh!" He presses a finger to his lips. "Your dad will hear."

"I don't care. I told him this morning that I smoked it."

"You *what?*" Hunter's face contorts with puzzlement akin to a puppy that's been chasing its own tail and can't understand why it's so hard to reach.

There are so many things I want to tell him, I can barely control myself.

"Can I ask you a question? It's important."

"Right now?"

"Yeah, right now." I stop moving. "Have you ever lived? Like, really lived?"

"Are you okay?" He reaches out to touch my forehead, suddenly serious. "Did something happen?"

"No. I'm fine, just listen." I wave my arm around, clutching the envelope. "I don't mean, pretending to live, you know, when you smile politely, say *hi* and *bye* and *thank you* and stuff like that. You get good grades, you do what your parents tell you to do, but you secretly hate your life. I mean, have you ever lived *for real?*" My hands shake from excitement and a surge of adrenaline.

"Hmmm." Hunter rubs his face.

"Have you ever felt like flying, like nothing mattered, nothing at all, except now, except you and this feeling of weightlessness that you hope will never end? Have you ever felt like there was no yesterday, and no tomorrow, only now? Have you?"

"You're stoned." He grins.

"No, no, I'm not, I swear. Well, I was, but not anymore.

Epilogue

Anyway, what I'm trying to say is..." I lick my lips. "I'm sixteen today, and I wanna start living. But I don't really know how, I've always only wanted to..." I stumble, afraid to say the word *die*.

"You always wanted to what?" He steps closer, taking my hand.

I lean on his shoulder and speak into his wet rain jacket. "I need your help." I raise my head and stare into his blue eyes. "Will you help me? I want to figure out how to live in the moment, find out what it means, make friends. I'm so lonely sometimes, it hurts. It doesn't matter if I'm around people, I still feel like an outcast. Whenever I..."

I pause for air.

"...whenever I go to school, and—"

"How about I help you shut up, for starters?" he says.

Before I can say anything else, he's kissing me. His damp jacket touches my skin, his warm hands cup my face. I try to mumble, to finish the sentence, but I can't. I'm drawn into the kiss, unraveling. My self-control evaporates. I grab his shoulders, and I claw at his back. I press him hard to me, curling my arms around him in a desperate grip. I lean into him, into the outline of his body, letting myself be carried away, letting myself be loved. All the while, I stare at the front door, remembering the morning my mother left me, realizing that I might never find out for sure what happened to her or her body. And I let it go.

I let it all go.

I close my eyes. One day, I will die. We all will. But, until then, I will live. No more thoughts of suicide, because life is beautiful, full of love.

It's all right here, in my heart.

About the Author

Ksenia was born in Moscow, Russia, and came to US in 1998 not knowing English, having studied architecture and not dreaming that one day she'd be writing. Siren Suicides, an urban fantasy set in Seattle, is her first novel. She lives in Seattle with her partner and their combined three kids in a house that they like to call The Loony Bin.

About the Cover

The new cover for this edition was designed by Anna Milioutina. Drawing for as long as she can remember, Anna has always been a creative mind and had very distinct plans for her adult life, all centering around art. Starting with a foundation in fine art, she soon realized that design was another passion, one she decided to pursue. She is enrolled at Chapman University as a Graphic Design major, set to graduate in 2016, and has been employed as a Graphic Design Assistant by the Art Department since Fall 2012. She currently lives in Orange, CA with her boyfriend.

About the Books

Siren Suicides was edited by Sarah Liu, who will never, ever smash three books into one again. Proofreading was done by Spencer Borup entirely in the bathtub. Final formatting was completed by Stuart Whitmore of Crenel Publishing. The main text is Adobe Garamond, while titles and chapter headings are Bitstream Futura. Final digital assembly was completed in Adobe InDesign.

You finished reading it!
And you're alive!
Please review it on
Amazon and Goodreads
and send me links.
Rosehead up next!

  Love,
  K.

Made in the USA
Lexington, KY
04 August 2017